# Goosebumps®

# Living Dummy Collection

# Goosebumps®

# Living Dummy Collection

## R.L. STINE

SCHOLASTIC INC.

New York Toronto London Auckland Sydney
Mexico City New Delhi Hong Kong Buenos Aires

# CONTENTS

Night of the Living Dummy            vii
Night of the Living Dummy II         137
Night of the Living Dummy III        261

# NIGHT OF THE LIVING DUMMY

"Mmmmm! Mmmm! Mmmmm!"

Kris Powell struggled to get her twin sister's attention.

Lindy Powell glanced up from the book she was reading to see what the problem was. Instead of her sister's pretty face, Lindy saw a round, pink bubble nearly the size of Kris's head.

"Nice one," Lindy said without much enthusiasm. With a sudden move, she poked the bubble and popped it.

"Hey!" Kris cried as the pink bubble gum exploded onto her cheeks and chin.

Lindy laughed. "Gotcha."

Kris angrily grabbed Lindy's paperback and slammed it shut. "Whoops — lost your place!" she exclaimed. She knew her sister hated to lose her place in a book.

Lindy grabbed the book back with a scowl. Kris struggled to pull the pink gum off her face.

"That was the biggest bubble I ever blew," she

1

said angrily. The gum wasn't coming off her chin.

"I've blown much bigger than that," Lindy said with a superior sneer.

"I don't *believe* you two," their mother muttered, making her way into their bedroom and dropping a neatly folded pile of laundry at the foot of Kris's bed. "You even compete over bubble gum?"

"We're not competing," Lindy muttered. She tossed back her blonde ponytail and returned her eyes to her book.

Both girls had straight blonde hair. But Lindy kept hers long, usually tying it behind her head or on one side in a ponytail. And Kris had hers cut very short.

It was a way for people to tell the twins apart, for they were nearly identical in every other way. Both had broad foreheads and round, blue eyes. Both had dimples in their cheeks when they smiled. Both blushed easily, large pink circles forming on their pale cheeks.

Both thought their noses were a little too wide. Both wished they were a little taller. Lindy's best friend, Alice, was nearly three inches taller, even though she hadn't turned twelve yet.

"Did I get it all off?" Kris asked, rubbing her chin, which was red and sticky.

"Not all," Lindy told her, glancing up. "There's some in your hair."

"Oh, great," Kris muttered. She grabbed at her

hair, but couldn't find any bubble gum.

"Gotcha again," Lindy said, laughing. "You're too easy!"

Kris uttered an angry growl. "Why are you always so mean to me?"

"Me? Mean?" Lindy looked up in wide-eyed innocence. "I'm an angel. Ask anyone."

Exasperated, Kris turned back to her mother, who was stuffing socks into a dresser drawer. "Mom, when am I going to get my own room?"

"On the Twelfth of Never," Mrs. Powell replied, grinning.

Kris groaned. "That's what you always say."

Her mother shrugged. "You know we don't have a spare inch, Kris." She turned to the bedroom window. Bright sunlight streamed through the filmy curtains. "It's a beautiful day. What are you two doing inside?"

"Mom, we're not little girls," Lindy said, rolling her eyes. "We're twelve. We're too old to go out and play."

"Did I get it all?" Kris asked, still scraping pink patches of bubble gum off her chin.

"Leave it. It improves your complexion," Lindy told her.

"I wish you girls would be nicer to each other," Mrs. Powell said with a sigh.

They suddenly heard shrill barking coming from downstairs. "What's Barky excited about now?" Mrs. Powell fretted. The little black terrier was

3

always barking about something. "Why not take Barky for a walk?"

"Don't feel like it," Lindy muttered, nose in her book.

"What about those beautiful new bikes you got for your birthdays?" Mrs. Powell said, hands on hips. "Those bikes you just couldn't live without. You know, the ones that have been sitting in the garage since you got them."

"Okay, okay. You don't have to be sarcastic, Mom," Lindy said, closing her book. She stood up, stretched, and tossed the book onto her bed.

"You want to?" Kris asked Lindy.

"Want to what?"

"Go for a bike ride. We could ride to the playground, see if anyone's hanging out at school."

"You just want to see if Robby is there," Lindy said, making a face.

"So?" Kris said, blushing.

"Go on. Get some fresh air," Mrs. Powell urged. "I'll see you later. I'm off to the supermarket."

Kris peered into the dresser mirror. She had gotten most of the gum off. She brushed her short hair back with both hands. "Come on. Let's go out," she said. "Last one out is a rotten egg." She darted to the doorway, beating her sister by half a step.

As they burst out the back door, with Barky yipping shrilly behind them, the afternoon sun was high in a cloudless sky. The air was still and dry. It felt more like summer than spring.

Both girls were wearing shorts and sleeveless T-shirts. Lindy bent to pull open the garage door, then stopped. The house next door caught her eye.

"Look — they've got the walls up," she told Kris, pointing across their back yard.

"That new house is going up so quickly. It's amazing," Kris said following her sister's gaze.

The builders had knocked down the old house during the winter. The new concrete foundation had been put down in March. Lindy and Kris had walked around on it when no workers were there, trying to figure out where the different rooms would go.

And now the walls had been built. The construction suddenly looked like a real house, rising up in the midst of tall stacks of lumber, a big mound of red-brown dirt, a pile of concrete blocks, and an assortment of power saws, tools, and machinery.

"No one's working today," Lindy said.

They took a few steps toward the new house. "Who do you think will move in?" Kris wondered. "Maybe some great-looking guy our age. Maybe great-looking twin guys!"

"Yuck!" Lindy made a disgusted face. "Twin guys? How drippy can you get! I can't believe you and I are in the same family."

Kris was used to Lindy's sarcasm. Both girls liked being twins and hated being twins at the same time. Because they shared nearly everything — their looks, their clothing, their room — they were closer than most sisters ever get.

But because they were so much alike, they also managed to drive each other crazy a lot of the time.

"No one's around. Let's check out the new house," Lindy said.

Kris followed her across the yard. A squirrel, halfway up the wide trunk of a maple tree, watched them warily.

They made their way through an opening in the low shrubs that divided the two yards. Then, walking past the stacks of lumber and the tall mound of dirt, they climbed the concrete stoop.

A sheet of heavy plastic had been nailed over the opening where the front door would go. Kris pulled one end of the plastic up, and they slipped into the house.

It was dark and cool inside and had a fresh wood smell. The plaster walls were up but hadn't been painted.

"Careful," Lindy warned. "Nails." She pointed to the large nails scattered over the floor. "If you step on one, you'll get lockjaw and die."

"You wish," Kris said.

"I don't want you to die," Lindy replied. "Just get lockjaw." She snickered.

"Ha-ha," Kris said sarcastically. "This must be the living room," she said, making her way carefully across the front room to the fireplace against the back wall.

"A cathedral ceiling," Lindy said, staring up at the dark, exposed wooden beams above their heads. "Neat."

"This is bigger than our living room," Kris remarked, peering out the large picture window to the street.

"It smells great," Lindy said, taking a deep breath. "All the sawdust. It smells so piney."

They made their way through the hall and explored the kitchen. "Are those wires on?" Kris asked, pointing to a cluster of black electrical wires suspended from the ceiling beams.

"Why don't you touch one and find out?" Lindy suggested.

"You first," Kris shot back.

"The kitchen isn't very big," Lindy said, bending down to stare into the holes where the kitchen cabinets would go.

She stood up and was about to suggest they check out the upstairs when she heard a sound. "Huh?" Her eyes widened in surprise. "Is someone in here?"

Kris froze in the middle of the kitchen.

They both listened.

Silence.

Then they heard soft, rapid footsteps. Close by. Inside the house.

"Let's go!" Lindy whispered.

Kris was already ducking under the plastic, heading out the doorway opening. She leapt off the back stoop and started running toward their back yard.

Lindy stopped at the bottom of the stoop and turned back to the new house. "Hey — look!" she called.

A squirrel came flying out a side window. It landed on the dirt with all four feet moving and scrambled toward the maple tree in the Powells' yard.

Lindy laughed. "Just a dumb squirrel."

Kris stopped near the low shrubs. "You sure?" She hesitated, watching the windows of the new house. "That was a pretty loud squirrel."

When she turned back from the house, she was surprised to find that Lindy had disappeared.

"Hey — where'd you go?"

"Over here," Lindy called. "I see something!"

It took Kris a while to locate her sister. Lindy was half-hidden behind a large black trash Dumpster at the far end of the yard.

Kris shielded her eyes with one hand to see better. Lindy was bent over the side of the Dumpster. She appeared to be rummaging through some trash.

"What's in there?" Kris called.

Lindy was tossing things around and didn't seem to hear her.

"What *is* it?" Kris called, taking a few reluctant steps toward the Dumpster.

Lindy didn't reply.

Then, slowly, she pulled something out. She started to hold it up. Its arms and legs dangled down limply. Kris could see a head with brown hair.

A head? Arms and legs?

"Oh, no!" Kris cried aloud, raising her hands to her face in horror.

## 2

A child?

Kris uttered a silent gasp, staring in horror as Lindy lifted him out of the trash Dumpster.

She could see his face, frozen in a wide-eyed stare. His brown hair stood stiffly on top of his head. He seemed to be wearing some sort of gray suit.

His arms and legs dangled lifelessly.

"Lindy!" Kris called, her throat tight with fear. "Is it — is he . . . *alive?*"

Her heart pounding, Kris started to run to her sister. Lindy was cradling the poor thing in her arms.

"Is he alive?" Kris repeated breathlessly.

She stopped short when her sister started to laugh.

"No, Not alive!" Lindy called gleefully.

And then Kris realized that it wasn't a child after all. "A dummy!" she shrieked.

Lindy held it up. "A ventriloquist's dummy,"

she said. "Someone threw him out. Do you believe it? He's in perfect shape."

It took Lindy a while to notice that Kris was breathing hard, her face bright red. "Kris, what's your problem? Oh, wow. Did you think he was a real kid?" Lindy laughed scornfully.

"No. Of course not," Kris insisted.

Lindy held the dummy up and examined his back, looking for the string to pull to make his mouth move. "I *am* a real kid!" Lindy made him say. She was speaking in a high-pitched voice through gritted teeth, trying not to move her lips.

"Dumb," Kris said, rolling her eyes.

"I am *not* dumb. You're dumb!" Lindy made the dummy say in a high, squeaky voice. When she pulled the string in his back, the wooden lips moved up and down, clicking as they moved. She moved her hand up his back and found the control to make his painted eyes shift from side to side.

"He's probably filled with bugs," Kris said, making a disgusted face. "Throw him back, Lindy."

"No way," Lindy insisted, rubbing her hand tenderly over the dummy's wooden hair. "I'm keeping him."

"She's keeping me," she made the dummy say.

Kris stared suspiciously at the dummy. His brown hair was painted on his head. His blue eyes moved only from side to side and couldn't blink. He had bright red painted lips, curved up into an

11

eerie smile. The lower lip had a chip on one side so that it didn't quite match the upper lip.

The dummy wore a gray, double-breasted suit over a white shirt collar. The collar wasn't attached to a shirt. Instead, the dummy's wooden chest was painted white. Big brown leather shoes were attached to the ends of his thin, dangling legs.

"My name is Slappy," Lindy made the dummy say, moving his grinning mouth up and down.

"Dumb," Kris repeated, shaking her head. "Why Slappy?"

"Come over here and I'll slap you!" Lindy made him say, trying not to move her lips.

Kris groaned. "Are we going to ride our bikes to the playground or not, Lindy?"

"Afraid poor Robby misses you?" Lindy made Slappy ask.

"Put that ugly thing down," Kris replied impatiently.

"I'm not ugly," Slappy said in Lindy's squeaky voice, sliding his eyes from side to side. "You're ugly!"

"Your lips are moving," Kris told Lindy. "You're a lousy ventriloquist."

"I'll get better," Lindy insisted.

"You mean you're really keeping it?" Kris cried.

"I like Slappy. He's cute," Lindy said, cuddling the dummy against the front of her T-shirt.

12

"I'm cute," she made him say. "And you're ugly."

"Shut up," Kris snapped to the dummy.

"You shut up!" Slappy replied in Lindy's tight, high-pitched voice.

"What do you want to keep him for?" Kris asked, following her sister toward the street.

"I always liked puppets," Lindy recalled. "Remember those marionettes I used to have? I played with them for hours at a time. I made up long plays with them."

"I always played with the marionettes, too," Kris remembered.

"You got the strings all tangled up," Lindy said, frowning. "You weren't any good at it."

"But what are you going to *do* with this dummy?" Kris demanded.

"I don't know. Maybe I'll work up an act," Lindy said thoughtfully, shifting Slappy to her other arm. "I'll bet I could earn some money with him. You know. Appear at kids' birthday parties. Put on shows."

"Happy birthday!" she made Slappy declare. "Hand over some money!"

Kris didn't laugh.

The two girls walked along the street in front of their house. Lindy cradled Slappy in her arms, one hand up his back.

"I think he's creepy," Kris said, kicking a large

13

pebble across the street. "You should put him back in the Dumpster."

"No way," Lindy insisted.

"No way," she made Slappy say, shaking his head, his glassy blue eyes moving from side to side. "I'll put *you* in the Dumpster!"

"Slappy sure is mean," Kris remarked, frowning at Lindy.

Lindy laughed. "Don't look at me," she teased. "Complain to Slappy."

Kris scowled.

"You're jealous," Lindy said. "Because I found him and you didn't."

Kris started to protest, but they both heard voices. Kris looked up to see the two Marshall kids from down the block running toward them. They were cute, red-headed kids that Lindy and Kris sometimes baby-sat for.

"What's that?" Amy Marshall asked, pointing at Slappy.

"Does he talk?" her younger brother, Ben, asked, staying several feet away, an uncertain expression on his freckled face.

"Hi, I'm Slappy!" Lindy made the dummy call out. She cradled Slappy in one arm, making him sit up straight, his arms dangling at his sides.

"Where'd you get him?" Amy asked.

"Do his eyes move?" Ben asked, still hanging back.

"Do *your* eyes move?" Slappy asked Ben.

14

Both Marshall kids laughed. Ben forgot his reluctance. He stepped up and grabbed Slappy's hand.

"Ouch! Not so hard!" Slappy cried.

Ben dropped the hand with a gasp. Then he and Amy collapsed in gleeful laughter.

"Ha-ha-ha-ha!" Lindy made Slappy laugh, tilting his head back and opening his mouth wide.

The two kids thought that was a riot. They laughed even harder.

Pleased by the response she was getting, Lindy glanced at her sister. Kris was sitting on the curb, cradling her head in her hands, a dejected look on her face.

She's jealous, Lindy realized. Kris sees that the kids really like Slappy and that I'm getting all the attention. And she's totally jealous.

I'm *definitely* keeping Slappy! Lindy told herself, secretly pleased at her little triumph.

She stared into the dummy's bright blue painted eyes. To her surprise, the dummy seemed to be staring back at her, a twinkle of sunlight in his eyes, his grin wide and knowing.

"Who was that on the phone?" Mr. Powell asked, shoveling another forkful of spaghetti into his mouth.

Lindy slipped back into her place at the table. "It was Mrs. Marshall. Down the block."

"Does she want you to baby-sit?" Mrs. Powell asked, reaching for the salad bowl. She turned to Kris. "Don't you want any salad?"

Kris wiped spaghetti sauce off her chin with her napkin. "Maybe later."

"No," Lindy answered. "She wants me to perform. At Amy's birthday party. With Slappy."

"Your first job," Mr. Powell said, a smile crossing his slender face.

"Amy and Ben liked Slappy so much, they insisted on him," Lindy said. "Mrs. Marshall is going to pay me twenty dollars."

"That's great!" their mother exclaimed. She passed the salad bowl across the table to her husband.

16

It had been a week since Lindy rescued Slappy from the trash Dumpster. Every day after school, she had spent hours up in her room rehearsing with him, working on his voice, practicing not moving her lips, thinking up jokes to perform with him.

Kris kept insisting the whole thing was dumb. "I can't believe you're being such a nerd," she told her sister. She refused to be an audience for Lindy's routines.

But when Lindy brought Slappy into school on Friday, Kris's attitude began to change. A group of kids had gathered around Lindy outside her locker.

As Lindy made Slappy talk for them, Kris watched from down the hall. She's going to make a total fool of herself, Kris thought.

But to her surprise, the kids hooted and howled. They thought Slappy was a riot. Even Robby Martin, the guy Kris had had a crush on for two years, thought Lindy was terrific.

Watching Robby laugh along with the other kids made Kris think hard. Becoming a ventriloquist might be fun.

And profitable. Lindy was going to earn twenty dollars at the Marshalls' birthday party. And when word got around, she'd probably perform at a lot of parties and earn even more money.

After dinner that evening, Lindy and Kris washed and dried the dishes. Then Lindy asked her parents if she could practice her new comedy routine on them. She hurried up to her room to get Slappy.

Mr. and Mrs. Powell took a seat on the living room couch. "Maybe Lindy will be a TV star," Mrs. Powell said.

"Maybe," Mr. Powell agreed, settling back on the couch, a pleased smile on his face. Barky yapped and climbed between Mr. and Mrs. Powell, his tiny stub of a tail wagging furiously.

"You know you're not allowed on the couch," Mrs. Powell said, sighing. But she made no move to push Barky off.

Kris sat down away from the others, on the floor by the steps, cradling her chin in her hands.

"You're looking glum this evening," her father remarked.

"Can I get a dummy, too?" Kris asked. She hadn't really planned to say it. The question just popped out of her mouth.

Lindy came back into the room, carrying Slappy around the waist. "Ready?" she asked. She pulled a dining room chair into the center of the living room and sat down on it.

"Well, can I?" Kris repeated.

"You really want one, too?" Mrs. Powell asked, surprised.

"Want *what*?" Lindy asked, confused.

"Kris says she wants a dummy, too," Mrs. Powell reported.

"No way," Lindy said heatedly. "Why do you want to be such a copycat?"

"It looks like fun," Kris replied, her cheeks turning bright pink. "If you can do it, I can do it, too," she added shrilly.

"You always copy everything I do," Lindy protested angrily. "Why don't you find something of your own for once? Go upstairs and work on your junk jewelry collection. That's *your* hobby. Let *me* be the ventriloquist."

"Girls" — Mr. Powell started, raising a hand for quiet — "please, don't fight over a dummy."

"I really think I'd be better at it," Kris said. "I mean, Lindy isn't very funny."

"Everyone thinks I'm funny," Lindy insisted.

"That's not very nice, Kris," Mrs. Powell scolded.

"Well, I just think if Lindy has one, I should be able to have one, too," Kris said to her parents.

"Copycat," Lindy repeated, shaking her head. "You've been putting me down all week. You said it was nerdy. But I know why you changed your mind. You're upset because I'm going to earn some money and you're not."

"I really wish you two wouldn't argue about *everything*," Mr. Powell said disgustedly.

"Well, can I have a dummy?" Kris asked him.

"They're expensive," Mr. Powell replied, glancing at his wife. "A good one will cost more than a hundred dollars. I really don't think we can afford to buy one now."

"Why don't you both share Slappy?" Mrs. Powell suggested.

"Huh?" Lindy's mouth dropped open in protest.

"You two always share everything," Mrs. Powell continued. "So why don't you share Slappy?"

"But, Mom — " Lindy whined unhappily.

"Excellent idea," Mr. Powell interrupted. He motioned to Kris. "Try it out. After you share him for a while, I'm sure one of you will lose interest in him. Maybe even both of you."

Kris climbed to her feet and walked over to Lindy. She reached out for the dummy. "I don't mind sharing," she said quietly, searching her sister's eyes for approval of the idea. "Can I hold him for just a second?"

Lindy held onto Slappy tightly.

Suddenly the dummy's head tilted back and his mouth opened wide. *"Beat it, Kris!"* he snarled in a harsh raspy voice. *"Get lost, you stupid moron!"*

Before Kris could back away, Slappy's wooden hand shot up, and he slapped her hard across the face.

# 4

"Ow!"

Kris screamed and raised her hand to her cheek, which was bright pink. She stepped back. "Stop it, Lindy! That *hurt!*"

"Me?" Lindy cried. "I didn't do it! Slappy did!"

"Don't be dumb," Kris protested, rubbing her cheek. "You really hurt me."

"But I didn't do it!" Lindy cried. She turned Slappy's face toward her. "Why were you so rude to Kris?"

Mr. Powell jumped up from the couch. "Stop acting dumb and apologize to your sister," he ordered.

Lindy bowed Slappy's head. "I'm sorry," she made the dummy say.

"No. In your own voice," Mr. Powell insisted, crossing his arms in front of his chest. "Slappy didn't hurt Kris. You did."

"Okay, okay," Lindy muttered, blushing. She avoided Kris's angry stare. "I'm sorry. Here." She dumped Slappy into Kris's arms.

Kris was so surprised, she nearly dropped the dummy. Slappy was heavier than she'd imagined.

"Now what am I supposed to do with him?" Kris asked Lindy.

Lindy shrugged and crossed the room to the couch, where she dropped down beside her mother.

"Why'd you make such a fuss?" Mrs. Powell whispered, leaning close to Lindy. "That was so babyish."

Lindy blushed. "Slappy is *mine*! Why can't something be mine for once?"

"Sometimes you girls are so nice to each other, and sometimes . . ." Mrs. Powell's voice trailed off.

Mr. Powell took a seat on the padded arm of the chair across the room.

"How do I make his mouth work?" Kris asked, tilting the dummy upside down to examine its back.

"There's a string in his back, inside the slit in his jacket," Lindy told her grudgingly. "You just pull it."

I don't want Kris to work Slappy, Lindy thought unhappily.

I don't want to share Slappy.

Why can't I have something that just belongs

to me? Why do I have to share everything with her?

Why does Kris always want to copy me?

She gritted her teeth and waited for her anger to fade.


Later that night, Kris sat straight up in bed. She'd had a bad dream.

I was being chased, she remembered, her heart still pounding. Chased by what? By whom?

She couldn't remember.

She glanced around the shadowy room, waiting for her heartbeat to return to normal. The room felt hot and stuffy, even though the window was open and the curtains were fluttering.

Lindy lay sound asleep on her side in the twin bed next to Kris's. She was snoring softly, her lips slightly parted, her long hair falling loose about her face.

Kris glanced at the clock-radio on the bed table between the two twin beds. It was nearly three in the morning.

Even though she was now wide awake, the nightmare wouldn't completely fade away. She still felt uncomfortable, a little frightened, as if she were still being chased by someone or something. The back of her neck felt hot and prickly.

She turned and fluffed up her pillow, propping it higher on the headboard. As she lay back on it, something caught her eye.

Someone sitting in the chair in front of the bedroom window. Someone staring at her.

After a sharp intake of breath, she realized it was Slappy.

Yellow moonlight poured over him, making his staring eyes glow. He was sitting up in the chair, tilted to the right at a slight angle, one arm resting on the slender arm of the chair.

His mouth locked in a wide, mocking grin, his eyes seemed to be staring right at Kris.

Kris stared back, studying the dummy's expression in the eerie yellow moonlight. Then, without thinking, without even realizing what she was doing, she climbed silently out of bed.

Her foot got tangled in the bedsheet and she nearly tripped. Kicking the sheet away, she made her way quickly across the room to the window.

Slappy stared up at her as her shadow fell over him. His grin seemed to grow wider as Kris leaned closer.

A gust of wind made the soft curtains flutter against her face. Kris pushed them away and peered down at the dummy's painted head.

She reached a hand out and rubbed his wooden hair, shining in the moonlight. His head felt warm, warmer than she'd imagined.

Kris quickly jerked her hand away.

*What was that sound?*

Had Slappy snickered? Had he laughed at her? No. Of course not.

Kris realized she was breathing hard.

Why am I so freaked out by this stupid dummy? she thought.

In the bed behind her, Lindy made a gurgling sound and rolled onto her back.

Kris stared hard into Slappy's big eyes, gleaming in the light from the window. She waited for him to blink or to roll his eyes from side to side.

She suddenly felt foolish.

He's just a stupid wooden dummy, she told herself.

She reached out and pushed him over.

The stiff body swung to the side. The hard head made a soft *clonk* as it hit the wooden arm of the chair.

Kris stared down at him, feeling strangely satisfied, as if she'd somehow taught him a lesson.

The curtains rustled against her face again. She pushed them away.

Feeling sleepy, she started back to bed.

She had only gone one step when Slappy reached up and grabbed her wrist.

## 5

"Oh!" As the hand tightened around her wrist, Kris cried out and spun around.

To her surprise, Lindy was crouched beside her. Lindy had a tight grip on Kris's wrist.

Kris jerked her hand from Lindy's grasp.

Moonlight through the window lit up Lindy's devilish grin. "Gotcha again!" she declared.

"You didn't scare me!" Kris insisted. But her voice came out a trembling whisper.

"You jumped a mile!" Lindy exclaimed gleefully. "You really thought the dummy grabbed you."

"Did not!" Kris replied. She hurried to her bed.

"What were you doing up, anyway?" Lindy demanded. "Were you messing with Slappy?"

"No. I . . . uh . . . had a bad dream," Kris told her. "I just went to look out the window."

Lindy snickered. "You should've seen the look on your face."

"I'm going back to sleep. Leave me alone," Kris

snapped. She pulled the covers up to her chin.

Lindy pushed the dummy back to a sitting position. Then she returned to her bed, still chuckling over the scare she'd given her sister.

Kris rearranged her pillows, then glanced across the room to the window. The dummy's face was half covered in shadow now. But the eyes glowed as if he were alive. And they stared into hers as if they were trying to tell her something.

*Why does he have to grin like that?* Kris asked herself, trying to rub away the prickly feeling on the back of her neck.

She pulled up the sheet, settled into the bed, and turned on her side, away from the wide, staring eyes.

But even with her back turned, she could feel them gazing at her. Even with her eyes closed and the covers pulled up to her head, she could picture the shadowy, distorted grin, the unblinking eyes. Staring at her. Staring. Staring.

She drifted into an uncomfortable sleep, drifted into another dark nightmare. Someone was chasing her. Someone very evil was chasing her.

But who?

On Monday afternoon, Lindy and Kris both stayed after school to rehearse for the spring concert. It was nearly five when they arrived home, and they were surprised to see their dad's car in the driveway.

"You're home so early!" Kris exclaimed, finding him in the kitchen helping their mother prepare dinner.

"I'm leaving tomorrow for a sales conference in Portland," Mr. Powell explained, peeling an onion over the sink with a small paring knife. "So I only worked half a day today."

"What's for dinner?" Lindy asked.

"Meat loaf," Mrs. Powell replied, "if your father ever gets the onion peeled."

"There's a trick to not crying when you peel an onion," Mr. Powell said, tears rolling down his cheeks. "Wish I knew it."

"How was chorus rehearsal?" Mrs. Powell asked, kneading a big ball of red ground beef in her hands.

"Boring," Lindy complained, opening the refrigerator and taking out a can of Coke.

"Yeah. We're doing all these Russian and Yugoslavian songs," Kris said. "They're so sad. They're all about sheep or something. We don't really know what they're about. There's no translation."

Mr. Powell rushed to the sink and began splashing cold water on his red, runny eyes. "I can't take this!" he wailed. He tossed the half-peeled onion back to his wife.

"Crybaby," she muttered, shaking her head.

Kris headed up the stairs to drop her backpack in her room. She tossed it onto the desk she shared with Lindy, then turned to go back downstairs.

But something by the window caught her eye.

Spinning around, she gasped.

"Oh, no!" The startled cry escaped her lips.

Kris raised her hands to her cheeks and stared in disbelief.

Slappy was propped up in the chair in front of the window, grinning at her with his usual wide-eyed stare. And seated beside him was another dummy, also grinning at her.

And they were holding hands.

"What's going on here?" Kris cried aloud.

# 6

"Do you like him?"

At first, Kris thought that Slappy had asked the question.

She gaped in stunned disbelief.

"Well? What do you think of him?"

It took Kris a long moment to realize that the voice was coming from behind her. She turned to find her father standing in the doorway, still dabbing at his eyes with a wet dishtowel.

"The — the new dummy?" Kris stammered.

"He's for you," Mr. Powell said, stepping into the room, the wet towel pressed against both eyes.

"Really?" Kris hurried over to the chair and picked the new dummy up to examine him.

"There's a tiny pawnshop on the corner across from my office," Mr. Powell said, lowering the towel. "I was walking past and, believe it or not, this guy was in the window. He was cheap, too. I think the pawnbroker was glad to get rid of him."

30

"He's . . . cute," Kris said, searching for the right word. "He looks just like Lindy's dummy, except his hair is bright red, not brown."

"Probably made by the same company," Mr. Powell said.

"His clothes are better than Slappy's," Kris said, holding the dummy out at arm's length to get a good view. "I hate that stupid gray suit on Lindy's dummy."

The new dummy wore blue denim jeans and a red-and-green flannel shirt. And instead of the formal-looking, shiny brown shoes, he had white high-top sneakers on his feet.

"So you like him?" Mr. Powell asked, smiling.

"I *love* him!" Kris cried happily. She crossed the room and gave her dad a hug.

Then she picked up the dummy and ran out of the room, down the stairs, and into the kitchen. "Hey, everybody! Meet Mr. Wood!" she declared happily, holding the grinning dummy up in front of her.

Barky yapped excitedly, leaping up to nip at the dummy's sneakers. Kris pulled her dummy away.

"Hey!" Lindy cried in surprise. "Where'd you get that?"

"From Daddy," Kris said, her grin wider than the dummy's. "I'm going to start practicing with him after dinner, and I'm going to be a better ventriloquist than you."

"Kris!" Mrs. Powell scolded. "Everything isn't a competition, you know!"

"I already have a job with Slappy," Lindy said with a superior sneer. "And you're just getting started. You're just a beginner."

"Mr. Wood is much better-looking than Slappy," Kris said, mirroring her twin's sneer. "Mr. Wood is cool-looking. That gray suit on your dummy is the pits."

"You think that ratty old shirt is cool-looking?" Lindy scoffed, making a disgusted face. "Yuck. That old dummy probably has worms!"

"*You* have worms!" Kris exclaimed.

"Your dummy won't be funny," Lindy said nastily, "because you don't have a sense of humor."

"Oh, yeah?" Kris replied, tossing Mr. Wood over her shoulder. "I *must* have a sense of humor. I put up with *you*, don't I?"

"Copycat! Copycat!" Lindy cried angrily.

"Out of the kitchen!" Mrs. Powell ordered with an impatient shriek. "Out! Get out! You two are impossible! The dummies have better personalities than either of you!"

"Thanks, Mom," Kris said sarcastically.

"Call me for dinner," Lindy called back. "I'm going upstairs to practice my act with Slappy for the birthday party on Saturday."

It was the next afternoon, and Kris was sitting at the dressing table she shared with Lindy. Kris rummaged in the jewelry box and pulled out another string of brightly colored beads. She slipped them over her head and untangled them from the other three strands of beads she was wearing. Then she gazed at herself in the mirror, shaking her head to better see the long, dangly earrings.

I love my junk jewelry collection, she thought, digging into the depths of the wooden jewelry box to see what other treasures she could pull out.

Lindy had no interest in the stuff. But Kris could spend hours trying on the beads, fingering the dozens of little charms, running her fingers over the plastic bracelets, jangling the earrings. Her jewelry collection always cheered her up.

She shook her head again, making the long earrings jangle. A knock on the bedroom door made her spin around.

"Hey, Kris, how's it going?" Her friend Cody Matthews stepped into the room. He had straight, white-blond hair, and pale gray eyes in a slender, serious face. Cody always looked as if he were deep in thought.

"You ride your bike over?" Kris asked, removing several strands of beads at once and tossing them into the jewelry box.

"No. Walked," Cody replied. "Why'd you call? You just want to hang out?"

"No." Kris jumped to her feet. She walked over to the chair by the window and grabbed up Mr. Wood. "I want to practice my act."

Cody groaned. "I'm the guinea pig?"

"No. The audience. Come on."

She led him out to the bent old maple tree in the middle of her back yard. The afternoon sun was just beginning to lower itself in the clear, spring-blue sky.

She raised one foot against the tree trunk and propped Mr. Wood on her knee. Cody sprawled on his back in the shade. "Tell me if this is funny," she instructed.

"Okay. Shoot," Cody replied, narrowing his eyes in concentration.

Kris turned Mr. Wood to face her. "How are you today?" she asked him.

"Pretty good. Knock wood," she made the dummy say.

She waited for Cody to laugh, but he didn't. "Was that funny?" she asked.

"Kinda," he replied without enthusiasm. "Keep going."

"Okay." Kris lowered her head so that she was face-to-face with her dummy. "Mr. Wood," she said, "why were you standing in front of the mirror with your eyes closed?"

"Well," answered the dummy in a high-pitched, squeaky voice, "I wanted to see what I look like when I'm asleep!"

Kris tilted the dummy's head back and made him look as if he were laughing. "How about that joke?" she asked Cody.

Cody shrugged. "Better, I guess."

"Aw, you're no help!" Kris screamed angrily. She lowered her arms, and Mr. Wood crumpled onto her lap. "You're supposed to tell me if it's funny or not."

"I guess *not*," Cody said thoughtfully.

Kris groaned. "I need some good joke books," she said. "That's all. Some good joke books with some really funny jokes. Then I'd be ready to perform. Because I'm a pretty good ventriloquist, right?"

"I guess," Cody replied, pulling up a handful of grass and letting the moist, green blades sift through his fingers.

"Well, I don't move my lips very much, *do* I?" Kris demanded.

"Not too much," Cody allowed. "But you don't really throw your voice."

"No one can throw her voice," Kris told him. "It's just an illusion. You make people *think* you're throwing your voice. You don't *really* throw it."

"Oh," Cody said, pulling up another handful of grass.

Kris tried out several more jokes. "What do you think?" she asked Cody.

"I think I have to go home," Cody said. He tossed a handful of grass at her.

Kris brushed the green blades off Mr. Wood's wooden head. She rubbed her hand gently over the dummy's painted red hair. "You're hurting

35

Mr. Wood's feelings," she told Cody.

Cody climbed to his feet. "Why do you want to mess with that thing, anyway?" he asked, pushing his white-blond hair back off his forehead.

"Because it's fun," Kris replied.

"Is that the real reason?" Cody demanded.

"Well . . . I guess I want to show Lindy that I'm better at it than she is."

"You two are *weird!*" Cody declared. "See you in school." He gave her a little wave, then turned and headed for his home down the block.

Kris pulled down the blankets and climbed into bed. Pale moonlight filtered in through the bedroom window.

Yawning, she glanced at the clock-radio. Nearly ten. She could hear Lindy brushing her teeth in the bathroom across the hall.

Why does Lindy always hum when she brushes her teeth? Kris wondered. How can one twin sister do so many annoying things?

She gave Mr. Wood one last glance. He was propped in the chair in front of the window, his hands carefully placed in his lap, his white sneakers hanging over the chair edge.

He looks like a real person, Kris thought sleepily.

Tomorrow I'm going to check out some good joke books from the library at school. I can be funnier than Lindy. I *know* I can.

She settled back sleepily on her pillow. I'll be asleep as soon as we turn off the lights, she thought.

A few seconds later, Lindy entered the room, wearing her nightshirt and carrying Slappy under one arm. "You asleep?" she asked Kris.

"Almost," Kris replied, yawning loudly. "I've been studying for the math final all night. Where've you been?"

"Over at Alice's," Lindy told her, setting Slappy down in the chair beside Mr. Wood. "Some kids were over, and I practiced my act for them. They laughed so hard, I thought they'd split a gut. When Slappy and I did our rap routine, Alice spit her chocolate milk out her nose. What a riot!"

"That's nice," Kris said without enthusiasm. "Guess you and Slappy are ready for Amy's birthday party on Saturday."

"Yeah," Lindy replied. She placed Slappy's arm around Mr. Wood's shoulder. "They look so cute together," she said. Then she noticed the clothing neatly draped over the desk chair. "What's that?" she asked Kris.

Kris raised her head from the pillow to see what her sister was pointing at. "My outfit for tomorrow," she told her. "We're having a dress-up party in Miss Finch's class. It's a farewell party. For Margot. You know. The student teacher."

Lindy stared at the clothes. "Your Betsey Johnson skirt? Your silk blouse?"

37

"We're supposed to get really dressed up," Kris said, yawning. "Can we go to sleep now?"

"Yeah. Sure." Lindy made her way to her bed, sat down, and clicked off the bed-table lamp. "Are you getting any better with Mr. Wood?" she asked, climbing between the sheets.

Kris was stung by the question. It was such an obvious put-down. "Yeah. I'm getting really good. I did some stuff for Cody. Out in the back yard. Cody laughed so hard, he couldn't breathe. Really. He was holding his sides. He said Mr. Wood and I should be on TV."

"Really?" Lindy replied after a long moment's hesitation. "That's weird. I never thought Cody had much of a sense of humor. He's always so grim. I don't think I've ever seen him laugh."

"Well, he was laughing at Mr. Wood and me," Kris insisted, wishing she were a better liar.

"Awesome," Lindy muttered. "I can't wait to see your act."

Neither can I, Kris thought glumly.

A few seconds later, they were both asleep.

Their mother's voice, calling from downstairs, awoke them at seven the next morning. Bright, morning-orange sunlight poured in through the window. Kris could hear birds chirping happily in the old maple tree.

"Rise and shine! Rise and shine!" Every morning, Mrs. Powell shouted up the same words.

Kris rubbed the sleep from her eyes, then stretched her arms high over her head. She glanced across the room, then uttered a quiet gasp. "Hey — what's going on?" She reached across to Lindy's bed and shook Lindy by the shoulder. "What's going on?"

"Huh?" Lindy, startled, sat straight up.

"What's the joke? Where is he?" Kris demanded.

"Huh?"

Kris pointed to the chair across the room.

Sitting straight up in the chair, Slappy grinned back at them, bathed in morning sunlight.

But Mr. Wood was gone.

# 7

Kris blinked several times and pushed herself up in bed with both hands. Her left hand tingled. She must have been sleeping on it, she realized.

"What? What's wrong?" Lindy asked, her voice fogged with sleep.

"Where's Mr. Wood?" Kris demanded impatiently. "Where'd you put him?"

"Huh? Put him?" Lindy struggled to focus her eyes. She saw Slappy sitting stiffly on the chair across the room. By himself.

"It's not funny," Kris snapped. She climbed out of bed, pulled down the hem of her nightshirt, and made her way quickly to the chair in front of the window. "Don't you ever get tired of playing stupid jokes?"

"Jokes? Huh?" Lindy lowered her feet to the floor.

Kris bent down to search the floor under the chair. Then she moved to the foot of the bed and

40

got down on her knees to search under both twin beds.

"Where *is* he, Lindy?" she asked angrily, on her knees at the foot of the bed. "I don't think this is funny. I really don't."

"Well, neither do I," Lindy insisted, standing up and stretching.

Kris climbed to her feet. Her eyes went wide as she spotted the missing dummy.

"Oh!"

Lindy followed her sister's startled gaze.

Mr. Wood grinned at them from the doorway. He appeared to be standing, his skinny legs bent at an awkward angle.

He was wearing Kris's dress-up clothes, the Betsey Johnson skirt and the silk blouse.

Her mouth wide open in surprise, Kris made her way quickly to the doorway. She immediately saw that the dummy wasn't really standing on his own. He had been propped up, the doorknob shoved into the opening in his back.

She grabbed the dummy by the waist and pulled him away from the door. "My blouse. It's all wrinkled," she cried, holding it so Lindy could see. She narrowed her eyes angrily at her sister. "This was so obnoxious of you, Lindy."

"Me?" Lindy shrieked. "I swear, Kris, I didn't do it. I slept like a rock last night. I didn't move. I didn't get up till you woke me. I didn't do it. Really!"

Kris stared hard at her sister, then lowered her eyes to the dummy.

In her blouse and skirt, Mr. Wood grinned up at her, as if enjoying her bewilderment.

"Well, Mr. Wood," Kris said aloud, "I guess you put on my clothes and walked to the door all by yourself!"

Lindy started to say something. But their mother's voice from downstairs interrupted. "Are you girls going to school today? Where *are* you? You're late!"

"Coming!" Kris called down, casting an angry glance at Lindy. She carefully set Mr. Wood down on his back on her bed and pulled her skirt and blouse off him. She looked up to see Lindy making a mad dash across the hall to be first in the bathroom.

Sighing, Kris stared down at Mr. Wood. The dummy grinned up at her, a mischievous grin.

"Well? What's going on?" she asked the dummy. "I didn't dress you up and move you. And Lindy swears *she* didn't do it."

*But if we didn't do it*, she thought, *who did?*

# 8

"Tilt his head forward," Lindy instructed. "That's it. If you bounce him up and down a little, it'll make it look like he's laughing."

Kris obediently bounced Mr. Wood on her lap, making him laugh.

"Don't move his mouth so much," Lindy told her.

"I think you're both crazy," Lindy's friend Alice said.

"So what else is new?" Cody joked.

All four of them were sitting in a small patch of shade under the bent old maple tree in the Powells' back yard. It was a hot Saturday afternoon, the sun high in a pale blue sky, streaks of yellow light filtering down through the shifting leaves above their heads.

Barky sniffed busily around the yard, his little tail wagging nonstop.

Kris sat on a folding chair, which leaned back

43

against the gnarled tree trunk. She had Mr. Wood on her lap.

Lindy and Alice stood at the edge of the shade, their hands crossed over their chests, watching Kris's performance with frowns of concentration on their faces.

Alice was a tall, skinny girl, with straight black hair down to her shoulders, a snub nose, and a pretty, heart-shaped mouth. She was wearing white shorts and a bright blue midriff top.

Cody was sprawled on his back in the grass, his hands behind his head, a long blade of grass between his teeth.

Kris was trying to show off her ventriloquist skills. But Lindy kept interrupting with "helpful" suggestions. When she wasn't making suggestions, Lindy was nervously glancing at her watch. She didn't want to be late for her job at Amy's birthday party at two o'clock.

"I think you're way weird," Alice told Lindy.

"Hey, no way," Lindy replied. "Slappy is a lot of fun. And I'm going to make a lot of money with him. And maybe I'll be a comedy star or something when I'm older." She glanced at her watch again.

"Well, everyone at school thinks that both of you are weird," Alice said, swatting a fly off her bare arm.

"Who cares?" Lindy replied sharply. "They're all weird, too."

"And so are you," Kris made Mr. Wood say.

"I could see your lips move," Lindy told Kris.

Kris rolled her eyes. "Give me a break. You've been giving me a hard time all morning."

"Just trying to help," Lindy said. "You don't have to be so defensive, do you?"

Kris uttered an angry growl.

"Was that your stomach?" she made Mr. Wood say.

Cody laughed.

"At least *one* person thinks you're funny," Lindy said dryly. "But if you want to do parties, you really should get some better jokes."

Kris let the dummy slump to her lap. "I can't find any good joke books," she said dejectedly. "Where do you find your jokes?"

A superior sneer formed on Lindy's face. She tossed her long hair behind her shoulder. "I make up my own jokes," she replied snootily.

"You *are* a joke!" Cody said.

"Ha-ha. Remind me to laugh later," Lindy said sarcastically.

"I can't believe you don't have *your* dummy out here," Alice told Lindy. "I mean, don't you want to rehearse for the party?"

"No need," Lindy replied. "I've got my act down. I don't want to over-rehearse."

Kris groaned loudly.

"Some of the other parents are staying at the birthday party to watch Slappy and me," Lindy continued, ignoring Kris's sarcasm. "If the kids like me, their parents might hire me for *their* parties."

"Maybe you and Kris should do an act together," Alice suggested. "That could be really awesome."

"Yeah. What an act! Then there'd be *four* dummies!" Cody joked.

Alice was the only one to laugh.

Lindy made a face at Cody. "That might actually be fun," she said thoughtfully. And then she added, "When Kris is ready."

Kris drew in her breath and prepared to make an angry reply.

But before she could say anything, Lindy grabbed Mr. Wood from her hands. "Let me give you a few pointers," Lindy said, putting one foot on Kris's folding chair and arranging Mr. Wood on her lap. "You have to hold him up straighter, like this."

"Hey — give him back," Kris demanded, reaching for her dummy.

As she reached up, Mr. Wood suddenly lowered his head until he was staring down at her. *"You're a jerk!"* he rasped in Kris's face, speaking in a low, throaty growl.

"Huh?" Kris pulled back in surprise.

*"You're a stupid jerk!"* Mr. Wood repeated nastily in the same harsh growl.

"Lindy — stop it!" Kris cried.

46

Cody and Alice both stared in openmouthed surprise.

"*Stupid moron! Get lost! Get lost, stupid jerk!*" the dummy rasped in Kris's face.

"Whoa!" Cody exclaimed.

"Make him stop!" Kris screamed at her sister.

"I can't!" Lindy cried in a trembling voice. Her face became pale, her eyes wide with fear. "I can't make him stop, Kris! He — he's speaking for himself!"

The dummy glared at Kris, its grin ugly and evil.

"I — I can't make him stop. I'm not doing it," Lindy cried. Tugging with all her might, she pulled Mr. Wood out of Kris's face.

Cody and Alice flashed each other bewildered glances.

Frightened, Kris raised herself from the folding chair and backed up against the tree trunk. "He — he's talking on his own?" She stared hard at the grinning dummy.

"I — I think so. I'm . . . all mixed up!" Lindy declared, her cheeks bright pink.

Barky yipped and jumped on Lindy's legs, trying to get her attention. But she kept her gaze on Kris's frightened face.

"This is a joke — right?" Cody asked hopefully.

"What's going on?" Alice demanded, her arms crossed in front of her chest.

Ignoring them, Lindy handed Mr. Wood back

to Kris. "Here. Take him. He's yours. Maybe *you* can control him."

"But, Lindy — " Kris started to protest.

Lindy glared at her watch. "Oh, no! The party! I'm late!" Shaking her head, she took off toward the house. "Later!" she called without looking back.

"But Lindy — " Kris called.

The kitchen door slammed behind Lindy.

Holding Mr. Wood by the shoulders, Kris lowered her eyes to his face. He grinned up at her, a devilish grin, his eyes staring intently into hers.

Kris swung easily, leaning back and raising her feet into the air. The chains squeaked with every swing. The old back yard swingset, half covered with rust, hadn't been used much in recent years.

The early evening sun was lowering itself behind the house. The aroma of a roasting chicken floated out from the kitchen window. Kris could hear her mother busy in the kitchen preparing dinner.

Barky yapped beneath her. Kris dropped her feet to the ground and stopped the swing to avoid kicking him. "Dumb dog. Don't you know you could get hurt?"

She looked up to see Lindy come running up the driveway, holding Slappy under her arm. From the smile on Lindy's face, Kris knew at once that the birthday party had been a triumph. But she had to ask anyway. "How'd it go?"

"It was awesome!" Lindy exclaimed. "Slappy and I were *great!*"

Kris pulled herself off the swing and forced a smile to her face. "That's nice," she offered.

"The kids thought we were a riot!" Lindy continued. She pulled Slappy up. "Didn't they, Slappy?"

"They liked me. Hated you!" Slappy declared in Lindy's high-pitched voice.

Kris forced a laugh. "I'm glad it went okay," she said, trying hard to be a good sport.

"I did a sing-along with Slappy, and it went over really well. Then Slappy and I did our rap routine. What a hit!" Lindy gushed.

She's spreading it on a little thick, Kris thought bitterly. Kris couldn't help feeling jealous.

"The kids all lined up to talk to Slappy," Lindy continued. "Didn't they, Slappy?"

"Everyone loved me," she made the dummy say. "Where's my share of the loot?"

"So you got paid twenty dollars?" Kris asked, kicking at a clump of weeds.

"Twenty-five," Lindy replied. "Amy's mom said I was so good, she'd pay me extra. Oh. And guess what else? You know Mrs. Evans? The woman who always wears the leopardskin pants? You know — Anna's mom? She asked me to do Anna's

50

party next Sunday. She's going to pay me *thirty* dollars! I'm going to be rich!"

"Wow. Thirty dollars," Kris muttered, shaking her head.

"I get twenty. You get ten," Lindy made Slappy say.

"I have to go tell Mom the good news!" Lindy said. "What have you been doing all afternoon?"

"Well, after you left, I was pretty upset," Kris replied, following Lindy to the house. "You know. About Mr. Wood. I — I put him upstairs. Alice and Cody went home. Then Mom and I went to the mall."

His tail wagging furiously, Barky ran right over their feet, nearly tripping both of them. "Barky, look out!" Lindy yelled.

"Oh. I nearly forgot," Kris said, stopping on the back stoop. "Something good happened."

Lindy stopped, too. "Something good?"

"Yeah. I ran into Mrs. Berman at the mall." Mrs. Berman was their music teacher and organizer of the spring concert.

"Thrills," Lindy replied sarcastically.

"And Mrs. Berman asked if Mr. Wood and I wanted to be master of ceremonies for the spring concert." Kris smiled at her sister.

Lindy swallowed hard. "She asked *you* to host the concert?"

"Yeah. I get to perform with Mr. Wood in front

51

of everyone!" Kris gushed happily. She saw a flash of jealousy on Lindy's face, which made her even happier.

Lindy pulled open the screen door. "Well, good luck," she said dryly. "With that weird dummy of yours, you'll *need* it."

Dinner was spent talking about Lindy's performance at Amy Marshall's birthday party. Lindy and Mrs. Powell chatted excitedly. Kris ate in silence.

"At first I thought the whole thing was strange, I have to admit," Mrs. Powell said, scooping ice cream into bowls for dessert. "I just couldn't believe you'd be interested in ventriloquism, Lindy. But I guess you have a flair for it. I guess you have some talent."

Lindy beamed. Mrs. Powell normally wasn't big on compliments.

"I found a book in the school library about ventriloquism," Lindy said. "It had some pretty good tips in it. It even had a comedy routine to perform." She glanced at Kris. "But I like making up my own jokes better."

"You should watch your sister's act," Mrs. Powell told Kris, handing her a bowl of ice cream. "I mean, you could probably pick up some pointers for the concert at school."

"Maybe," Kris replied, trying to hide how annoyed she was.

After dinner, Mr. Powell called from Portland, and they all talked with him. Lindy told him about her success with Slappy at the birthday party. Kris told him about being asked to host the concert with Mr. Wood. Her father promised he wouldn't schedule any road trips so that he could attend the concert.

After watching a video their mother had rented at the mall, the two sisters went up to their room. It was a little after eleven.

Kris clicked on the light. Lindy followed her in.

They both glanced across the room to the chair where they kept the two dummies — and gasped.

"Oh, no!" Lindy cried, raising one hand to her wide open mouth.

Earlier that night, the dummies had been placed side by side in a sitting position.

But now Slappy was upside down, falling out of the chair, his head on the floor. His brown shoes had been pulled off his feet and tossed against the wall. His suit jacket had been pulled halfway down his arms, trapping his hands behind his back.

"L-look!" Kris stammered, although her sister was already staring in horror at the scene. "Mr. Wood — he's . . ." Kris's voice caught in her throat.

Mr. Wood was sprawled on top of Slappy. His hands were wrapped around Slappy's throat, as if he were strangling him.

# 10

"I — I don't believe this!" Kris managed to whisper. She turned and caught the frightened expression on Lindy's face.

"What's going *on?*" Lindy cried.

Both sisters hurried across the room. Kris grabbed Mr. Wood by the back of the neck and pulled him off the other dummy. She felt as if she were separating two fighting boys.

She held Mr. Wood up in front of her, examining him carefully, staring at his face as if half-expecting him to talk to her.

Then she lowered the dummy and tossed it facedown onto her bed. Her face was pale and taut with fear.

Lindy stooped and picked up Slappy's brown shoes from the floor. She held them up and studied them, as if they would offer a clue as to what had happened.

"Kris — did you do this?" Lindy asked softly.

"Huh? Me?" Kris reacted with surprise.

"I mean, I *know* you're jealous of Slappy and me — " Lindy started.

"Whoa. Wait a minute," Kris replied angrily in a shrill, trembling voice. "I didn't do this, Lindy. Don't accuse me."

Lindy glared at her sister, studying her face. Then her expression softened and she sighed. "I don't get. I just don't get it. Look at Slappy. He's nearly been torn apart."

She set the shoes down on the chair and picked the dummy up gently as if picking up a baby. Holding him in one hand, she struggled to pull his suit jacket up with the other.

Kris heard her sister mutter something. It sounded like "Your dummy is evil."

"What did you say?" Kris demanded.

"Nothing," Lindy replied, still struggling with the jacket. "I'm . . . uh . . . I'm kind of scared about this," Lindy confessed, blushing, avoiding Kris's eyes.

"Me, too," Kris admitted. "Something weird is going on. I think we should tell Mom."

Lindy buttoned the jacket. Then she sat down on the bed with Slappy on her lap and started to replace the dummy's shoes. "Yeah. I guess we should," she replied. "It — it's just so creepy."

Their mother was in bed, reading a Stephen King novel. Her bedroom was dark except for a tiny reading lamp on her headboard that threw down a narrow triangle of yellow light.

Mrs. Powell uttered a short cry as her two daughters appeared out of the shadows. "Oh. You startled me. This is such a scary book, and I think I was just about to fall asleep."

"Can we talk to you?" Kris asked eagerly in a low whisper.

"Something weird is going on," Lindy added.

Mrs. Powell yawned and closed her book. "What's wrong?"

"It's about Mr. Wood," Kris said. "He's been doing a lot of strange things."

"Huh?" Mrs. Powell's eyes opened wide. She looked pale and tired under the harsh light from the reading lamp.

"He was strangling Slappy," Lindy reported. "And this afternoon, he said some really gross things. And — "

"Stop!" Mrs. Powell ordered, raising one hand. "Just stop."

"But, Mom — " Kris started.

"Give me a break, girls," their mother said wearily. "I'm tired of your silly competitions."

"You don't understand," Lindy interrupted.

"Yes, I *do* understand," Mrs. Powell said sharply. "You two are even competing with those ventriloquist dummies."

"Mom, please!"

"I want it to stop right now," Mrs. Powell

56

insisted, tossing the book onto her bed table. "I mean it. I don't want to hear another word from either of you about those dummies. If you two have problems, settle it between yourselves."

"Mom, listen — "

"And if you can't settle it, I'll take the dummies away. Both of them. I'm serious." Mrs. Powell reached above her head and clicked off the reading light, throwing the room into darkness. "Good night," she said.

The girls had no choice but to leave the room. They slunk down the hall in silence.

Kris hesitated at the doorway to their bedroom. She expected to find Mr. Wood strangling Slappy again. She breathed a sigh of relief when she saw the two dummies on the bed where they had been left.

"Mom wasn't too helpful," Lindy said dryly, rolling her eyes. She picked up Slappy and started to arrange him in the chair in front of the window.

"I think she was asleep and we woke her up," Kris replied.

She picked up Mr. Wood and started toward the chair with him — then stopped. "You know what? I think I'm going to put him in the closet tonight," she said thoughtfully.

"Good idea," Lindy said, climbing into bed.

Kris glanced down at the dummy, half-expecting him to react. To complain. To start calling her names.

But Mr. Wood grinned up at her, his painted eyes dull and lifeless.

Kris felt a chill of fear.

I'm becoming afraid of a stupid ventriloquist's dummy, she thought.

I'm shutting him up in the closet tonight because I'm afraid.

She carried Mr. Wood to the closet. Then, with a groan, she raised him high above her head and slid him onto the top shelf. Carefully closing the closet door, listening for the click, she made her way to her bed.

She slept fitfully, tossing on top of the covers, her sleep filled with disturbing dreams. She awoke to find her nightshirt completely twisted, cutting off the circulation to her right arm. She struggled to straighten it, then fell back to sleep.

She awoke early, drenched in sweat. The sky was still dawn-gray outside the window.

The room felt hot and stuffy. She sat up slowly, feeling weary, as if she hadn't slept at all.

Blinking away the sleep, her eyes focused on the chair in front of the window.

There sat Slappy, exactly where Lindy had placed him.

And beside him sat Mr. Wood, his arm around Slappy's shoulder, grinning triumphantly at Kris as if he had just pulled off a wonderful joke.

# 11

"Now, Mr. Wood, do you go to school?"

"Of course I do. Do you think I'm a dummy?"

"And what's your favorite class?"

"Wood shop, of course!"

"What project are you building in shop class, Mr. Wood?"

"I'm building a *girl* dummy! What else? Ha-ha! Think I want to spend the rest of my life on *your* lap?!"

Kris sat in front of the dressing table mirror with Mr. Wood on her lap, studying herself as she practiced her routine for the school concert.

Mr. Wood had been well-behaved for two days. No frightening, mysterious incidents. Kris was beginning to feel better. Maybe everything would go okay from now on.

She leaned close to the mirror, watching her lips as she made the dummy talk.

The b's and the m's were impossible to pronounce without moving her lips. She'd just have to avoid those sounds as best she could.

I'm getting better at switching from Mr. Wood's voice back to mine, she thought happily. But I've got to switch faster. The faster he and I talk, the funnier it is.

"Let's try it again, Mr. Wood," she said, pulling her chair closer to the mirror.

"Work, work, work," she made the dummy grumble.

Before she could begin the routine, Lindy came rushing breathlessly into the room. Kris watched her sister in the mirror as she came up behind her, her long hair flying loosely over her shoulders, an excited smile on her face.

"Guess what?" Lindy asked.

Kris started to reply, but Lindy didn't give her a chance.

"Mrs. Petrie was at Amy Marshall's birthday party," Lindy gushed excitedly. "She works for Channel Three. You know. The TV station. And she thinks I'm good enough to go on *Talent Search*, the show they have every week."

"Huh? Really?" was all Kris could manage in reply.

Lindy leapt excitedly in the air and cheered. "Slappy and I are going to be on TV!" she cried. "Isn't that *fabulous*?"

Staring at her sister's jubilant reflection in the mirror, Kris felt a stab of jealousy.

"I've got to tell Mom!" Lindy declared. "Hey,

61

Mom! Mom!" She ran from the room. Kris heard her shouting all the way down the stairs.

"Aaaaaargh!" Kris couldn't hold it in. She uttered an angry cry.

"Why does everything good happen to Lindy?" Kris screamed aloud. "I'm hosting a stupid concert for maybe a hundred parents — and she's going to be on TV! I'm just as good as she is. Maybe better!"

In a rage, she raised Mr. Wood high over her head and slammed him to the floor.

The dummy's head made a loud *clonk* as it hit the hardwood floor. The wide mouth flew open as if about to scream.

"Oh." Kris struggled to regain her composure.

Mr. Wood, crumpled at her feet, stared up at her accusingly.

Kris lifted him up and cradled the dummy against her. "There, there, Mr. Wood," she whispered soothingly. "Did I hurt you? Did I? I'm so sorry. I didn't mean to."

The dummy continued to stare up at her. His painted grin hadn't changed, but his eyes seemed cold and unforgiving.

It was a still night. No breeze. The curtains in front of the open bedroom window didn't flutter or move. Pale silver moonlight filtered in, creating long, purple shadows that appeared to creep across the girls' bedroom.

Lindy had been sleeping fitfully, a light sleep filled with busy, colorful dreams. She was startled awake by a sound. A gentle *thud*.

"Huh?" she raised her head from the damp pillow and turned.

Someone was moving in the darkness.

The sounds she'd heard were footsteps.

"Hey!" she whispered, wide awake now. "Who is it?"

The figure turned in the doorway, a shadow against even blacker shadows. "It's only me," came a whispered reply.

"Kris?"

"Yeah. Something woke me up. My throat is sore," Kris whispered from the doorway. "I'm going down to the kitchen for a glass of water."

She disappeared into the shadows. Her head still raised off the pillow, Lindy listened to her footsteps padding down the stairs.

When the sounds faded, Lindy shut her eyes and lowered her head to the pillow.

A few seconds later, she heard Kris's scream of horror.

# 12

Her heart pounding, Lindy struggled out of bed. The sheet tangled around her legs, and she nearly fell.

Kris's bloodcurdling scream echoed in her ears.

She practically leapt down the dark stairway, her bare feet thudding hard on the thin carpet of the steps.

It was dark downstairs, except for a thin sliver of yellow light from the kitchen.

"Kris — Kris — are you okay?" Lindy called, her voice sounding small and frightened in the dark hallway.

"Kris?"

Lindy stopped at the kitchen doorway.

What was that eerie light?

It took her a while to focus. Then she realized she was staring at the dim yellow light from inside the refrigerator.

The refrigerator door was wide open.

And . . . the refrigerator was empty.

"What — what's going on here?"

She took a step into the kitchen. Then another. Something cold and wet surrounded her foot.

Lindy gasped and, looking down, saw that she had stepped into a wide puddle.

An overturned milk carton beside her foot revealed that the puddle was spilled milk.

She raised her eyes to Kris, who was standing in darkness across the room, her back against the wall, her hands raised to her face in horror.

"Kris, what on earth — "

The scene was coming into focus now. It was all so weird, so . . . *wrong*. It was taking Lindy a long time to see the whole picture.

But, now, following Kris's horrified stare, Lindy saw the mess on the floor. And realized why the refrigerator was empty.

Everything inside it had been pulled out and dumped on the kitchen floor. An orange juice bottle lay on its side in a puddle of orange juice. Eggs were scattered everywhere. Fruits and vegetables were strewn over the floor.

"Ohh!" Lindy moaned in utter disbelief.

Everything seemed to sparkle and gleam.

What was all that shiny stuff among the food? Kris's jewelry!

There were earrings and bracelets and strands of beads tossed everywhere, mixed with the spilled, strewn food like some kind of bizarre salad.

"Oh, no!' Lindy shrieked as her eyes came to rest on the figure on the floor.

Sitting upright in the middle of the mess was Mr. Wood, grinning gleefully at her. He had several strands of beads around his neck, long, dangling earrings hanging from his ears, and a platter of leftover chicken on his lap.

# 13

"Kris, are you *okay?*" Lindy cried, turning her eyes away from the grinning, jewelry-covered dummy.

Kris didn't seem to hear her.

"Are you okay?" Lindy repeated the question.

"Wh-what's going on?" Kris stammered, her back pressed against the wall, her expression taut with terror. "Who — who *did* this? Did Mr. Wood — ?"

Lindy started to reply. But their mother's howl of surprise from the doorway cut off her words. "Mom — " Lindy cried, spinning around.

Mrs. Powell clicked on the ceiling light. The kitchen seemed to flare up. All three of them blinked, struggling to adjust to the sudden brightness.

"What on earth!" Mrs. Powell cried. She started

to call to her husband, then remembered he wasn't home. "I — I don't believe this!"

Barky came bounding into the room, his tail wagging. He lowered his head and started to lick up some spilled milk.

"Out you go," Mrs. Powell said sternly. She picked up the dog, carried him out, and closed the kitchen door. Then she strode into the center of the room, shaking her head, her bare feet narrowly missing the puddle of milk.

"I came down for a drink, and I — I found this mess," Kris said in a trembling voice. "The food. My jewelry. Everything . . ."

"Mr. Wood did it," Lindy accused. "Look at him!"

"*Stop it! Stop it!*" Mrs. Powell screamed. "I've had enough."

Mrs. Powell surveyed the mess, frowning and tugging at a strand of blonde hair. Her eyes stopped on Mr. Wood, and she uttered a groan of disgust.

"I knew it," she said in a low voice, raising her eyes accusingly to the two girls. "I knew this had something to do with those ventriloquist dummies."

"Mr. Wood did it, Mom," Kris said heatedly, stepping away from the wall, her hands tensed into fists. "I know it sounds dumb, but — "

"Stop it," Mrs. Powell ordered, narrowing her

eyes. "This is just sick. Sick!" She stared hard at the jewel-bedecked dummy, who grinned up at her over the big platter of chicken.

"I'm going to take the dummies away from you both," Mrs. Powell said, turning back to Lindy and Kris. "This whole thing has just gotten out of control."

"No!" Kris cried.

"That's not fair!" Lindy declared.

"I'm sorry. They have to be put away," Mrs. Powell said firmly. She let her eyes move over the cluttered floor, and let out another weary sigh. "Look at my kitchen."

"But I didn't do anything!" Lindy screamed.

"I need Mr. Wood for the spring concert!" Kris protested. "Everyone is counting on me, Mom."

Mrs. Powell glanced from one to the other. Her eyes stayed on Kris. "That's *your* dummy on the floor, right?"

"Yeah," Kris told her. "But I didn't do this. I swear!"

"You both swear you didn't do it, right?" Mrs. Powell said, suddenly looking very tired under the harsh ceiling light.

"Yes," Lindy answered quickly.

"Then you both lose your dummies. I'm sorry," Mrs. Powell said. "One of you is lying. I — I really can't believe this."

A heavy silence blanketed the room as all three Powells stared down in dismay at the mess on the floor.

Kris was the first to speak. "Mom, what if Lindy and I clean everything up?"

Lindy caught on quickly. Her face brightened. "Yeah. What if we put everything back. Right now. Make the kitchen just like normal. Make it spotless. Can we keep our dummies?"

Mrs. Powell shook her head. "No. I don't think so. Look at this mess. All the vegetables are spoiled. And the milk."

"We'll replace it all," Kris said quickly. "With our allowance. And we'll clean it up perfectly. Please. If we do that, give us one more chance?"

Mrs. Powell twisted her face in concentration, debating with herself. She stared at her daughters' eager faces. "Okay," she replied finally. "I want the kitchen spotless when I come down in the morning. All the food, all the jewelry. Everything back where it goes."

"Okay," both girls said in unison.

"And I don't want to see either of those dummies down here in my kitchen again," Mrs. Powell demanded. "If you can do that, I'll give you one more chance."

"Great!" both girls cried at once.

"And I don't want to hear any more arguments

about those dummies," Mrs. Powell continued. "No more fights. No more competing. No more blaming everything on the dummies. I don't want to hear *anything* about them. Ever."

"You won't," Kris promised, glancing at her sister.

"Thanks, Mom," Lindy said. "You go to bed. We'll clean up." She gave her mother a gentle shove toward the doorway.

"Not another word," Mrs. Powell reminded them.

"Right, Mom," the twins agreed.

Their mother disappeared toward her room. They began to clean up. Kris pulled a large garbage bag from the drawer and held it while Lindy tossed in empty cartons and spoiled food.

Kris carefully collected her jewelry and carried it upstairs.

Neither girl spoke. They worked in silence, picking up, cleaning, and mopping until the kitchen was clean. Lindy closed the refrigerator door. She yawned loudly.

Kris inspected the floor on her hands and knees, making sure it was spotless. Then she picked up Mr. Wood. He grinned back at her as if it was all a big joke.

This dummy has been nothing but trouble, Kris thought.

Nothing but trouble.

She followed Lindy out of the kitchen, clicking off the light as she left. The two girls climbed the stairs silently. Neither of them had spoken a word.

Pale moonlight filtered into their room through the open window. The air felt hot and steamy.

Kris glanced at the clock. It was a little past three in the morning.

Slappy sat slumped in the chair in front of the window, moonlight shining on his grinning face. Lindy, yawning, climbed into bed, pushed down the blanket, and pulled up the sheet. She turned her face away from her sister.

Kris lowered Mr. Wood from her shoulder. *You're nothing but trouble*, she thought angrily, holding him in front of her and staring at his grinning face.

Nothing but trouble.

Mr. Wood's wide, leering grin seemed to mock her.

A chill of fear mixed with her anger.

I'm beginning to hate this dummy, she thought.

Fear him and hate him.

Angrily, she pulled open the closet door and tossed the dummy into the closet. It fell in a crumpled heap on the closet floor.

Kris slammed the closet door shut.

Her heart thudding, she climbed into bed and pulled up the covers. She suddenly felt very tired. Her entire body ached from weariness.

She buried her face in the pillow and shut her eyes.

She had just about fallen asleep when she heard the tiny voice.

"Let me out! Let me out of here!" it cried. A muffled voice, coming from inside the closet.

# 14

"Let me out! Let me out!" the high-pitched voice called angrily.

Kris sat up with a jolt. Her entire body convulsed in a shudder of fear.

Her eyes darted to the other bed. Lindy hadn't moved.

"Did — did you hear it?" Kris stammered.

"Hear what?" Lindy asked sleepily.

"The voice," Kris whispered. "In the closet."

"Huh?" Lindy asked sleepily. "What are you talking about? It's three in the morning. Can't we get some sleep?"

"But, Lindy — " Kris lowered her feet to the floor. Her heart was thudding in her chest. "Wake up. Listen to me! Mr. Wood was calling to me. He was *talking*!"

Lindy raised her head and listened.

Silence.

"I don't hear anything, Kris. Really. Maybe you were dreaming."

"No!" Kris shrieked, feeling herself lose control. "It wasn't a dream! I'm so scared, Lindy. I'm just so *scared!*"

Suddenly Kris was trembling all over, and hot tears were pouring down her cheeks.

Lindy stood up and moved to the edge of her sister's bed.

"Something h-horrible is going on here, Lindy," Kris stammered through her tears.

"And I know who's doing it," Lindy whispered, leaning over her twin, putting a comforting hand on her quivering shoulder.

"Huh?"

"Yes. I know who's been doing it all," Lindy whispered. "I know who it is."

"Who?" Kris asked breathlessly.

"Who?" Kris repeated, letting the tears run down her cheeks. "Who?"

"*I* have," Lindy said. Her smile spread into a grin almost as wide as Slappy's. She closed her eyes and laughed.

"Huh?" Kris didn't understand. "What did you say?"

"I said I have been doing it," Lindy repeated. "Me. Lindy. It was all a joke, Kris. I gotcha again." She nodded her head as if confirming her words.

Kris gaped at her twin in disbelief. "It was all a joke?"

Lindy kept nodding.

"You moved Mr. Wood during the night? You dressed him in my clothes and made him say those gross things to me? You put him in the kitchen? You made that horrible mess?"

Lindy chuckled. "Yeah. I really scared you, didn't I?"

Kris balled her hands into angry fists. "But —
but — " she sputtered. *"Why?"*

"For fun," Lindy replied, dropping back onto
her bed, still grinning.

"Fun?"

"I wanted to see if I could scare you,"
Lindy explained. "It was just a joke. You know.
I can't *believe* you fell for that voice in the
closet just now! I must be a really good ventriloquist!"

"But, Lindy — "

"You really believed Mr. Wood was alive or
something!" Lindy said, laughing, enjoying her
victory. "You're such a nit!"

"Nit?"

"Half a nitwit!" Lindy burst into wild laughter.

"It isn't funny," Kris said softly.

"I know," Lindy replied. "It's a riot! You
should've seen the look on your face when you saw
Mr. Wood downstairs in your precious beads and
earrings!"

"How — how did you ever *think* of such a mean
joke?" Kris demanded.

"It just came to me," Lindy answered with some
pride. "When you got your dummy."

"You didn't want me to get a dummy," Kris said
thoughtfully.

"You're right," Lindy quickly agreed. "I wanted
something that would be mine, for a change. I'm
so tired of you being a copycat. So — "

"So you thought of this mean joke," Kris accused.

Lindy nodded.

Kris strode angrily to the window and pressed her forehead against the glass. "I — I can't believe I was so stupid," she muttered.

"Neither can I," Lindy agreed, grinning again.

"You really made me start thinking that Mr. Wood was alive or something," Kris said, staring out the window to the back yard below. "You really made me afraid of him."

"Aren't I brilliant!" Lindy proclaimed.

Kris turned to face her sister. "I'm never speaking to you again," she said angrily.

Lindy shrugged. "It was just a joke."

"No," Kris insisted. "It was too mean to be just a joke. I'm never speaking to you again. Never."

"Fine," Lindy replied curtly. "I thought you had a sense of humor. Fine." She slid into bed, her back to Kris, and pulled the covers up over her head.

*I've got to find a way to pay her back for this,* Kris thought. *But how?*

# 16

After school a few days later, Kris walked home with Cody. It was a hot, humid afternoon. The trees were still, and seemed to throw little shade on the sidewalk. The air above the pavement shimmered in the heat.

"Wish we had a swimming pool," Kris muttered, pulling her backpack off her shoulder.

"I wish you had one, too," Cody said, wiping his forehead with the sleeve of his red T-shirt.

"I'd like to dive into an enormous pool of iced tea," Kris said, "like in the TV commercials. It always looks so cold and refreshing."

Cody made a face. "Swim in iced tea? With ice cubes and lemon?"

"Forget it," Kris muttered.

They crossed the street. A couple of kids they knew rode by on bikes. Two men in white uniforms were up on ladders, leaning against the corner house, painting the gutters.

"Bet they're hot," Cody remarked.

"Let's change the subject," Kris suggested.

"How are you doing with Mr. Wood?" Cody asked.

"Not bad," Kris said. "I think I've got some pretty good jokes. I should be ready for the concert tomorrow night."

They stopped at the corner and let a large blue van rumble past.

"Are you talking to your sister?" Cody asked as they crossed the street. The bright sunlight made his white-blond hair glow.

"A little," Kris said, making a face. "I'm talking to her. But I haven't forgiven her."

"That was such a dumb stunt she pulled," Cody said sympathetically. He wiped the sweat off his forehead with the sleeve of his T-shirt.

"It just made me feel like such a dork," Kris admitted. "I mean, I was so stupid. She really had me believing that Mr. Wood was doing all that stuff." Kris shook her head. Thinking about it made her feel embarrassed all over again.

Her house came into view. She unzipped the back compartment of her backpack and searched for the keys.

"Did you tell your mom about Lindy's practical joke?" Cody asked.

Kris shook her head. "Mom is totally disgusted. We're not allowed to mention the dummies to her. Dad got home from Portland last night, and Mom told him what was going on. So we're not allowed

80

to mention the dummies to him, either!" She found the keys and started up the drive. "Thanks for walking home with me."

"Yeah. Sure." Cody gave her a little wave and continued on toward his house up the street.

Kris pushed the key into the front door lock. She could hear Barky jumping and yipping excitedly on the other side of the door. "I'm coming, Barky," she called in. "Hold your horses."

She pushed open the door. Barky began leaping on her, whimpering as if she'd been away for months. "Okay, okay!" she cried laughing.

It took several minutes to calm the dog down. Then Kris got a snack from the kitchen and headed up to her room to practice with Mr. Wood.

She hoisted the dummy up from the chair where it had spent the day beside Lindy's dummy. A can of Coke in one hand, the dummy over her shoulder, she headed to the dressing table and sat down in front of the mirror.

This was the best time of day to rehearse, Kris thought. No one was home. Her parents were at work. Lindy was at some after-school activity.

She arranged Mr. Wood on her lap. "Time to go to work," she made him say, reaching into his back to move his lips. She made his eyes slide back and forth.

A button on his plaid shirt had come unbuttoned. Kris leaned him down against the dressing table and started to fasten it.

Something caught her eye. Something yellow inside the pocket.

"Weird," Kris said aloud. "I never noticed anything in there."

Slipping two fingers into the slender pocket, she pulled out a yellowed sheet of paper, folded up.

Probably just the receipt for him, Kris thought.

She unfolded the sheet of paper and held it up to read it.

It wasn't a receipt. The paper contained a single sentence handwritten very cleanly in bold black ink. It was in a language Kris didn't recognize.

"Did someone send you a love note, Mr. Wood?" she asked the dummy.

It stared up at her lifelessly.

Kris lowered her eyes to the paper and read the strange sentence out loud:

"Karru marri odonna loma molonu karrano."

What language is *that*? Kris wondered.

She glanced down at the dummy and uttered a low cry of surprise.

Mr. Wood appeared to blink.

But that wasn't possible — *was* it?

Kris took a deep breath, then let it out slowly.

The dummy stared up at her, his painted eyes as dull and wide open as ever.

Let's not get paranoid, Kris scolded herself.

"Time to work, Mr. Wood," she told him. She folded up the piece of yellow paper and slipped it back into his shirt pocket. Then she raised him to

82

a sitting position, searching for the eye and mouth controls with her hand.

"How are things around *your* house, Mr. Wood?"

"Not good, Kris. I've got termites. I need termites like I need another hole in my head! Haha!"

"Lindy! Kris! Could you come downstairs, please!" Mr. Powell called from the foot of the stairs.

It was after dinner, and the twins were up in their room. Lindy was sprawled on her stomach on the bed, reading a book for school. Kris was in front of the dressing table mirror, rehearsing quietly with Mr. Wood for tomorrow night's concert.

"What do you want, Dad?" Lindy shouted down, rolling her eyes.

"We're kind of busy," Kris shouted, shifting the dummy on her lap.

"The Millers are here, and they're dying to see your ventriloquist acts," their father shouted up.

Lindy and Kris both groaned. The Millers were the elderly couple who lived next door. They were very nice people, but very boring.

The twins heard Mr. Powell's footsteps on the stairs. A few seconds later, he poked his head into their room. "Come on, girls. Just put on a short show for the Millers. They came over for coffee, and we told them about your dummies."

"But I have to rehearse for tomorrow night," Kris insisted.

"Rehearse on them," her father suggested. "Come on. Just do five minutes. They'll get a real kick out of it."

Sighing loudly, the girls agreed. Carrying their dummies over their shoulders, they followed their father down to the living room.

Mr. and Mrs. Miller were side by side on the couch, coffee mugs in front of them on the low coffee table. They smiled and called out cheerful greetings as the girls appeared.

Kris was always struck by how much the Millers looked alike. They both had slender, pink faces topped with spongy white hair. They both wore silver-framed bifocals, which slipped down on nearly identical, pointy noses. They both had the same smile. Mr. Miller had a small, gray mustache. Lindy always joked that he grew it so the Millers could tell each other apart.

Is *that* what happens to you when you've been married a long time? Kris found herself thinking. You start to look exactly alike?

The Millers were even dressed alike, in loose-fitting tan Bermuda shorts and white cotton sports shirts.

"Lindy and Kris took up ventriloquism a few weeks ago," Mrs. Powell was explaining, twisting herself forward to see the girls from the armchair. She motioned them to the center of the room. "And they both seem to have some talent for it."

"Have you girls ever heard of Bergen and McCarthy?" Mrs. Miller asked, smiling.

"Who?" Lindy and Kris asked in unison.

"Before your time," Mr. Miller said, chuckling. "They were a ventriloquist act."

"Can you do something for us?" Mrs. Miller asked, picking up her coffee mug and setting it in her lap.

Mr. Powell pulled a dining room chair into the center of the room. "Here. Lindy, why don't you go first?" He turned to the Millers. "They're very good. You'll see," he said.

Lindy sat down and arranged Slappy on her lap. The Millers applauded. Mrs. Miller nearly spilled her coffee, but she caught the mug just in time.

"Don't applaud — just throw money!" Lindy made Slappy say. Everyone laughed as if they'd never heard that before.

Kris watched from the stairway as Lindy did a short routine. Lindy was really good, she had to admit. Very smooth. The Millers were laughing so hard, their faces were bright red. An identical shade of red. Mrs. Miller kept squeezing her husband's knee when she laughed.

Lindy finished to big applause. The Millers gushed about how wonderful she was. Lindy told them about the TV show she might be on, and they promised they wouldn't miss it. "We'll tape it," Mr. Miller said.

Kris took her place on the chair and sat Mr. Wood up in her lap. "This is Mr. Wood," she told the Millers. "We're going to be the hosts of the spring concert at school tomorrow night. So I'll give you a preview of what we're going to say."

"That's a nice-looking dummy," Mrs. Miller said quietly.

*"You're a nice-looking dummy, too!"* Mr. Wood declared in a harsh, raspy growl of a voice.

Kris's mother gasped. The Millers' smiles faded.

Mr. Wood leaned forward on Kris's lap and stared at Mr. Miller. *"Is that a mustache, or are you eating a rat?"* he asked nastily.

Mr. Miller glanced uncomfortably at his wife, then forced a laugh. They both laughed.

*"Don't laugh so hard. You might drop your false teeth!"* Mr. Wood shouted. *"And how do you get your teeth that disgusting shade of yellow? Does your bad breath do that?"*

"Kris!" Mrs. Powell shouted. "That's enough!"

The Millers' faces were bright red now, their expressions bewildered.

"That's not funny. Apologize to the Millers," Mr. Powell insisted, crossing the room and standing over Kris.

"I — I didn't say any of it!" Kris stammered. "Really, I — "

"Kris — apologize!" her father demanded angrily.

Mr. Wood turned to the Millers. *"I'm sorry,"* he rasped. *"I'm sorry you're so ugly! I'm sorry you're so old and stupid, too!"*

The Millers stared at each other unhappily. "I don't get her humor," Mrs. Miller said.

"It's just crude insults," Mr. Miller replied quietly.

"Kris — what is *wrong* with you!" Mrs. Powell demanded. She had crossed the room to stand beside her husband. "Apologize to the Millers right now! I don't *believe* you!"

"I — I — " Gripping Mr. Wood tightly around the waist, Kris rose to her feet. "I — I — " She tried to utter an apology, but no words would come out.

"Sorry!" she finally managed to scream. Then, with an embarrassed cry, she turned and fled up the stairs, tears streaming down her face.

# 17

"You *have* to believe me!" Kris cried in a trembling voice. "I really didn't say any of those things. Mr. Wood was talking by himself!"

Lindy rolled her eyes. "Tell me another one," she muttered sarcastically.

Lindy had followed Kris upstairs. Down in the living room, her parents were still apologizing to the Millers. Now, Kris sat on the edge of her bed, wiping tears off her cheeks. Lindy stood with her arms crossed in front of the dressing table.

"I don't make insulting jokes like that," Kris said, glancing at Mr. Wood, who lay crumpled in the center of the floor where Kris had tossed him. "You know that isn't my sense of humor."

"So why'd you do it?" Lindy demanded. "Why'd you want to make everyone mad?"

"But I *didn't!*" Kris shrieked, tugging at the sides of her hair. "Mr. Wood said those things! I didn't!"

"How can you be such a copycat?" Lindy asked

disgustedly. "I already *did* that joke, Kris. Can't you think of something original?"

"It's not a joke," Kris insisted. "Why don't you believe me?"

"No way," Lindy replied, shaking her head, her arms still crossed in front of her chest. "No way I'm going to fall for the same gag."

"Lindy, please!" Kris pleaded. "I'm frightened. I'm really frightened."

"Yeah. Sure," Lindy said sarcastically. "I'm shaking all over, too. Wow. You really fooled me, Kris. Guess you showed me you can play funny tricks, too."

"Shut up!" Kris snapped. More tears formed in the corners of her eyes.

"Very good crying," Lindy said. "But it doesn't fool me, either. And it won't fool Mom and Dad." She turned and picked up Slappy. "Maybe Slappy and I should practice some jokes. After your performance tonight, Mom and Dad might not let you do the concert tomorrow night."

She slung Slappy over her shoulder and, stepping over the crumpled form of Mr. Wood, hurried from the room.

It was hot and noisy backstage in the auditorium. Kris's throat was dry, and she kept walking over to the water fountain and slurping mouthfuls of the warm water.

The voices of the audience on the other side of

the curtain seemed to echo off all four walls and the ceiling. The louder the noise became as the auditorium filled, the more nervous Kris felt.

How am I ever going to do my act in front of all those people? she asked herself, pulling the edge of the curtain back a few inches and peering out. Her parents were off to the side, in the third row.

Seeing them brought memories of the night before flooding back to Kris. Her parents had grounded her for two weeks as punishment for insulting the Millers. They almost hadn't let her come to the concert.

Kris stared at the kids and adults filing into the large auditorium, recognizing a lot of faces. She realized her hands were ice cold. Her throat was dry again.

Don't think of it as an audience, she told herself. Think of it as a bunch of kids and parents, most of whom you know.

Somehow that made it worse.

She let go of the curtain, hurried to get one last drink from the fountain, then retrieved Mr. Wood from the table she had left him on.

It suddenly grew quiet on the other side of the curtain. The concert was about to begin.

"Break a leg!" Lindy called across to her as she hurried to join the other chorus members.

"Thanks," Kris replied weakly. She pulled up

Mr. Wood and straightened his shirt. "Your hands are clammy!" she made him say.

"No insults tonight," Kris told him sternly.

To her shock, the dummy blinked.

"Hey!" she cried. She hadn't touched his eye controls.

She had a stab of fear that went beyond stage fright. Maybe I shouldn't go on with this, she thought, staring intently at Mr. Wood, watching for him to blink again.

Maybe I should say I'm sick and not perform with him.

"Are you nervous?" a voice whispered.

"Huh?" At first, she thought it was Mr. Wood. But then she quickly realized that it was Mrs. Berman, the music teacher.

"Yeah. A little," Kris admitted, feeling her face grow hot.

"You'll be terrific," Mrs. Berman gushed, squeezing Kris's shoulder with a sweaty hand. She was a large, heavyset woman with several chins, a red lipsticked mouth, and flowing black hair. She was wearing a long, loose-fitting dress of red-and-blue flower patterns. "Here goes," she said, giving Kris's shoulder one more squeeze.

Then she stepped onstage, blinking against the harsh white light of the spotlight, to introduce Kris and Mr. Wood.

Am I really doing this? Kris asked herself.

*Can* I do this?

Her heart was pounding so hard, she couldn't hear Mrs. Berman's introduction. Then, suddenly, the audience was applauding, and Kris found herself walking across the stage to the microphone, carrying Mr. Wood in both hands.

Mrs. Berman, her flowery dress flowing around her, was heading offstage. She smiled at Kris and gave her an encouraging wink as they passed each other.

Squinting against the bright spotlight, Kris walked to the middle of the stage. Her mouth felt as dry as cotton. She wondered if she could make a sound.

A folding chair had been set up for her. She sat down, arranging Mr. Wood on her lap, then realized that the microphone was much too high.

This drew titters of soft laughter from the audience.

Embarrassed, Kris stood up and, holding Mr. Wood under one arm, struggled to lower the microphone.

"Are you having trouble?" Mrs. Berman called from the side of the stage. She hurried over to help Kris.

But before the music teacher got halfway across the stage, Mr. Wood leaned into the microphone. *"What time does the blimp go up?"* he rasped nastily, staring at Mrs. Berman's dress.

"What?" She stopped in surprise.

*"Your face reminds me of a wart I had removed!"* Mr. Wood growled at the startled woman.

Her mouth dropped open in horror. "Kris!"

*"If we count your chins, will it tell us your age?"*

There was laughter floating up from the audience. But it was mixed with gasps of horror.

"Kris — that's enough!" Mrs. Berman cried, the microphone picking up her angry protest.

*"You're more than enough! You're enough for two!"* Mr. Wood declared nastily. *"If you got any bigger, you'd need your own zip code!"*

"Kris — really! I'm going to ask you to apologize," Mrs. Berman said, her face bright red.

"Mrs. Berman, I — I'm not doing it!" Kris stammered. "I'm not saying these things!"

"Please apologize. To me and to the audience," Mrs. Berman demanded.

Mr. Wood leaned into the microphone. *"Apologize for THIS!"* he screamed.

The dummy's head tilted back. His jaw dropped. His mouth opened wide.

And a thick green liquid came spewing out.

"Yuck!" someone screamed.

It looked like pea soup. It spurted up out of Mr. Wood's open mouth like water rushing from a fire hose.

Voices screamed and cried out their surprise as the thick, green liquid showered over the people in the front rows.

"Stop it!"

"Help!"

"Somebody — turn it off!"

"It stinks!"

Kris froze in horror, staring as more and more of the disgusting substance poured from her dummy's gaping mouth.

A putrid stench — the smell of sour milk, of rotten eggs, of burning rubber, of decayed meat — rose up from the liquid. It puddled over the stage and showered over the front seats.

Blinded by the spotlight, Kris couldn't see the audience in front of her. But she could hear the choking and the gagging, the frantic cries for help.

"Clear the auditorium! Clear the auditorium!" Mrs. Berman was shouting.

Kris heard the rumble and scrape of people shoving their way up the aisles and out the doors.

"It stinks!"

"I'm sick!"

"Somebody — help!"

Kris tried to clamp her hand over the dummy's mouth. But the force of the putrid green liquid frothing and spewing out was too strong. It pushed her hand away.

Suddenly she realized she was being shoved from behind. Off the stage. Away from the shouting people fleeing the auditorium. Out of the glaring spotlight.

She was backstage before she realized that it was Mrs. Berman who was pushing her.

"I — I don't know how you did that. Or why!" Mrs. Berman shouted angrily, frantically wiping splotches of the disgusting green liquid off the front of her dress with both hands. "But I'm going to see that you're suspended from school, Kris! And if I have my way," she sputtered, "you'll be suspended for *life!*"

# 18

"That's right. Close the door," Mr. Powell said sternly, glaring with narrowed eyes at Kris.

He stood a few inches behind her, arms crossed in front of him, making sure she followed his instructions. She had carefully folded Mr. Wood in half and shoved him to the back of her closet shelf. Now she closed the closet, making sure it was completely shut, as he ordered.

Lindy watched silently from her bed, her expression troubled.

"Does the closet door lock?" Mr. Powell asked.

"No. Not really," Kris told him, lowering her head.

"Well, that will have to do," he said. "On Monday, I'm taking him back to the pawn shop. Do not take him out until then."

"But, Dad — "

He raised a hand to silence her.

"We have to talk about this," Kris pleaded. "You have to listen to me. What happened tonight — it wasn't a practical joke. I — "

Her father turned away from her, a scowl on his face. "Kris, I'm sorry. We'll talk tomorrow. Your mother and I — we're both too angry and too upset to talk now."

"But, Dad — "

Ignoring her, he stormed out of the room. She listened to his footsteps, hard and hurried, down the stairs. Then Kris slowly turned to Lindy. "Now do you believe me?"

"I — I don't know what to believe," Lindy replied. "It was just so . . . unbelievably gross."

"Lindy, I — I — "

"Daddy's right. Let's talk tomorrow," Lindy said. "I'm sure everything will be clearer and calmer tomorrow."

But Kris couldn't sleep. She shifted from side to side, uncomfortable, wide awake. She pulled the pillow over her face, held it there for a while, welcoming the soft darkness, then tossed it to the floor.

I'm never going to sleep again, she thought.

Every time she closed her eyes, she saw the hideous scene in the auditorium once again. She heard the astonished cries of the audience, the kids and their parents. And she heard the cries of shock turn to groans of disgust as the putrid gunk poured out over everyone.

Sickening. So totally sickening.

And everyone blamed her.

My life is ruined, Kris thought. I can never go back there again. I can never go to school. I can never show my face *anywhere.*

Ruined. My whole life. Ruined by that stupid dummy.

In the next bed, Lindy snored softly, in a slow, steady rhythm.

Kris turned her eyes to the bedroom window. The curtains hung down over the window, filtering the pale moonlight from outside. Slappy sat in his usual place in the chair in front of the window, bent in two, his head between his knees.

Stupid dummies, Kris thought bitterly. So stupid.

And now my life is ruined.

She glanced at the clock. One-twenty. Outside the window, she heard a low, rumbling sound. A soft whistle of brakes. Probably a large truck going by.

Kris yawned. She closed her eyes and saw the gross green gunk spewing out of Mr. Wood's mouth.

Will I see that every time I close my eyes? she wondered.

What on earth *was* it? How could everyone blame *me* for something so . . . so . . .

The rumbling of the truck faded into the distance.

But then Kris heard another sound. A rustling sound.

A soft footstep.

Someone was moving.

She sucked in her breath and held it, listening hard.

Silence now. Silence so heavy, she could hear the loud thudding of her heart.

Then another soft footstep.

A shadow moved.

The closet door swung open.

Or was it just shadows shifting?

No. Someone was moving. Moving from the open closet. Someone was creeping toward the bedroom door. Creeping so softly, so silently.

Her heart pounding, Kris pulled herself up, trying not to make a sound. Realizing that she'd been holding her breath, she let it out slowly, silently. She took another breath, then sat up.

The shadow moved slowly to the door.

Kris lowered her feet to the floor, staring hard into the darkness, her eyes staying with the silent, moving figure.

*What's happening?* she wondered.

The shadow moved again. She heard a scraping sound, the sound of a sleeve brushing the doorframe.

Kris pushed herself to her feet. Her legs felt shaky as she crept to the door, following the moving shadow.

Out into the hallway. Even darker out here because there were no windows.

Toward the stairway.

The shadow moved more quickly now.

Kris followed, her bare feet moving lightly over the thin carpet.

*What's happening? What's happening?*

She caught up to the shadowy figure on the landing. "Hey!" she called, her voice a tight whisper.

She grabbed the shoulder and turned the figure around.

And stared into the grinning face of Mr. Wood.

# 19

Mr. Wood blinked, then hissed at her, an ugly sound, a menacing sound. In the darkness of the stairwell, his painted grin became a threatening leer.

In her fright, Kris squeezed the dummy's shoulder, wrapping her fingers around the harsh fabric of his shirt.

"This — this is impossible!" she whispered.

He blinked again. He giggled. His mouth opened, making his grin grow wider.

He tried to tug out of Kris's grasp, but she hung on without even realizing she was holding him.

"But — you're a *dummy*!" she squealed.

He giggled again. "So are you," he replied. His voice was a deep growl, like the angry snarl of a large dog.

"You can't walk!" Kris cried, her voice trembling.

The dummy giggled its ugly giggle again.

"You can't be alive!" Kris exclaimed.

"Let go of me — *now!*" the dummy growled.

Kris held on, tightening her grip. "I'm dreaming," Kris told herself aloud. "I have to be dreaming."

"I'm not a dream. I'm a nightmare!" the dummy exclaimed, and tossed back his wooden head, laughing.

Still gripping the shoulder of the shirt, Kris stared through the darkness at the grinning face. The air seemed to grow heavy and hot. She felt as if she couldn't breathe, as if she were suffocating.

What was that sound?

It took her a while to recognize the strained gasps of her own breathing.

"Let go of me," the dummy repeated. "Or I'll throw you down the stairs." He tried once again to tug out of her grasp.

"No!" Kris insisted, holding tight. "I — I'm putting you back in the closet."

The dummy laughed, then pushed his painted face close to Kris's face. "You can't keep me there."

"I'm locking you in. I'm locking you in a box. In *something!*" Kris declared, panic clouding her thoughts.

The darkness seemed to descend over her, choking her, weighing her down.

"Let go of me." The dummy pulled hard.

102

Kris reached out her other hand and grabbed him around the waist.

"Let go of me," he snarled in his raspy, deep rumble of a voice. "I'm in charge now. You will listen to me. This is *my* house now."

He pulled hard.

Kris encircled his waist.

They both fell onto the stairs, rolling down a few steps.

"Let go!" the dummy ordered. He rolled on top of her, his wild eyes glaring into hers.

She pushed him off, tried to pin his arms behind his back.

He was surprisingly strong. He pulled back one arm, then shoved a fist hard into the pit of her stomach.

"Ohhh." Kris groaned, feeling the breath knocked out of her.

The dummy took advantage of her momentary weakness, and pulled free. Grasping the banister with one hand, he tried to pull himself past her and down the stairs.

But Kris shot out a foot and tripped him.

Still struggling to breathe, she pounced onto his back. Then she pulled him away from the banister and pushed him down hard onto a step.

"Oh!" Kris gasped loudly as the overhead hall light flashed on. She closed her eyes against the sudden harsh intrusion. The dummy struggled to pull out from under her, but she pushed down on his back with all her weight.

"Kris — what on earth — ?!" Lindy's startled voice called down from the top step.

"It's Mr. Wood!" Kris managed to cry up to her. "He's . . . *alive!*" She pushed down hard, sprawled over the dummy, keeping him pinned beneath her.

"Kris — what are you doing?" Lindy demanded. "Are you okay?"

"No!" Kris exclaimed. "I'm not okay! Please — Lindy! Go get Mom and Dad! Mr. Wood — he's alive!"

"It's just a dummy!" Lindy called down, taking a few reluctant steps toward her sister. "Get up, Kris! Have you lost your mind?"

"*Listen to me!*" Kris shrieked at the top of her lungs. "Get Mom and Dad! Before he escapes!"

But Lindy didn't move. She stared down at her sister, her long hair falling in tangles about her face, her features twisted in horror. "Get up, Kris," she urged. "Please — get up. Let's go back to bed."

"I'm *telling* you, he's *alive!*" Kris cried desperately. "You've got to believe me, Lindy. You've *got* to!"

The dummy lay lifelessly beneath her, his face buried in the carpet, his arms and legs sprawled out to the sides.

"You had a nightmare," Lindy insisted, climbing down step by step, holding her long nightshirt up above her ankles until she was standing right above Kris. "Come back to bed, Kris. It was just a nightmare. The horrible thing that happened at the concert — it gave you a nightmare, that's all."

Gasping for breath, Kris lifted herself up and twisted her head to face her sister. Grabbing the banister with one hand, she raised herself a little.

The instant she lightened up on him, the dummy grabbed the edge of the stair with both hands and pulled himself out from under her. Half-falling, half-crawling, he scrambled down the rest of the stairs.

"No! No! I don't *believe* it!" Lindy shrieked, seeing the dummy move.

"Go get Mom and Dad!" Kris said. "Hurry!"

Her mouth wide open in shocked disbelief, Lindy turned and headed back up the stairs, screaming for her parents.

Kris dived off the step, thrusting her arms in front of her.

She tackled Mr. Wood from behind, wrapping her arms around his waist.

His head hit the carpet hard as they both crumpled to the floor.

He uttered a low, throaty cry of pain. His eyes closed. He didn't move.

Dazed, her chest heaving, her entire body trembling, Kris slowly climbed to her feet. She quickly pressed a foot on the dummy's back to hold him in place.

"Mom and Dad — where *are* you?" she cried aloud. "Hurry."

The dummy raised its head. He let out an angry growl and started to thrash his arms and legs wildly.

Kris pressed her foot hard against his back.

"Let go!" he growled viciously.

Kris heard voices upstairs.

"Mom? Dad? Down here!" she called up to them.

Both of her parents appeared at the upstairs landing, their faces filled with worry.

"Look!" Kris cried, frantically pointing down to the dummy beneath her foot.

# 20

"Look at *what?*" Mr. Powell cried, adjusting his pajama top.

Kris pointed down to the dummy under her foot. "He — he's trying to get away," she stammered.

But Mr. Wood lay lifeless on his stomach.

"Is this supposed to be a joke?" Mrs. Powell demanded angrily, hands at the waist of her cotton nightgown.

"I don't get it," Mr. Powell said, shaking his head.

"Mr. Wood — he ran down the stairs," Kris said frantically. "He's been doing everything. He — "

"This isn't funny," Mrs. Powell said wearily, running a hand back through her blonde hair. "It isn't funny at all, Kris. Waking everyone up in the middle of the night."

"I really think you've lost your mind. I'm very worried about you," Mr. Powell added. "I mean, after what happened at school tonight — "

"Listen to me!" Kris shrieked. She bent down and pulled Mr. Wood up from the floor. Holding him by the shoulders, she shook him hard. "He moves! He runs! He talks! He — he's *alive!*"

She stopped shaking the dummy and let go. He slumped lifelessly to the floor, falling in an unmoving heap at her feet.

"I think maybe you need to see a doctor," Mr. Powell said, his face tightening with concern.

"No. I *saw* him, too!" Lindy said, coming to Kris's aid. "Kris is right. The dummy *did* move." But then she added, "I mean, I *think* it moved!"

You're a big help, Lindy, Kris thought, suddenly feeling weak, drained.

"Is this just another stupid prank?" Mrs. Powell asked angrily. "After what happened at school tonight, I'd think that would be enough."

"But, Mom — " Kris started, staring down at the lifeless heap at her feet.

"Back to bed," Mrs. Powell ordered. "There's no school tomorrow. We'll have plenty of time to discuss punishments for you two."

"*Me?*" Lindy cried, outraged. "What did *I* do?"

"Mom, we're telling the truth!" Kris insisted.

"I still don't get the joke," Mr. Powell said, shaking his head. He turned to his wife. "Were we supposed to believe her or something?"

"Get to bed. Both of you. Now!" their mother snapped. She and their father disappeared from the upstairs landing, heading angrily back down the hall to their room.

Lindy remained, one hand on the top of the banister, staring down regretfully at Kris.

"You believe me, don't you?" Kris called up to her.

"Yeah. I guess," Lindy replied doubtfully, lowering her eyes to the dummy at Kris's feet.

Kris looked down, too. She saw Mr. Wood blink. He started to straighten up.

"Whoa!" She uttered an alarmed cry and grabbed him by the neck. "Lindy — hurry!" she called. "He's moving again!"

"Wh-what should we do?" Lindy stammered, making her way hesitantly down the stairs.

"I don't know," Kris replied as the dummy thrashed his arms and legs against the carpet, trying desperately to free himself from her two-handed grip on his neck. "We've got to — "

"There's *nothing* you can do," Mr. Wood snarled. "You will be my slaves now. I'm alive once again! Alive!"

"But — how?" Kris demanded, staring at him in disbelief. "I mean, you're a dummy. How — ?"

The dummy snickered. "*You* brought me back to life," he told her in his raspy voice. "You read the ancient words."

The ancient words? What was he talking about? And then Kris remembered. She had read the

109

strange-sounding words from the sheet of paper in the dummy's shirt pocket.

"I am back, thanks to you," the dummy growled. "And now you and your sister will serve me."

As she stared in horror at the grinning dummy, an idea popped into Kris's mind.

The paper. She had tucked it back into his pocket.

If I read the words again, Kris thought, it will put him back to sleep.

She reached out and grabbed him. He tried to jerk away, but she was too quick.

The folded sheet of yellow paper was in her hand.

"Give me that!" he cried. He swiped at it, but Kris swung it out of his reach.

She unfolded it quickly. And before the dummy could grab the paper out of her hands, she read the strange words aloud:

"Karru marri odonna loma molonu karrano."

## 21

Both sisters stared at the dummy, waiting for him to collapse.

But he gripped the banister and tossed his head back in an amused, scornful laugh. "Those are the words of the ancient sorcerer to bring me to life!" he proclaimed. "Those aren't the words to kill me!"

*Kill him?*

Yes, Kris thought frantically. She tossed down the yellow paper disgustedly.

We have no choice.

"We have to kill him, Lindy."

"Huh?" Her sister's face filled with surprise.

Kris grabbed the dummy by the shoulders and held on tightly. "I'll hold him. You pull his head off."

Lindy was beside her now. She had to duck away from Mr. Wood's thrashing feet.

"I'll hold him still," Kris repeated. "Grab his head. Pull it off."

"You — you're sure?" Lindy hesitated, her features tight with fear.

*"Just do it!"* Kris screamed.

She let her hands slide down around Mr. Wood's waist.

Lindy grabbed his head in both hands.

*"Let go of me!"* the dummy rasped.

"Pull!" Kris cried to her terrified sister.

Holding the dummy tightly around the waist, she leaned back, pulling him away from her sister.

Lindy's hands were wrapped tightly around the dummy's head. With a loud groan, she pulled hard.

The head didn't come off.

Mr. Wood uttered a high-pitched giggle. "Stop. You're tickling me!" he rasped.

"Pull harder!" Kris ordered her sister.

Lindy's face was bright red. She tightened her grip on the head and pulled again, tugging with all her strength.

The dummy giggled his shrill, unpleasant giggle.

"It — it won't come off," Lindy said, sighing in defeat.

"Twist it off!" Kris suggested frantically.

The dummy thrashed out with his feet, kicking Kris in the stomach. But she held on. "Twist the head off!" she cried.

Lindy tried to turn the head.

The dummy giggled.

"It won't twist!" Lindy cried in frustration. She let go of the head and took a step back.

Mr. Wood raised his head, stared up at Lindy, and grinned. "You can't kill me. I have powers."

"What do we do?" Lindy cried, raising her eyes to Kris.

"This is my house now," the dummy rasped, grinning at Lindy as it struggled to wriggle out of Kris's arms. "You will do as I say now. Put me down."

"What do we *do*?" Lindy repeated.

"Take him upstairs. We'll *cut* his head off," Kris replied.

Mr. Wood swung his head around, his eyes stretched open in an evil glare.

"Ow!" Kris cried out in surprise as the dummy snapped his jaws over her arm, biting her. She pulled her arm away and, without thinking, slapped the dummy's wooden head with the palm of her hand.

The dummy giggled in response. "Violence! Violence!" he said in a mock scolding tone.

"Get those sharp scissors. In your drawer," Kris instructed her sister. "I'll carry him up to our room."

Her arm throbbed where he had bitten her. But she held onto him tightly and carried him up to their bedroom.

113

Lindy had already pulled the long metal scissors from the drawer. Her hand trembled as she opened and closed the blades.

"Below the neck," Kris said, holding Mr. Wood tightly by the shoulders.

He hissed furiously at her. She dodged as he tried to kick her with both sneakered feet.

Holding the scissors with two hands, Lindy tried cutting the head off at the neck. The scissors didn't cut, so she tried a sawing motion.

Mr. Wood giggled. "I told you. You can't kill me."

"It isn't going to work," Lindy cried, tears of frustration running down her cheeks. "Now what?"

"We'll put him in the closet. Then we can think," Kris replied.

"You have no need to think. You are my slaves," the dummy rasped. "You will do whatever I ask. I will be in charge from now on."

"No way," Kris muttered, shaking her head.

"What if we *won't* help you?" Lindy demanded.

The dummy turned to her, casting her a hard, angry stare. "Then I'll start hurting the ones you love," he said casually. "Your parents. Your friends. Or maybe that disgusting dog that's always yapping at me." He tossed back his head and a dry, evil laugh escaped his wooden lips.

"Lock him in the closet," Lindy suggested. "Till we figure out how to get rid of him."

"You *can't* get rid of me," Mr. Wood insisted. "Don't make me angry. I have powers. I'm warning you. I'm starting to get tired of your stupid attempts to harm me."

"The closet doesn't lock — remember?" Kris cried, struggling to hold onto the wriggling dummy.

"Oh. Wait. How about this?" Lindy hurried to the closet. She pulled out an old suitcase from the back.

"Perfect," Kris said.

"I'm warning you — " Mr. Wood threatened. "You are becoming very tiresome."

With a hard tug, he pulled himself free of Kris.

She dove to tackle him, but he darted out from under her. She fell facedown onto her bed.

The dummy ran to the center of the room, then turned his eyes to the doorway, as if trying to decide where to go. "You must do as I tell you," he said darkly, raising a wooden hand toward Lindy. "I will not run from you two. You are to be my slaves."

"No!" Kris cried, pushing herself up.

She and her sister both dove at the dummy. Lindy grabbed his arms. Kris ducked to grab his ankles.

Working together, they stuffed him into the open suitcase.

"You will regret this," he threatened, kicking his legs, struggling to hit them. "You will pay dearly for this. Now someone will die!"

He continued screaming after Kris latched the suitcase and shoved it into the closet. She quickly closed the closet door, then leaned her back against it, sighing wearily.

"Now what?" she asked Lindy.

# 22

"We'll bury him," Kris said.

"Huh?" Lindy stifled a yawn.

They had been whispering together for what seemed like hours. As they tried to come up with a plan, they could hear the dummy's muffled cries from inside the closet.

"We'll bury him. Under that huge mound of dirt," Kris explained, her eyes going to the window. "You know. Next door, at the side of the new house."

"Yeah. Okay. I don't know," Lindy replied. "I'm so tired, I can't think straight." She glanced at the bed table clock. It was nearly three-thirty in the morning. "I still think we should wake up Mom and Dad," Lindy said, fear reflected in her eyes.

"We can't," Kris told her. "We've been over that a hundred times. They won't believe us. If we wake them up, we'll be in even bigger trouble."

"How could we be in *bigger* trouble?" Lindy demanded, gesturing with her head to the closet where Mr. Wood's angry cries could still be heard.

"Get dressed," Kris said with renewed energy. "We'll bury him under all that dirt. Then we'll never have to think about him again."

Lindy shuddered and turned her eyes to her dummy, folded up in the chair. "I can't bear to look at Slappy anymore. I'm so sorry I got us interested in dummies."

"Ssshhh. Just get dressed," Kris said impatiently.

A few minutes later, the two girls crept down the stairs in the darkness. Kris carried the suitcase in both arms, trying to muffle the sound of Mr. Wood's angry protests.

They stopped at the bottom of the stairs and listened for any sign that they had awakened their parents.

Silence.

Lindy pulled open the front door and they slipped outside.

The air was surprisingly cool and wet. A heavy dew had begun to fall, making the front lawn glisten under the light of a half-moon. Blades of wet grass clung to their sneakers as they made their way to the garage.

As Kris held onto the suitcase, Lindy slowly, quietly, pulled open the garage door. When it was halfway up, she ducked and slipped inside.

A few seconds later she emerged, carrying a large snow shovel. "This should do it," she said, whispering even though no one was around.

Kris glanced down the street as they headed across the yard to the lot next door. The heavy morning dew misted the glow of the streetlamps, making the pale light appear to bend and flicker like candles. Everything seemed to shimmer under the dark purple sky.

Kris set the suitcase down beside the tall mound of dirt. "We'll dig right down here," she said, pointing toward the bottom of the mound. "We'll shove him in and cover him."

"I'm warning you," Mr. Wood threatened, listening inside the suitcase. "Your plan won't work. I have powers!"

"You dig first," Kris told her sister, ignoring the dummy's threat. "Then I'll take a turn."

Lindy dug into the pile and heaved up a shovelful of dirt. Kris shivered. The heavy dew felt cold and damp. A cloud floated over the moon, darkening the sky from purple to black.

"Let me out!" Mr. Wood called. "Let me out now, and your punishment won't be too severe."

"Dig faster," Kris whispered impatiently.

"I'm going as fast as I can," Lindy replied. She had dug a pretty good-sized square-shaped hole at the base of the mound. "How much deeper, do you think?"

"Deeper," Kris said. "Here. Watch the suitcase. I'll take a turn." She changed places with Lindy and started to dig.

Something scampered heavily near the low shrubs that separated the yards. Kris looked up, saw a moving shadow, and gasped.

"Raccoon, I think," Lindy said with a shudder. "Are we going to bury Mr. Wood in the suitcase, or are we going to take him out?"

"Think Mom will notice the suitcase is gone?" Kris asked, tossing a shovelful of wet dirt to the side.

Lindy shook her head. "We never use it."

"We'll bury him in the suitcase," Kris said. "It'll be easier."

"You'll be sorry," the dummy rasped. The suitcase shook and nearly toppled onto its side.

"I'm so sleepy," Lindy moaned, tossing her socks onto the floor, then sliding her feet under the covers.

"I'm wide awake," Kris replied, sitting on the edge of her bed. "I guess it's because I'm so happy. So happy we got rid of that awful creature."

"It's all so weird," Lindy said, adjusting her pillow behind her head. "I don't blame Mom or Dad for not believing it. I'm not sure I believe it, either."

"You put the shovel back where you found it?" Kris asked.

Lindy nodded. "Yeah," she said sleepily.

"And you closed the garage door?"

"Ssshhh. I'm asleep," Lindy said. "At least there's no school tomorrow. We can sleep late."

"I hope I can fall asleep," Kris said doubtfully. "I'm just so *pumped*. It's all like some kind of hideously gross nightmare. I just think . . . Lindy? Lindy — are you still awake?"

No. Her sister had fallen asleep.

Kris stared up at the ceiling. She pulled the blankets up to her chin. She still felt chilled. She couldn't shake the cold dampness of the early morning air.

After a short while, with thoughts of everything that had happened that night whirring crazily in her head, Kris fell asleep, too.

The rumble of machines woke her up at eight-thirty the next morning. Stretching, trying to rub the sleep from her eyes, Kris stumbled to the window, leaned over the chair holding Slappy, and peered out.

It was a gray, cloudy day. Two enormous yellow steamrollers were rolling over the lot next door behind the newly constructed house, flattening the land.

I wonder if they're going to flatten that big mound of dirt, Kris thought, staring down at them. That would really be *excellent*.

Kris smiled. She hadn't slept very long, but she felt refreshed.

Lindy was still sound asleep. Kris tiptoed past her, pulled her robe on, and headed downstairs.

"Morning, Mom," she called brightly, tying the belt to her robe as she entered the kitchen.

Mrs. Powell turned from the sink to face her. Kris was surprised to see an angry expression on her face.

She followed her mother's stare to the breakfast counter.

"Oh!" Kris gasped when she saw Mr. Wood. He was seated at the counter, his hands in his lap. His hair was matted with red-brown dirt, and he had dirt smears on his cheeks and forehead.

Kris raised her hands to her face in horror.

"I thought you were told never to bring that thing down here!" Mrs. Powell scolded. "What do I have to do, Kris?" She turned angrily back to the sink.

The dummy winked at Kris and flashed her a wide, evil grin.

## 23

As Kris stared in horror at the grinning dummy, Mr. Powell suddenly appeared in the kitchen doorway. "Ready?" he asked his wife.

Mrs. Powell hung the dishtowel on the rack and turned around, brushing a lock of hair off her forehead. "Ready. I'll get my bag." She brushed past him into the front hallway.

"Where are you going?" Kris cried, her voice revealing her alarm. She kept her eyes on the dummy at the counter.

"Just doing a little shopping at the garden store," her father told her, stepping into the room, peering out the kitchen window. "Looks like rain."

"Don't go!" Kris pleaded.

"Huh?" He turned toward her.

"Don't go — please!" Kris cried.

Her father's eyes landed on the dummy. He walked over to him. "Hey — what's the big idea?" her father asked angrily.

"I thought you wanted to take him back to the

pawn shop," Kris replied, thinking quickly.

"Not till Monday," her father replied. "Today is Saturday, remember?"

The dummy blinked. Mr. Powell didn't notice.

"Do you have to go shopping now?" Kris asked in a tiny voice.

Before her father could answer, Mrs. Powell reappeared in the doorway. "Here. Catch," she called, and tossed the car keys to him. "Let's go before it pours."

Mr. Powell started to the door. "Why don't you want us to go?" he asked.

"The dummy — " Kris started. But she knew it was hopeless. They'd never listen. They'd never believe her. "Never mind," she muttered.

A few seconds later, she heard their car back down the driveway. They were gone.

And she was alone in the kitchen with the grinning dummy.

Mr. Wood turned toward her slowly, swiveling the tall counter stool. His big eyes locked angrily on Kris's.

"I warned you," he rasped.

Barky came trotting into the kitchen, his toenails clicking loudly on the linoleum. He sniffed the floor as he ran, searching for breakfast scraps someone might have dropped.

"Barky, where've you been?" Kris asked, glad to have company.

124

The dog ignored her and sniffed under the stool Mr. Wood sat on.

"He was upstairs, waking me up," Lindy said, rubbing her eyes as she walked into the kitchen. She was wearing white tennis shorts and a sleeveless magenta T-shirt. "Stupid dog."

Barky licked at a spot on the linoleum.

Lindy cried out as she spotted Mr. Wood. "Oh, no!"

"I'm back," the dummy rasped. "And I'm very unhappy with you two slaves."

Lindy turned to Kris, her mouth open in surprise and terror.

Kris kept her eyes trained on the dummy. *What does he plan to do?* she wondered. *How can I stop him?*

Burying him under all that dirt hadn't kept him from returning. Somehow he had freed himself from the suitcase and pulled himself out.

Wasn't there any way to defeat him? Any way at all?

Grinning his evil grin, Mr. Wood dropped down to the floor, his sneakers thudding hard on the floor. "I'm very unhappy with you two slaves," he repeated in his growly voice.

"What are you going to do?" Lindy cried in a shrill, frightened voice.

"I have to punish you," the dummy replied. "I have to prove to you that I am serious."

"Wait!" Kris cried.

But the dummy moved quickly. He reached down and grabbed Barky by the neck with both hands.

As the dummy tightened his grip, the frightened terrier began to howl in pain.

# 24

"I warned you," Mr. Wood snarled over the howls of the little black terrier. "You will do as I say — or one by one, those you love will suffer!"

"No!" Kris cried.

Barky let out a high-pitched *whelp*, a bleat of pain that made Kris shudder.

"Let go of Barky!" Kris screamed.

The dummy giggled.

Barky uttered a hoarse gasp.

Kris couldn't stand it any longer. She and Lindy leapt at the dummy from two sides. Lindy tackled his legs. Kris grabbed Barky and tugged.

Lindy dragged the dummy to the floor. But his wooden hands held a tight grip on the dog's throat.

Barky's howls became a muffled whimper as he struggled to breathe.

"Let go! Let *go!*" Kris shrieked.

"I *warned* you!" the dummy snarled as Lindy held tight to his kicking legs. "The dog must die now!"

"No!" Kris let go of the gasping dog. She slid her hands down to the dummy's wrists. Then with a fierce tug, she pulled the wooden hands apart.

Barky dropped to the floor, wheezing. He scampered to the corner, his paws sliding frantically over the smooth floor.

"You'll pay now!" Mr. Wood growled. Jerking free from Kris, he swung his wooden hand up, landing a hard blow on Kris's forehead.

She cried out in pain and raised her hands to her head.

She heard Barky yipping loudly behind her.

"Let go of me!" Mr. Wood demanded, turning back to Lindy, who still held onto his legs.

"No way!" Lindy cried. "Kris — grab his arms again."

Her head still throbbing, Kris lunged forward to grab the dummy's arms.

But he lowered his head as she approached and clamped his wooden jaws around her wrist.

"Owww!" Kris howled in pain and pulled back.

Lindy lifted the dummy up by the legs, then slammed his body hard against the floor. He uttered a furious growl and tried to kick free of her.

Kris lunged again, and this time grabbed one arm, then the other. He lowered his head to bite once more, but she dodged away and pulled his arms tight behind his back.

"I'm warning you!" he bellowed. "I'm warning you!"

Barky yipped excitedly, hopping up on Kris.

"What do we *do* with him?" Lindy cried, shouting over the dummy's angry threats.

"Outside!" Kris yelled, pressing the arms more tightly behind Mr. Wood's back.

She suddenly remembered the two steamrollers she had seen moving over the yard next door, flattening the ground. "Come on," she urged her sister. "We'll crush him!"

"I'm warning you! I have powers!" the dummy screamed.

Ignoring him, Kris pulled open the kitchen door and they carried their wriggling captive outside.

The sky was charcoal-gray. A light rain had begun to fall. The grass was already wet.

Over the low shrubs that separated the yards, the girls could see the two enormous yellow steamrollers, one in the back, one at the side of the next door lot. They looked like huge, lumbering animals, their giant black rollers flattening everything in their path.

"This way! Hurry!" Kris shouted to her sister, holding the dummy tightly as she ran. "Toss him under that one!"

"Let me go! Let me go, slaves!" the dummy screamed. "This is your last chance!" He swung his head hard, trying to bite Kris's arm.

Thunder rumbled, low in the distance.

The girls ran at full speed, slipping on the wet

grass as they hurried toward the fast-moving steamroller.

They were just a few yards away from the enormous machine when they saw Barky. His tail wagging furiously, he scampered ahead of them.

"Oh, no! How'd he get out?" Lindy cried.

Gazing back at them, his tongue hanging out of his mouth, prancing happily in the wet grass, the dog was running right into the path of the rumbling bulldozer.

"No, Barky!" Kris shrieked in horror. "No! Barky — no!"

## 25

Letting go of Mr. Wood, both girls dove toward the dog. Hands outstretched, they slid on their stomachs on the wet grass.

Unaware of any problem, enjoying the game of tag, Barky scampered away.

Lindy and Kris rolled out of the path of the steamroller.

"Hey — get away from there!" the angry operator shouted through the high window of the steamroller. "Are you girls crazy?"

They leapt to their feet and turned back to Mr. Wood.

The rain began to come down a little harder. A jagged streak of white lightning flashed high in the sky.

"I'm free!" the dummy cried, hands raised victoriously above his head. "Now you will pay!"

"Get him!" Kris shouted to her sister.

The rain pelted their hair and shoulders. The two girls lowered their heads, leaned into the rain, and began to chase after the dummy.

Mr. Wood turned and started to run.

He never saw the other steamroller.

The gigantic black wheel rolled right over him, pushing him onto his back, then crushing him with a loud *crunch*.

A loud *hiss* rose up from under the machine, like air escaping from a large balloon.

The steamroller appeared to rock back and forth.

A strange green gas spurted up from beneath the wheel, into the air, spreading out in an eerie, mushroom-shaped cloud.

Barky stopped scampering and stood frozen in place, his eyes following the green gas as it floated up against the nearly black sky.

Lindy and Kris stared in open mouthed wonder.

Pushed by the wind and the rain, the green gas floated over them.

"Yuck! It stinks!" Lindy declared.

It smelled like rotten eggs.

Barky uttered a low whimper.

The steamroller backed up. The driver jumped out and came running toward them. He was a short, stocky man with big, muscular arms bulging out from the sleeves of his T-shirt. His face was bright red under a short, blond flattop, his eyes wide with horror.

"A kid?" he cried. "I — I ran over a kid?"

"No. He was a dummy," Kris told him. "He wasn't alive."

He stopped. His face faded from red to flour-white. He uttered a loud, grateful sigh. "Oh, man," he moaned. "Oh, man. I thought it was a kid."

He took a deep breath and let it out slowly. Then he bent to examine the area beneath his wheel. As the girls came near, they saw the remains of the dummy, crushed flat inside its jeans and flannel shirt.

"Hey, I'm real sorry," the man said, wiping his forehead with his T-shirt sleeve as he straightened up to face them. "I couldn't stop in time."

"That's okay," Kris said, a wide smile forming on her face.

"Yeah. Really. It's okay," Lindy quickly agreed.

Barky moved close to sniff the crushed dummy.

The man shook his head. "I'm so relieved. It looked like it was running. I really thought it was a kid. I was so scared."

"No. Just a dummy," Kris told him.

"Whew!" The man exhaled slowly. "Close one." His expression changed. "What are you girls doing out in the rain, anyway?"

Lindy shrugged. Kris shook her head. "Just walking the dog."

The man picked up the crushed dummy. The

head crumbled to powder as he lifted it. "You want this thing?"

"You can throw it in the trash," Kris told him.

"Better get out of the rain," he told them. "And don't scare me like that again."

The girls apologized, then headed back to the house. Kris cast a happy grin at her sister. Lindy grinned back.

I may grin forever, Kris thought. I'm so happy. So relieved.

They wiped their wet sneakers on the mat, then held the kitchen door open for Barky. "Wow. What a morning!" Lindy declared.

They followed the dog into the kitchen. Outside, a flash of bright lightning was followed by a roar of thunder.

"I'm drenched," Kris said. "I'm going up to get changed."

"Me, too." Lindy followed her up the stairs.

They entered their bedroom to find the window wide open, the curtains slapping wildly, rain pouring in. "Oh, no!" Kris hurried across the room to shut the window.

As she leaned over the chair to grab the window frame, Slappy reached up and grabbed her arm.

"Hey, slave — is that other guy gone?" the dummy asked in a throaty growl. "I thought he'd never leave!"

# NIGHT OF THE
# LIVING DUMMY II

# 1

My name is Amy Kramer, and every Thursday night I feel a little dumb. That's because Thursday is "Family Sharing Night" at my house.

Sara and Jed think it's dumb, too. But Mom and Dad won't listen to our complaints. "It's the most important night of the week," Dad says.

"It's a family tradition," Mom adds. "It's something you kids will always remember."

Right, Mom. It's something I'll always remember as really painful and embarrassing.

You've probably guessed that on Family Sharing Night, every member of the Kramer family — except for George, our cat — has to share something with the rest of the family

It isn't so bad for my sister, Sara. Sara is fourteen — two years older than me — and she's a genius painter. Really. One of her paintings was chosen for a show at the art museum downtown. Sara may go to a special arts high school next year.

So Sara always shares some sketches she's working on. Or a new painting.

And Family Sharing Night isn't so bad for Jed, either. My ten-year-old brother is such a total goof. He doesn't care what he shares. One Thursday night, he burped really loud and explained that he was sharing his dinner.

Jed laughed like a lunatic.

But Mom and Dad didn't think it was funny. They gave Jed a stern lecture about taking Family Sharing Night more seriously.

The next Thursday night, my obnoxious brother shared a note that David Miller, a kid at my school, had written to me. A very personal note! Jed found the note in my room and decided to share it with everyone.

Nice?

I wanted to die. I really did.

Jed just thinks he's so cute and adorable, he can get away with anything. He thinks he's really special.

I think it's because he's the only redhead in the family. Sara and I both have straight black hair, dark green eyes, and very tan skin. With his pale skin, freckled face, and curly red hair, Jed looks like he comes from another family!

And sometimes Sara and I both wish he did.

Anyway, I'm the one with the most problems on Family Sharing Night. Because I'm not really talented the way Sara is. And I'm not a total goof like Jed.

So I never really know what to share.

I mean, I have a seashell collection, which I keep in a jar on my dresser. But it's really kind of boring to hold up shells and talk about them. And we haven't been to the ocean for nearly two years. So my shells are kind of old, and everyone has already seen them.

I also have a really good collection of CDs. But no one else in my family is into Bob Marley and reggae music. If I start to share some music with them, they all hold their ears and complain till I shut it off.

So I usually make up some kind of a story — an adventure story about a girl who survives danger after danger. Or a wild fairy tale about princesses who turn into tigers.

After my last story, Dad had a big smile on his face. "Amy is going to be a famous writer," he announced. "She's so good at making up stories." Dad gazed around the room, still smiling. "We have such a talented family!" he exclaimed.

I knew he was just saying that to be a good parent. To "encourage" me. Sara is the real talent in our family. Everyone knows that.

Tonight, Jed was the first to share. Mom and Dad sat on the living room couch. Dad had taken out a tissue and was squinting as he cleaned his glasses. Dad can't stand to have the tiniest speck of dust on his glasses. He cleans them about twenty times a day.

I settled in the big brown armchair against the wall. Sara sat cross-legged on the carpet beside my chair.

"What are you going to share tonight?" Mom asked Jed. "And I hope it isn't another horrible burp."

"That was so gross!" Sara moaned.

"Your face is gross!" Jed shot back. He stuck out his tongue at Sara.

"Jed, please — give us a break tonight," Dad muttered, slipping his glasses back on, adjusting them on his nose. "Don't cause trouble."

"She started it," Jed insisted, pointing at Sara.

"Just share something," I told Jed, sighing.

"I'm going to share your freckles," Sara told him. "I'm going to pull them off one by one and feed them to George."

Sara and I laughed. George didn't glance up. He was curled up, napping on the carpet beside the couch.

"That's not funny, girls," Mom snapped. "Stop being mean to your brother."

"This is supposed to be a family night," Dad wailed. "Why can't we be a family?"

"We are!" Jed insisted.

Dad frowned and shook his head. He looks like

an owl when he does that. "Jed, are you going to share something?" he demanded weakly.

Jed nodded. "Yeah." He stood in the center of the room and shoved his hands into his jeans pockets. He wears loose, baggy jeans about ten sizes too big. They always look as if they're about to fall down. Jed thinks that's cool.

"I . . . uh . . . learned to whistle through my fingers," he announced.

"Wow," Sara muttered sarcastically.

Jed ignored her. He pulled his hands from his pockets. Then he stuck his two little fingers into the sides of his mouth — and let out a long, shrill whistle.

He whistled through his fingers two more times. Then he took a deep bow. The whole family burst into loud applause.

Jed, grinning, took another low bow.

"Such a talented family!" Dad declared. This time, he meant it as a joke.

Jed dropped down on the floor beside George, startling the poor cat awake.

"Your turn next, Amy," Mom said, turning to me. "Are you going to tell us another story?"

"Her stories are too long!" Jed complained.

George climbed unsteadily to his feet and moved a few feet away from Jed. Yawning, the cat dropped on to his stomach beside Mom's feet.

"I'm not going to tell a story tonight," I

143

announced. I picked up Dennis from behind my armchair.

Sara and Jed both groaned.

"Hey — give me a break!" I shouted. I settled back on the edge of the chair, fixing my dummy on my lap. "I thought I'd talk to Dennis tonight," I told Mom and Dad.

They had half-smiles on their faces. I didn't care. I'd been practicing with Dennis all week. And I wanted to try out my new comedy routine with him.

"Amy is a lousy ventriloquist," Jed chimed in. "You can see her lips move."

"Be quiet, Jed. I think Dennis is funny," Sara said. She scooted toward the couch so she could see better.

I balanced Dennis on my left knee and wrapped my fingers around the string in his back that worked his mouth. Dennis is a very old ventriloquist's dummy. The paint on his face is faded. One eye is almost completely white. His turtleneck sweater is torn and tattered.

But I have a lot of fun with him. When my five-year-old cousins come to visit, I like to entertain them with Dennis. They squeal and laugh. They think I'm a riot.

I think I'm getting much better with Dennis. Despite Jed's complaints.

I took a deep breath, glanced at Mom and Dad, and began my act.

"How are you tonight, Dennis?" I asked.

*"Not too well,"* I made the dummy reply in a high, shrill voice. Dennis's voice.

"Really, Dennis? What's wrong?"

*"I think I caught a bug."*

"You mean you have the flu?" I asked him.

*"No. Termites!"*

Mom and Dad laughed. Sara smiled. Jed groaned loudly.

I turned back to Dennis. "Well, have you been to a doctor?" I asked him.

*"No. A carpenter!"*

Mom and Dad smiled at that one, but didn't laugh. Jed groaned again. Sara stuck her finger down her throat, pretending to puke.

"No one liked that joke, Dennis," I told him.

*"Who's joking?"* I made Dennis reply.

"This is lame," I heard Jed mutter to Sara. She nodded her head in agreement.

"Let's change the subject, Dennis," I said, shifting the dummy to my other knee. "Do you have a girlfriend?"

I leaned Dennis forward, trying to make him nod his head yes. But his head rolled right off his shoulders.

The wooden head hit the floor with a *thud* and bounced over to George. The cat leaped up and scampered away.

Sara and Jed collapsed in laughter, slapping each other high fives.

145

I jumped angrily to my feet. "Dad!" I screamed. "You *promised* you'd buy me a new dummy!"

Jed scurried over to the rug and picked up Dennis's head. He pulled the string, making the dummy's mouth move. "Amy reeks! Amy reeks!" Jed made the dummy repeat over and over.

"Give me that!" I grabbed the head angrily from Jed's hand.

"Amy reeks! Amy reeks!" Jed continued chanting.

"That's enough!" Mom shouted, jumping up off the couch.

Jed retreated back to the wall.

"I've been checking the stores for a new dummy," Dad told me, pulling off his glasses again and examining them closely. "But they're all so expensive."

"Well, how am I ever going to get better at this?" I demanded. "Dennis's head falls off every time I use him!"

"Do your best," Mom said.

What did *that* mean? I always hated it when she said that.

"Instead of Family Sharing Night, we should call this the Thursday Night Fights," Sara declared.

Jed raised his fists. "Want to fight?" he asked Sara.

"It's your turn, Sara," Mom replied, narrowing

her eyes at Jed. "What are you sharing tonight?"

"I have a new painting," Sara announced. "It's a watercolor."

"Of what?" Dad asked, settling his glasses back on his face.

"Remember that cabin we had in Maine a few summers ago?" Sara replied, tossing back her straight black hair. "The one overlooking the dark rock cliff? I found a snapshot of it, and I tried to paint it."

I suddenly felt really angry and upset. I admit it. I was jealous of Sara.

Here she was, about to share another beautiful watercolor. And here I was, rolling a stupid wooden dummy head in my lap.

It just wasn't fair!

"You'll have to come to my room to see it," Sara was saying. "It's still wet."

We all stood up and trooped to Sara's room.

My family lives in a long, one-story ranch-style house. My room and Jed's room are at the end of one hallway. The living room, dining room, and kitchen are in the middle. Sara's room and my parents' room are down the other hall, way at the other end of the house.

I led the way down the hall. Behind me, Sara was going on and on about all the trouble she'd had with the painting and how she'd solved the problems.

"I remember that cabin so well," Dad said.

"I can't wait to see the painting," Mom added.

I stepped into Sara's room and clicked on the light.

Then I turned to the easel by the window that held the painting — and let out a scream of horror.

# 2

My mouth dropped open in shock. I stared at the painting, unable to speak.

When Sara saw it, she let out a shriek. "I — I don't *believe* it!" she screamed. "Who *did* that?"

Someone had painted a yellow-and-black smile face in the corner of her painting. Right in the middle of the black rock cliff.

Mom and Dad stepped up to the easel, fretful expressions on their faces. They studied the smile face, then turned to Jed.

Jed burst out laughing. "Do you like it?" he asked innocently.

"Jed — how *could* you!" Sara exploded. "I'll kill you! I really will!"

"The painting was too dark," Jed explained with a shrug. "I wanted to brighten it up."

"But . . . but . . . but . . ." my sister sputtered. She balled her hands into fists, shook them at Jed, and uttered a loud cry of rage.

"Jed — what were you doing in Sara's room?" Mom demanded.

Sara doesn't like for anyone to go into her precious room without a written invitation!

"Young man, you know you're never allowed to touch your sister's paintings," Dad scolded.

"I can paint, too," Jed replied. "I'm a good painter."

"Then do your own paintings!" Sara snapped. "Don't sneak in here and mess up my work!"

"I didn't sneak," Jed insisted. He sneered at Sara. "I was just trying to help."

"You were not!" Sara screamed, angrily tossing her black hair over her shoulder. "You ruined my painting!"

"Your painting reeks!" Jed shot back.

"*Enough!*" Mom shouted. She grabbed Jed by both shoulders. "Jed — look at me! You don't seem to see how serious this is. This is the worst thing you've ever done!"

Jed's smile finally faded.

I took another glance at the ugly smile face he had slopped on to Sara's watercolor. Since he's the baby in the family, Jed thinks he can get away with anything.

But I knew that this time he had gone too far.

After all, Sara is the star of the family. She's the talented one. The one with the painting that hung in a museum. Messing with Sara's precious painting was bound to get Jed in major trouble.

Sara is so stuck-up about her paintings. A few times, I even thought about painting something funny on one of them. But of course I only *thought* it. I would *never* do anything that horrible.

"You don't have to be jealous of your sister's work," Dad was telling Jed. "We're all talented in this family."

"Oh, sure," Jed muttered. He has this weird habit. Whenever he's in trouble, he doesn't say he's sorry. Instead, he gets really angry. "What's *your* talent, Dad?" Jed demanded, sneering.

Dad's jaw tightened. He narrowed his eyes at Jed. "We're not discussing me," he said in a low voice. "But I'll tell you. My talent is my Chinese cooking. You see, there are all kinds of talents, Jed."

Dad considers himself a Master of the Wok. Once or twice a week, he chops a ton of vegetables into little pieces and fries them up in the electric wok Mom got him for Christmas.

We pretend it tastes great.

No point in hurting Dad's feelings.

"Is Jed going to be punished or not?" Sara demanded in a shrill voice.

She had opened her box of watercolor paints and was rolling a brush in the black. Then she began painting over the smile face with quick, furious strokes.

151

"Yes, Jed is going to be punished," Mom replied, glaring at him. Jed lowered his eyes to the floor. "First he's going to apologize to Sara."

We all waited.

It took Jed a while. But he finally managed to mutter, "Sorry, Sara."

He started to leave the room, but Mom grabbed his shoulders again and pulled him back. "Not so fast, Jed," she told him. "Your punishment is you can't go to the movies with Josh and Matt on Saturday. And . . . no video games for a week."

"Mom — give me a break!" Jed whined.

"What you did was really bad," Mom said sternly. "Maybe this punishment will make you realize how horrible it was."

"But I *have* to go to the movies!" Jed protested.

"You can't," Mom replied softly. "And no arguing, or I'll add on to your punishment. Now go to your room."

"I don't think it's enough punishment," Sara said, dabbing away at her painting.

"Keep out of it, Sara," Mom snapped.

"Yeah. Keep out of it," Jed muttered. He stomped out of the room and down the long hall to his room.

Dad sighed. He swept a hand back over his bald head. "Family Sharing Night is over," he said sadly.

\* \* \*

152

I stayed in Sara's room and watched her repair the painting for a while. She kept tsk-tsking and shaking her head.

"I have to make the rocks much darker, or the paint won't cover the stupid smile face," she explained unhappily. "But if I make the rocks darker, I have to change the sky. The whole balance is ruined."

"I think it looks pretty good," I told her, trying to cheer her up.

"How could Jed do that?" Sara demanded, dipping her brush in the water jar. "How could he sneak in here and totally destroy a work of art?"

I was feeling sorry for Sara. But that remark made me lose all sympathy. I mean, why couldn't she just call it a watercolor painting? Why did she have to call it "a work of art"?

Sometimes she is so stuck-up and so in love with herself, it makes me sick.

I turned and left the room. She didn't even notice.

I went down the hall to my room and called my friend Margo. We talked for a while about stuff. And we made plans to get together the next day.

As I talked on the phone, I could hear Jed in his room next door. He was pacing back and forth, tossing things around, making a lot of noise.

Sometimes I spell the word "Jed" B-R-A-T.

Margo's dad made her get off the phone. He's

real strict. He never lets her talk for more than ten or fifteen minutes.

I wandered into the kitchen and made myself a bowl of Frosted Flakes. My favorite late snack. When I was a little kid, I used to have a bowl of cereal every night before bed. And I just never got out of the habit.

I rinsed out the bowl. Then I said good night to Mom and Dad and went to bed.

It was a warm spring night. A soft breeze fluttered the curtains over the window. Pale light from a big half-moon filled the window and spilled on to the floor.

I fell into a deep sleep as soon as my head hit the pillow.

A short while later, something woke me up. I'm not sure what.

Still half asleep, I blinked my eyes open and raised myself on my pillow. I struggled to see clearly.

The curtains flapped over the window.

I felt as if I were still asleep, dreaming.

But what I saw in the window snapped me awake.

The curtains billowed, then lifted away.

And in the silvery light, I saw a face.

An ugly, grinning face in my bedroom window. Staring through the darkness at me.

The curtains flapped again.

The face didn't move.

"Who — ?" I choked out, squeezing the sheet up to my chin.

The eyes stared in at me. Cold, unblinking eyes. Dummy eyes.

Dennis.

Dennis stared blankly at me, his white eye catching the glow of the moonlight.

I let out an angry roar, tossed off the sheet, and bolted out of bed. To the window.

I pushed away the billowing curtains and grabbed Dennis's head off the window ledge. "Who put you there?" I demanded, holding the head between my hands. "Who did it, Dennis?"

I heard soft laughter behind me. From the hallway.

I flew across the room, the head still in my hands. I pulled open my bedroom door.

Jed held his hand over his mouth, muffling his laughter. "Gotcha!" he whispered gleefully.

"Jed — you creep!" I cried. I let the dummy head drop to the floor. Then I grabbed Jed's pajama pants with both hands and jerked them up as high as I could — nearly to his chin!

He let out a gasp of pain and stumbled back against the wall.

"Why did you do that?" I demanded in an angry whisper. "Why did you put the dummy head on my window ledge?"

Jed tugged his pajama pants back into place. "To pay you back," he muttered.

"Huh? Me?" I shrieked. "I didn't do anything to you. What did *I* do?"

"You didn't stick up for me," he grumbled, scratching his red curly hair. His eyes narrowed at me. "You didn't say anything to help me out. You know. About Sara's painting."

"Excuse me?" I cried. "How could I help you out? What could I say?"

"You could have said it was no big deal," Jed replied.

"But it *was* a big deal!" I told him. "You know how seriously Sara takes her paintings." I shook my head. "I'm sorry, Jed. But you deserve to be punished. You really do."

He stared at me across the dim hallway, thinking about what I'd said. Then an evil smile spread slowly over his freckled face. "Hope I didn't scare you too much, Amy." He snickered. Then he picked Dennis's head up off the carpet and tossed it at me.

I caught it in one hand. "Go to sleep, Jed," I told him. "And don't mess with Dennis again!"

I stepped back into my room and closed the door. I tossed Dennis's head onto a pile of clothes on my desk chair. Then I climbed wearily back into bed.

So much trouble around here tonight, I thought, shutting my eyes, trying to relax.

So much trouble . . .

Two days later, Dad brought home a present for me.

A new ventriloquist's dummy.

That's when the *real* trouble began.

# 4

Margo came over the next afternoon. Margo is real tiny, sort of like a mini-person. She has a tiny face, and is very pretty, with bright blue eyes, and delicate features.

Her blond hair is very light and very fine. She let it grow this year. It's just about down to her tiny little waist.

She's nearly a foot shorter than me, even though we both turned twelve in February. She's very smart and very popular. But the boys like to make fun of her soft, whispery voice.

Today she was wearing a bright blue tank top tucked into white tennis shorts. "I bought the new Beatles collection," she told me as she stepped into the house. She held up a CD box.

Margo loves the Beatles. She doesn't listen to any of the new groups. In her room, she has an entire shelf of Beatles CDs and tapes. And she has Beatles posters on her walls.

We went to my room and put on the CD. Margo settled on the bed. I sprawled on the carpet across from her.

"My dad almost didn't let me come over," Margo told me, pushing her long hair behind her shoulder. "He thought he might need me to work at the restaurant."

Margo's dad owns a huge restaurant downtown called The Party House. It's not really a restaurant. It's a big, old house filled with enormous rooms where people can hold parties.

A lot of kids have birthday parties there. And there are bar mitzvahs and confirmations and wedding receptions there, too. Sometimes there are six parties going on at once!

One Beatles song ended. The next song, "Love Me Do," started up.

"I *love* this song!" Margo exclaimed. She sang along with it for a while. I tried singing with her, but I'm totally tone deaf. As my dad says, I can't carry a tune in a wheelbarrow.

"Well, I'm glad you didn't have to work today," I told Margo.

"Me, too," Margo sighed. "Dad always gives me the worst jobs. You know. Clearing tables. Or putting away dishes. Or wrapping up garbage bags. Yuck."

She started singing again — and then stopped. She sat up on the bed. "Amy, I almost forgot. Dad may have a job for you."

"Excuse me?" I replied. "Wrapping up garbage bags? I don't think so, Margo."

"No. No. Listen," Margo pleaded excitedly in her mouselike voice. "It's a good job. Dad has a bunch of birthday parties coming up. For teeny tiny kids. You know. Two-year-olds. Maybe three- or four-year-olds. And he thought you could entertain them."

"Huh?" I stared at my friend. I still didn't understand. "You mean, sing or something?"

"No. With Dennis," Margo explained. She twisted a lock of hair around in her fingers and bobbed her head in time to the music as she talked. "Dad saw you with Dennis at the sixth-grade talent night. He was really impressed."

"He was? I was terrible that night!" I replied.

"Well, Dad didn't think so. He wonders if you'd like to come to the birthday parties and put on a show with Dennis. The little kids will love it. Dad said he'd even pay you."

"Wow! That's cool!" I replied. What an exciting idea.

Then I remembered something.

I jumped to my feet, crossed the room to the chair, and held up Dennis's head. "One small problem," I groaned.

Margo let go of her hair and made a sick face. "His head? Why did you take off his head?"

"I didn't," I replied. "It fell off. Every time I use Dennis, his head falls off."

"Oh." Margo uttered a disappointed sigh. "The head looks weird all by itself. I don't think little kids would like it if it fell off."

"I don't think so," I agreed.

"It might frighten them or something," Margo said. "You know. Give them nightmares. Make them think their own head might fall off."

"Dennis is totally wrecked. Dad promised me a new dummy. But he hasn't been able to find one."

"Too bad," Margo replied. "You'd have fun performing for the kids."

We listened to more Beatles music. Then Margo had to go home.

A few minutes after she left, I heard the front door slam.

"Hey, Amy! Amy — are you home?" I heard Dad call from the living room.

"Coming!" I called. I made my way to the front of the house. Dad stood in the entryway, a long carton under his arm, a smile on his face.

He handed the carton to me. "Happy Unbirthday!" he exclaimed.

"Dad! Is it — ?" I cried. I tore open the carton. "Yes!" A new dummy!

I lifted him carefully out of the carton.

The dummy had wavy brown hair painted on top of his wooden head. I studied his face. It was kind of strange. Kind of intense. His eyes were bright blue — not faded like Dennis's. He had bright red painted lips, curved up into an eerie

161

smile. His lower lip had a chip on one side so that it didn't quite match the other lip.

As I pulled him from the box, the dummy appeared to stare into my eyes. The eyes sparkled. The grin grew wider.

I felt a sudden chill. Why does this dummy seem to be laughing at me? I wondered.

I held him up, examining him carefully. He wore a gray, double-breasted suit over a white shirt collar. The collar was stapled to his neck. He didn't have a shirt. Instead, his wooden chest had been painted white.

Big, black leather shoes were attached to the ends of his thin, dangling legs.

"Dad — he's great!" I exclaimed.

"I found him in a pawnshop," Dad said, picking up the dummy's hand and pretending to shake hands with it. "How do you do, Slappy."

"Slappy? Is that his name?"

"That's what the man in the store said," Dad replied. He lifted Slappy's arms, examining his suit. "I don't know why he sold Slappy so cheaply. He practically *gave* the dummy away!"

I turned the dummy around and looked for the string in his back that made the mouth open and close. "He's excellent, Dad," I said. I kissed my dad on the cheek. "Thanks."

"Do you really like him?" Dad asked.

Slappy grinned up at me. His blue eyes stared

into mine. He seemed to be waiting for an answer, too.

"Yes. He's awesome!" I said. "I like his serious eyes. They look so real."

"The eyes move," Dad said. "They're not painted on like Dennis's. They don't blink, but they move from side to side."

I reached my hand inside the dummy's back. "How do you make his eyes move?" I asked.

"The man showed me," Dad said. "It's not hard. First you grab the string that works the mouth."

"I've got that," I told him.

"Then you move your hand up into the dummy's head. There is a little lever up there. Do you feel it? Push on it. The eyes will move in the direction you push."

"Okay. I'll try," I said.

Slowly I moved my hand up inside the dummy's back. Through the neck. And into his head.

I stopped and let out a startled cry as my hand hit something soft.

Something soft and warm.

His brain!

# 5

"Ohhh." I uttered a sick moan and jerked my hand out as fast as I could.

I could still feel the soft, warm mush on my fingers.

"Amy — what's wrong?" Dad cried.

"His — his brains — !" I choked out, feeling my stomach lurch.

"Huh? What are you *talking* about?" Dad grabbed the dummy from my hands. He turned it over and reached into the back.

I covered my mouth with both hands and watched him reach into the head. His eyes widened in surprise.

He struggled with something. Then pulled his hand out.

"Yuck!" I groaned. "What's *that*?"

Dad stared down at the mushy, green and purple and brown object in his hand. "Looks like someone left a sandwich in there!" he exclaimed.

Dad's whole face twisted in disgust. "It's all

164

moldy and rotten. Must have been in there for months!"

"Yuck!" I repeated, holding my nose. "It really stinks! Why would someone leave a sandwich in a dummy's head?"

"Beats me," Dad replied, shaking his head. "And it looks like there are wormholes in it!"

"Yuuuuuck!" we both cried in unison.

Dad handed Slappy back to me. Then he hurried into the kitchen to get rid of the rotted, moldy sandwich.

I heard him run the garbage disposal. Then I heard water running as he washed his hands. A few seconds later, Dad returned to the living room, drying his hands on a dish towel.

"Maybe we'd better examine Slappy closely," he suggested. "We don't want any more surprises — *do* we!"

I carried Slappy into the kitchen, and we stretched him out on the counter. Dad examined the dummy's shoes carefully. They were attached to the legs and didn't come off.

I put my finger on the dummy's chin and moved the mouth up and down. Then I checked out his wooden hands.

I unbuttoned the gray suit jacket and studied the dummy's painted shirt. Patches of the white paint had chipped and cracked. But it was okay.

"Everything looks fine, Dad," I reported.

He nodded. Then he smelled his fingers. I guess

he hadn't washed away all of the stink from the rotted sandwich.

"We'd better spray the inside of his head with disinfectant or perfume or something," Dad said.

Then, as I was buttoning up the jacket, something caught my eye.

Something yellow. A slip of paper poking up from the jacket pocket.

It's probably a sales receipt, I thought.

But when I pulled out the small square of yellow paper, I found strange writing on it. Weird words in a language I'd never seen before.

I squinted hard at the paper and slowly read the words out loud:

"Karru marri odonna loma molonu karrano."

I wonder what that means? I thought.

And then I glanced down at Slappy's face.

And saw his red lips twitch.

And saw one eye slowly close in a wink.

# 6

"D-d-dad!" I stuttered. "He — moved!"

"Huh?" Dad had gone back to the sink to wash his hands for a third time. "What's wrong with the dummy?"

"He moved!" I cried. "He *winked* at me!"

Dad came over to the counter, wiping his hands. "I told you, Amy — he can't blink. The eyes only move from side to side."

"No!" I insisted. "He winked. His lips twitched, and he winked."

Dad frowned and picked up the dummy head in both hands. He raised it to examine it. "Well . . . maybe the eyelids are loose," he said. "I'll see if I can tighten them up. Maybe if I take a screw-driver I can — "

Dad didn't finish his sentence.

Because the dummy swung his wooden hand up and hit Dad on the side of the head.

"Ow!" Dad cried, dropping the dummy back

onto the counter. Dad grabbed his cheek. "Hey — stop it, Amy! That hurt!"

"*Me?*" I shrieked. "I didn't do it!"

Dad glared at me, rubbing his cheek. It had turned bright red.

"The dummy did it!" I insisted. "I didn't touch him, Dad! I didn't move his hand!"

"Not funny," Dad muttered. "You know I don't like practical jokes."

I opened my mouth to answer, but no words came out. I decided I'd better just shut up.

Of course Dad wouldn't believe that the dummy had slapped him.

I didn't believe it myself.

Dad must have pulled too hard when he was examining the head. Dad jerked the hand up without realizing it.

That's how I explained it to myself.

What other explanation could there be?

I apologized to Dad. Then we washed Slappy's face with a damp sponge. We cleaned him up and sprayed disinfectant inside his head.

He was starting to look pretty good.

I thanked Dad again and hurried to my room. I set Slappy down on the chair beside Dennis. Then I phoned Margo.

"I got a new dummy," I told her excitedly. "I can perform for the kids' birthday parties. At The Party House."

"That's great, Amy!" Margo exclaimed. "Now all you need is an act."

She was right.

I needed jokes. A lot of jokes. If I was going to perform with Slappy in front of dozens of kids, I needed a long comedy act.

The next day after school, I hurried to the library. I took out every joke book I could find. I carried them home and studied them. I wrote down all the jokes I thought I could use with Slappy.

After dinner, I should have been doing my homework. Instead, I practiced with Slappy. I sat in front of the mirror and watched myself with him.

I tried hard to speak clearly but not move my lips. And I tried hard to move Slappy's mouth so that it really looked as if he were talking.

Working his mouth and moving his eyes at the same time was pretty hard. But after a while, it became easier.

I tried some knock-knock jokes with Slappy. I thought little kids might like those.

"Knock knock," I made Slappy say.

"Who's there?" I asked him, staring into his eyes as if I were really talking to him.

"Jane," Slappy said.

"Jane who?"

"Jane jer clothes. You stink!"

I practiced each joke over and over, watching

myself in the mirror. I wanted to be a really good ventriloquist. I wanted to be excellent. I wanted to be as good with Slappy as Sara is with her paints.

I practiced some more knock-knock jokes and some jokes about animals. Jokes I thought little kids would find funny.

I'll try them out on Family Sharing Night, I decided. It will make Dad happy to see how hard I'm working with Slappy. At least I know Slappy's head won't fall off.

I glanced across the room at Dennis. He looked so sad and forlorn, crumpled in the chair, his head tilted nearly sideways on his shoulders.

Then I propped Slappy up and turned back to the mirror.

"Knock knock."

"Who's there?"

"Wayne."

"Wayne who?"

"Wayne wayne, go away! Come again another day!"

On Thursday night, I was actually eager to finish dinner so that Sharing Night could begin. I couldn't wait to show my family my new act with Slappy.

We had spaghetti for dinner. I like spaghetti, but Jed always ruins it.

He's so gross. He sat across the table from me, and he kept opening his mouth wide, showing me a mouth full of chewed-up spaghetti.

Then he'd laugh because he cracks himself up. And spaghetti sauce would run down his chin.

By the time dinner was over, Jed had spaghetti sauce smeared all over his face and all over the tablecloth around his plate.

No one seemed to notice. Mom and Dad were too busy listening to Sara brag about her grades. For a change.

Report cards were being handed out tomorrow. Sara was sure she was getting all A's.

I was sure, too. Sure I *wasn't* getting all A's!

I'd be lucky to get a C in math. I really messed up the last two tests. And I probably wasn't going to do real well in science, either. My weather balloon project fell apart, so I hadn't handed it in yet.

I finished my spaghetti and mopped up some of the leftover sauce on my plate with a chunk of bread.

When I glanced up, Jed had stuck two carrot sticks in his nose. "Amy, check this out. I'm a walrus!" he cried, grinning. He let out a few *urk urk*s and clapped his hands together like a walrus.

"Jed — stop that!" Mom cried sharply. She made a disgusted face. "Get those out of your nose."

"Make him eat them, Mom!" I cried.

Jed stuck his tongue out at me. It was orange from the spaghetti sauce.

"Look at you. You're a mess!" Mom shouted at Jed. "Go get cleaned up. Now! Hurry! Wash all that sauce off your face."

Jed groaned. But he climbed to his feet and headed to the bathroom.

"Did he eat anything? Or did he just rub it all over himself?" Dad asked, rolling his eyes. Dad had some sauce on his chin, too, but I didn't say anything.

"You interrupted me," Sara said impatiently. "I was telling you about the State Art Contest. Remember? I sent my flower painting in for that?"

"Oh, yes," Mom replied. "Have you heard from the judges?"

I didn't listen to Sara's reply. My mind wandered. I started thinking again about how bad my report card was going to be. I had to force myself to stop thinking about it.

"Uh . . . I'll clear the dishes," I announced.

I started to stand up.

But I stopped with a startled cry when I saw the short figure creep into the living room.

A dummy!

My dummy.

He was crawling across the room!

# 7

I let out another cry. I pointed to the living room
with a trembling finger. "M-mom! Dad!" I stammered.

Sara was still talking about the art competition. But she turned to see what everyone was
gaping at.

The dummy's head popped out from behind the
armchair.

"It's Dennis!" I cried.

I heard muffled laughter. Jed's muffled
laughter.

The dummy reached up both hands and pulled
off his own head. And Jed's head popped up
through the green turtleneck. He still had spaghetti sauce smeared on his cheeks. He was laughing hard.

Everyone else started to laugh, too. Everyone
but me.

Jed had really frightened me.

He had pulled the neck of his sweater way up over his head. Then he had tucked Dennis's wooden head inside the turtleneck.

Jed was so short and thin. It really looked as if Dennis were creeping into the room.

"Stop laughing!" I shouted at my family. "It isn't funny!"

"I think it's *very* funny!" Mom cried. "What a crazy thing to think of!"

"Very clever," Dad added.

"It's not clever," I insisted. I glared furiously at my brother. "I always knew you were a dummy!" I screamed at him.

"Amy, you really were scared," Sara accused. "You nearly dropped your teeth!"

"Not true!" I sputtered. "I knew it was Dennis — I mean — Jed!"

Now everyone started laughing at *me*! I could feel my face getting hot, and I knew I was blushing.

That made them all laugh even harder.

Nice family, huh?

I climbed to my feet, walked around the table, and took Dennis's head away from Jed. "Don't go in my room," I told him through clenched teeth. "And don't mess with my stuff." I stomped away to put the dummy head back in my room.

"It was just a joke, Amy," I heard Sara call after me.

"Yeah. It was just a joke," Jed repeated nastily. "Ha-ha!" I shouted back at them. "What a riot!"

My anger had faded away by the time we started Family Sharing Night. We settled in the living room, taking our usual places.

Mom volunteered to go first. She told a funny story about something that had happened at work.

Mom works in a fancy women's clothing store downtown. She told us about a really big woman who came into the store and insisted on trying on only tiny sizes.

The woman ripped every piece of clothing she tried on — and then bought them all! "They're not for me," the woman explained. "They're for my sister!"

We all laughed. But I was surprised Mom told that story. Because Mom is pretty chubby. And she's very sensitive about it.

About as sensitive as Dad is about being bald.

Dad was the next to share. He brought out his guitar, and we all groaned. Dad thinks he's a great singer. But he's nearly as tone deaf as I am.

He loves singing all these old folk songs from the sixties. There's supposed to be some kind of message in them. But Sara, Jed, and I have no idea what he's singing about.

Dad strummed away and sang something about

not working on Maggie's farm anymore. At least, I *think* that's what he was saying.

We all clapped and cheered. But Dad knew we didn't really mean it.

It was Jed's turn next. But he insisted that he had already shared. "Dressing up like Dennis — that was it," he said.

No one wanted to argue with him. "Your turn, Amy," Mom said, leaning against Dad on the couch. Dad fiddled with his glasses, then settled back.

I picked up Slappy and arranged him on my lap. I was feeling a little nervous. I wanted to do a good job and impress them with my new comedy act.

I'd been practicing all week, and I knew the jokes by heart. But as I slipped my hand into Slappy's back and found the string, my stomach felt all fluttery.

I cleared my throat and began.

"This is Slappy, everyone," I said. "Slappy, say hi to my family."

"*Hi to my family!*" I made Slappy say. I made his eyes slide back and forth.

They all chuckled.

"This dummy is much better!" Mom commented.

"But it's the same old ventriloquist," Sara said cruelly.

I glared at her.

"Just joking! Just joking!" my sister insisted.

"I think that dummy reeks," Jed chimed in.

"Give Amy a break," Dad said sharply. "Go ahead, Amy."

I cleared my throat again. It suddenly felt very dry. "Slappy and I are going to tell some knock-knock jokes," I announced. I turned to face Slappy and made him turn his head to me. "Knock knock," I said.

*"Knock it off!"* came the harsh reply.

Slappy spun around to face my Mom. *"Hey — don't break the sofa, fatso!"* he rasped. *"Why don't you skip the French fries and have a salad once in a while?"*

"Huh?" Mom gasped in shock. "Amy — "

"Amy, that's not funny!" Dad cried angrily.

*"What's your problem, baldy?"* Slappy shouted. *"Is that your head — or are you hatching an ostrich egg on your neck?"*

"That's enough, Amy!" Dad cried, jumping to his feet. "Stop it — right now!"

"But — but — Dad — !" I sputtered.

*"Why don't you put an extra hole in your head and use it for a bowling ball?"* Slappy screamed at Dad.

"Your jokes are horrible!" Mom exclaimed. "They're hurtful and insulting."

"It's not funny, Amy!" Dad fumed. "It's not funny to hurt people's feelings."

"But, Dad — " I replied. "I didn't say any of

that! It wasn't me! It was Slappy! Really! I wasn't saying it! I wasn't!"

Slappy raised his head. His red-lipped grin appeared to spread. His blue eyes sparkled. *"Did I mention you are all ugly?"* he asked.

# 8

Everyone started shouting at once.

I stood up and dropped Slappy facedown on the armchair.

My legs were trembling. My entire body was shaking.

What's going on here? I asked myself. I didn't say those things. I really didn't.

But Slappy can't be talking on his own — *can* he?

Of course not, I realized.

But what did that mean? Did that mean I was saying those horrible, insulting things to my parents without even knowing it?

Mom and Dad stood side by side, staring at me angrily, demanding to know why I insulted them.

"Did you really think that was funny?" Mom asked. "Didn't you think it would hurt my feelings to call me fatso?"

Meanwhile, Jed was sprawled on his back in the

179

middle of the floor, giggling like a moron. He thought the whole thing was a riot.

Sara sat cross-legged against the wall, shaking her head, her black hair falling over her face. "You're in major trouble," she muttered. "What's your problem, Amy?"

I turned to Mom and Dad. My hands were balled into tight fists. I couldn't stop shaking.

"You've got to believe me!" I shrieked. "I didn't say those things! I really didn't!"

"Yeah. Right. Slappy is a baaad dude!" Jed chimed in, grinning.

"Everybody, just be quiet!" Dad screamed. His face turned bright red.

Mom squeezed his arm. She didn't like it when he got too angry or excited. I guess she worried he might totally explode or something.

Dad crossed his arms in front of his chest. I saw that he had a sweat stain on the chest of his polo shirt. His face was still red.

The room suddenly fell silent.

"Amy, we're *not* going to believe you," Dad said softly.

"But — but — but — "

He raised a hand to silence me.

"You're a wonderful storyteller, Amy," Dad continued. "You make up wonderful fantasies and fairy tales. But we're not going to believe this one. I'm sorry. We're not going to believe that your dummy spoke up on his own."

"But he *did!*" I screamed. I felt like bursting out in sobs. I bit my lip hard, trying to force them back.

Dad shook his head. "No, Slappy didn't insult us. You said those things, Amy. You did. And now I want you to apologize to your mother and me. Then I want you to take your dummy and go to your room."

There was no way they'd ever believe me. No way. I wasn't sure I believed it myself.

"Sorry," I muttered, still holding back the tears. "Really. I'm sorry."

With an unhappy sigh, I lifted Slappy off the chair. I carried him around the waist so that his arms and legs dangled toward the floor. "Good night," I said. I walked slowly toward my room.

"What about my turn?" I heard Sara ask.

"Sharing Night is over," Dad replied grumpily. "You two — get lost. Leave your mom and me alone."

Dad sounded really upset.

I didn't blame him.

I stepped into my room and closed the door behind me. Then I lifted Slappy up, holding him under the shoulders. I raised his face to mine.

His eyes seemed to stare into my face.

Such cold blue eyes, I thought.

His bright red lips curled up into that smirking grin. The smile suddenly seemed evil. Mocking.

As if Slappy were laughing at me.

181

But of course that was impossible. My wild imagination was playing tricks on me, I decided.

Frightening tricks.

Slappy was just a dummy, after all. Just a hunk of painted wood.

I stared hard into those cold blue eyes. "Slappy, look at all the trouble you caused me tonight," I told him.

Thursday night had been awful. Totally awful.

But Friday turned out to be much worse.

# 9

First I dropped my tray in the lunchroom. The trays were all wet, and mine just slipped out of my hand.

The plates clattered on the floor, and my lunch spilled all over my new white sneakers. Everyone in the lunchroom clapped and cheered.

Was I embarrassed? Take three guesses.

Later that afternoon, report cards were handed out.

Sara came home grinning and singing. Nothing makes her more happy than being perfect. And her report card was perfect. All A's.

She insisted on showing it to me three times. She showed it to Jed three times, too. And we both had to tell her how wonderful she was each time.

I'm being unfair to Sara.

She was happy and excited. And she had a right to be. Her report card was perfect — *and* her flower painting won the blue ribbon in the State Art Contest.

So I shouldn't blame her for dancing around the house and singing at the top of her lungs.

She wasn't trying to rub it in. She wasn't trying to make me feel like a lowly slug because my report card had two C's. One in math and one in science.

It wasn't Sara's fault that I had received my worst report card ever.

So I tried to hold back my jealous feelings and not strangle her the tenth time she told me about the art prize. But it wasn't easy.

The worst part of my report card wasn't the two C's. It was the little note Miss Carson wrote at the bottom.

It said: *Amy isn't working to the best of her ability. If she worked harder, she could do much better than this.*

I don't think teachers should be allowed to write notes on report cards. I think getting grades is bad enough.

I tried to make up some kind of story to explain the two C's to my parents. I planned to tell them that *everyone* in the class got C's in math and science. "Miss Carson didn't have time to grade our papers. So she gave us all C's — just to be fair."

It was a good story. But not a great story.

No way Mom and Dad would buy that one.

I paced back and forth in my room, trying to think of a better story. After a while, I noticed Slappy staring at me.

He sat in the chair beside Dennis, grinning and staring.

Slappy's eyes weren't following me as I paced — were they?

I felt a chill run down my back.

It really seemed as if the eyes were watching me, moving as I moved.

I darted to the chair and turned Slappy so that his back was to me. I didn't have time to think about a stupid dummy. My parents would be home from work any minute. And I needed a good story to explain my awful report card.

Did I come up with one? No.

Were my parents upset? Yes.

Mom said she would help me get better organized. Dad said he would help me understand my math problems. The last time Dad helped me with my math, I nearly flunked!

Even Jed — the total goof-off — got a better report card than me. They don't give grades in the lower school. The teacher just writes a report about you.

And Jed's report said that he was a great kid and a really good student. That teacher must be *sick*!

I stared at Jed across the dinner table. He opened his mouth wide to show me a mouth full of chewed-up peas.

Sick!

"You reek," he said to me. For no reason at all. Sometimes I wonder why families were invented.

Saturday morning, I called Margo. "I can't come over," I told her with a sigh. "My parents won't let me."

"My report card wasn't too good, either," Margo replied. "Miss Carson wrote a note at the bottom. She said I talk too much in class."

"Miss Carson talks too much," I said bitterly.

As I chatted with Margo, I stared at myself in the dresser mirror. I look too much like Sara, I thought. Why do I have to look like her twin? Maybe I'll cut my hair really short. Or get a tattoo.

I wasn't thinking too clearly.

I was too angry that my parents weren't allowing me to go over to Margo's house.

"This is bad news," Margo said. "I wanted to talk to you about performing with Slappy at my dad's place."

"I know," I replied sadly. "But they're not letting me go anywhere until my science project is finished."

"You still haven't turned that in?" Margo demanded.

"I kind of forgot about it," I confessed. "I did the project part — for the second time. I just have to write the report."

"Well, I told you, Daddy has a birthday party for a dozen three-year-olds next Saturday," Margo said. "And he wants you and Slappy to entertain them."

"As soon as I finish the science report, I'm going to start rehearsing," I promised. "Tell your dad not to worry, Margo. Tell him I'll be great."

We chatted for a few more minutes. Then my mom shouted for me to get off the phone. I talked for a little while longer — until Mom shouted a second time. Then I said good-bye to Margo and hung up.

I slaved over my computer all morning and most of the afternoon. And I finished the science report.

It wasn't easy. Jed kept coming into my room, begging me to play a Nintendo game with him. "Just one!" And I had to keep tossing him out.

When I finally finished writing the paper, I printed it out and read it one more time. I thought it was pretty good.

What it needs is a really great-looking cover, I decided.

I wanted to get a bunch of colored markers and do a really bright cover. But my markers were all dried up.

I tossed them into the trash and made my way

to Sara's room. I knew that she had an entire drawer filled with colored markers.

Sara was at the mall with a bunch of her friends. Miss Perfect could go out and spend Saturday doing whatever she wanted. Because she was perfect.

I knew she wouldn't mind if I borrowed a few markers.

Jed stopped me outside her door. "One game of Battle Chess!" he pleaded. "Just one game!"

"No way," I told him. I placed my hand on top of his head. His red, curly hair felt so soft. I pushed him out of my way. "You always murder me at Battle Chess. And I'm not finished with my work yet."

"Why are you going in Sara's room?" he demanded.

"None of your business," I told him.

"You reek," he said. "You double reek, Amy."

I ignored him and made my way into Sara's room to borrow the markers.

I spent nearly an hour making the cover. I filled it with molecules and atoms, all in different colors. Miss Carson will be impressed, I decided.

Sara returned home just as I finished. She was carrying a big shopping bag filled with clothes she'd bought at Banana Republic.

She started to her room with the bag. "Mom — come see what I bought," she called.

Mom appeared, carrying a stack of freshly laundered towels.

"Can I see, too?" I called. I followed them to Sara's room.

But Sara stopped at her door.

The bag fell from her hand.

And she let out a scream.

Mom and I crowded behind her. We peered into the bedroom.

What a mess!

Someone had overturned about a dozen jars of paint. Reds, yellows, blues. The paint had spread over Sara's white carpet, like a big, colorful mud puddle.

I gasped and blinked several times. It was unreal!

"I don't believe it!" Sara kept shrieking. "I don't believe it!"

"The carpet is ruined!" Mom exclaimed, taking one step into the room.

The emptied paint jars were on their sides, strewn around the room.

"Jed!" Mom shouted angrily. "Jed — get in here! Now!"

We turned to see Jed right behind us in the hall. "You don't have to shout," he said softly.

Mom narrowed her eyes angrily at my brother. "Jed — how *could* you?" she demanded through clenched teeth.

"Excuse me?" He gazed up at her innocently.

"Jed — don't lie!" Sara screamed. "Did you do this? Did you go in my room again?"

"No way!" Jed protested, shaking his head. "I didn't go in your room today, Sara. Not once. But I saw Amy go in. And she wouldn't tell me why."

# 10

Sara and Mom both turned accusing eyes on me.

"How could you?" Sara screamed, walking around the big paint puddle. "How *could* you?"

"Whoa! Wait! I didn't! I didn't!" I cried frantically.

"I asked Amy why she was going in here," Jed chimed in. "And she said it was none of my business."

"Amy!" Mom cried. "I'm horrified. I'm truly horrified. This — this is *sick!*"

"Yes, it's sick," Sara repeated, shaking her head. "All of my poster paint. All of it. What a mess. I know why you did it. It's because you're jealous of my perfect report card."

"*But I didn't do it!*" I wailed. "I didn't! I didn't! I didn't!"

"Amy — no one else could have," Mom replied. "If Jed didn't do it, then — "

"But I only came in here to borrow markers!"

I cried in a trembling voice. "That's all. I needed markers."

"Amy — " Mom started, pointing to the huge paint puddle.

"I'll show you!" I cried. "I'll show you what I borrowed."

I ran to my room. My hands were shaking as I scooped Sara's markers off my desk. My heart pounded.

How could they accuse me of something so terrible? I asked myself.

Is that what everyone thinks of me? That I'm such a monster?

That I'm so jealous of my sister, I'd pour out all her paints and ruin her rug?

Do they really think I'm crazy?

I ran back to Sara's room, carrying the markers in both hands. Jed sat on Sara's bed, staring down at the thick red, blue, and yellow puddle.

Mom and Sara stood over it, gazing down and shaking their heads. Mom kept making clucking noises with her tongue. She kept pressing her hands against her cheeks.

"Here! See?" I cried. I shoved the markers toward them. "That's why I came in here. I'm not lying!"

Some of the markers fell out of my hands. I bent to pick them up.

"Amy, there were only three of us home this afternoon," Mom said. She was trying to keep her voice low and calm. But she spoke through gritted teeth. "You, me, and Jed."

"I know — " I started.

Mom raised a hand to silence me. "I certainly didn't do this horrible thing," Mom continued. "And Jed says that he didn't do it. So . . ." Her voice trailed off.

"Mom — I'm not a sicko!" I shrieked. "I'm not!"

"You'll feel better if you confess," Mom said. "Then we can talk about this calmly, and — "

"*But I didn't do it!*" I raged.

With a cry of anger, I flung the markers to the floor. Then I spun around, bolted from Sara's room, and ran down the long hall to my room.

I slammed the door and threw myself facedown onto my bed. I started sobbing loudly. I don't know how long I cried.

Finally, I stood up. My face was sopping wet, and my nose was running. I started to the dresser to get a tissue.

But something caught my eye.

Hadn't I turned Slappy around so that his back was turned to me?

Now he was sitting facing me, staring up at me, his red-lipped grin wider than ever.

Did I turn him back around? Did I?

I didn't remember.

And what did I see on Slappy's shoes?

I wiped the tears from my eyes with the backs of my hands. Then I took a few steps toward the dummy, squinting hard at his big leather shoes.

What *was* that on his shoes?

Red and blue and yellow . . . paint?

Yes.

With a startled gasp, I grabbed both shoes by the heels and raised them close to my face.

Yes.

Drips of paint on Slappy's shoes.

"Slappy — what is going on here?" I asked out loud. "What is going on?"

# 11

When Dad came home and saw Sara's room, he nearly exploded.

I was actually worried about him. His face turned as red as a tomato. His chest started heaving in and out. And horrible gurgling noises came up from his throat.

The whole family gathered in the living room. We took our Sharing Night places. Only, this wasn't Family Sharing Night. This was What Are We Going To Do About Amy Night.

"Amy, first you have to tell us the truth," Mom said. She sat stiffly on the couch, squeezing her hands together in her lap.

Dad sat on the other end of the couch, tapping one hand nervously against the couch arm, chewing his lower lip. Jed and Sara sat on the floor against the wall.

"I *am* telling the truth," I insisted shrilly. I slumped in the armchair across from them. My hair fell over my forehead, but I didn't bother to brush it back. My white T-shirt had tear stains on the front, still damp. "If you would only listen to me," I pleaded."

"Okay, we're listening," Mom replied.

"When I went into my room," I started, "there were splashes of paint on Slappy's shoes. And — "

"Enough!" Dad cried, jumping to his feet.

"But, Dad — " I protested.

"Enough!" he insisted. He pointed a finger at me. "No more wild stories, young lady. Storytime is over. We don't want to hear about paint stains on Slappy. We want an explanation for the crime that was committed in Sara's room today."

"But I *am* giving an explanation!" I wailed. "Why did Slappy have paint on his shoes? Why?"

Dad dropped back onto the couch with a sigh. He whispered something to Mom. She whispered back.

I thought I heard them mention the word "doctor."

"Are you — are you going to take me to a psychiatrist?" I asked timidly.

"Do you think you need one?" Mom replied, staring hard at me.

I shook my head. "No."

"Your father and I will talk about this," Mom said. "We will figure out the best thing to do."

The best thing to do?
They grounded me for two weeks. No movies.

No friends over. No trips to the mall. No trips anywhere.

I heard them talking about finding me a counselor. But they didn't say anything about it to me.

All week, I could feel them watching me. Studying me as if I were some kind of alien creature.

Sara was pretty cold to me. Her room had to be emptied out and a new rug installed. She wasn't happy about it.

Even Jed treated me differently. He kind of tiptoed around me and kept his distance, as if I had a bad cold or something. He didn't tease me, or tell me that I reek, or call me names.

I really missed it. No kidding.

How did I feel? I felt miserable.

I wanted to get sick. I wanted to catch a really bad stomach flu or something so they'd all feel sorry for me and stop treating me like a criminal.

One good thing: They said I could perform with Slappy at The Party House on Saturday.

Whenever I picked Slappy up, I felt a little weird. I remembered the paint on his shoes and the mess in my sister's room.

But I couldn't come up with one single explanation. So I practiced with Slappy every night.

I had put a lot of good jokes together. Silly jokes I thought little three-year-olds would find funny.

And I studied myself in the mirror. I was getting better at not moving my lips. And it was getting easier to make Slappy's mouth and eyes move correctly.

"Knock knock," I made Slappy say.

"Who's there?" I asked.

"Eddie."

"Eddie who?" I asked.

"Eddie-body got a tissue? I hab a teddible cold!"

And then I pulled back Slappy's head, opened his mouth really wide, and jerked his whole body as I made him sneeze and sneeze and sneeze.

I thought that would really crack up the three-year-olds.

Every night, I worked and worked on our comedy act. I worked so hard.

I didn't know that the act would never go on.

On Saturday afternoon, Mom dropped me off at The Party House. "Have a good show!" she called as she drove away.

I carried Slappy carefully in my arms. Margo met me at the door. She greeted me with an excited smile.

"Just in time!" she cried. "The kids are almost all here. They're total animals!"

"Oh, great!" I muttered, rolling my eyes.

"They're total animals, but they're so cute!" Margo added.

She led me through the twisting hallway to the party room in back. Clusters of red and yellow balloons covered the ceiling. I saw a brightly decorated table, all yellow and red. A balloon on a string floated up from each chair around the table. Each balloon had the name of a guest on it.

The kids really were cute. They were dressed mostly in jeans and bright T-shirts. Two of the girls wore frilly party dresses.

I counted ten of them, all running wildly, chasing each other in the huge room.

Their mothers were grouped around a long table against the back wall. Some of them were sitting down. Some were standing, huddled together, chatting. Some were calling to their kids to stop being so wild.

"I'm helping out, pouring the punch and stuff," Margo told me. "Dad wants you to do your act first thing. You know. To quiet the kids down."

I swallowed hard. "First thing, huh?"

I had been excited. I could barely choke down my tuna fish sandwich at lunch. But now I began to feel nervous. I had major fluttering in my stomach.

Margo led me to the front of the room. I saw a low wooden platform there, painted bright blue. That was the stage.

Seeing the stage made my heart start to pound. My mouth suddenly felt very dry.

Could I really step up on that stage and do my act in front of all these people? Kids and mothers?

1 had forgotten that the mothers would all be there. Seeing adults in the audience made me even more nervous.

"Here is the birthday girl," a woman's voice said.

I turned to see a smiling mother. She held the hand of a beautiful little girl. The girl gazed up at me with sparkling blue eyes. She had straight black hair, a lot like mine, only silkier and finer. She had a bright yellow ribbon in her hair. It matched her short yellow party dress and yellow sneakers.

"This is Alicia," the mother announced.

"Hi. I'm Amy," I replied.

"Alicia would like to meet your dummy," the woman said.

"Is he real?" Alicia asked.

I didn't know how to answer that question. "He's a real dummy," I told Alicia.

I propped Slappy up in my arms and slipped my hand into his back. "This is Slappy," I told the little girl. "Slappy, this is Alicia."

"How do you do?" I made Slappy say.

Alicia and her mother both laughed. Alicia stared up at the dummy with her sparkling blue eyes.

"How old are you?" I made Slappy say.

Alicia held up three fingers. "I'm fffree," she told him.

"Would you like to shake hands with Slappy?" I asked.

Alicia nodded.

I lowered the dummy a little. I pushed forward Slappy's right hand. "Go ahead," I urged Alicia. "Take his hand."

Alicia reached up and grabbed Slappy's hand. She giggled.

"Happy Birthday," Slappy said.

Alicia shook his hand gently. Then she started to back away.

"We can't wait to see your show," Alicia's mother said to me. "I know the kids are going to love it."

"I hope so!" I replied. My stomach fluttered again. I was still really nervous.

"Let go!" Alicia cried. She tugged at Slappy's hand. She giggled. "He won't let go!"

Alicia's mom laughed. "What a funny dummy!" She grabbed Alicia's other hand. "Let go of the dummy, honey. We have to get everyone in their seats for the show."

Alicia tugged a little harder. "But he won't let go of *me*, Mommy!" she cried. "He wants to shake hands!"

Alicia gave a hard tug. But her tiny hand was still wrapped up inside Slappy's. She giggled. "He likes me. He won't let go."

"Oh, look," her mother said, glancing to the

door. "Phoebe and Jennifer just arrived. Let's go say hi."

Alicia tried to follow her mom, but Slappy held tight to her hand. Alicia's smile faded. "Let *go!*" she insisted.

I saw that several kids had gathered around. They watched Alicia tug at Slappy's hand.

"Let go! Let me go!" Alicia cried angrily.

I leaned over to examine Slappy's hand. To my surprise, it appeared that his hand had clenched tightly around hers.

Alicia gave a hard tug. "Ow! He's hurting me, Mommy!"

More kids came over to watch. Some of them were laughing. Two little dark-haired boys exchanged frightened glances.

"Please — make him let go!" Alicia wailed. She tugged again and again.

I froze in panic. My mind whirred. I tried to think of what to do.

Had Alicia gotten her hand caught somehow?

Slappy's hand couldn't really close around hers — could it?

Alicia's mother was staring at me angrily. "Please let Alicia's hand out," she said impatiently.

"He's hurting me!" Alicia cried. "Ow! He's squeezing my hand!"

The room grew very quiet. The other kids were

all watching now. Their eyes wide. Their expressions confused.

I didn't know what to do. I had no control for Slappy's hands.

My heart pounded in my chest. I tried to make a joke of it. "Slappy really likes you!" I told Alicia.

But the little girl was sobbing now. Little tears rolled down her cheeks. "Mommy — make him stop!"

I pulled my hand out from Slappy's back. I grabbed his wooden hand between my hands. "Let go of her, Slappy!" I demanded.

I tried pulling the fingers open.

But I couldn't budge them.

"What is wrong?" Alicia's mother was screaming. "Is her hand caught? What are you doing to her?"

"He's hurting me!" Alicia wailed. "Owwww! He's squeezing me!"

Several kids were crying now. Mothers rushed across the room to comfort them.

Alicia's sobs rose up over the frightened cries of the other three-year-olds. The harder she tugged, the tighter the wooden hand squeezed.

"Let go, Slappy!" I shrieked, pulling his fingers. "Let go! Let go!"

"I don't understand!" Alicia's mother cried. She began frantically tugging my arm. "What are you doing? Let her go! Let her go!"

"Owwwww!" Alicia uttered a high, heartbreaking wail. "Make him stop! It hurts! It hurts!"

And then Slappy suddenly tilted his head back. His eyes opened wide, and his mouth opened in a long, evil laugh.

# 12

I burst into the house and let the screen door slam behind me. I had taken the city bus to Logan Street. Then I had run the six blocks to my house with Slappy hanging over my shoulder.

"Amy, how did it go?" Mom called from the kitchen. "Did you get a ride? I thought we were supposed to come pick you up."

I didn't answer her. I was sobbing too hard. I ran down the hall to my room and slammed the door.

I hoisted Slappy off my shoulder and tossed him into the closet. I never wanted to see him again. Never.

I caught a glimpse of myself in the dresser mirror. My cheeks were swollen and puffy from crying. My eyes were red. My hair was wet and tangled, and matted to my forehead.

I took several deep breaths and tried to stop crying.

I kept hearing that poor little girl's screams in

my ears. Slappy finally let go of her after he uttered his ugly laugh.

But Alicia couldn't stop crying. She was so frightened! And her little hand was red and swollen.

The other kids were all screaming and crying, too.

Alicia's mother was furious. She called Margo's dad out from the kitchen. She was shaking and sputtering with anger. She said she was going to sue The Party House.

Margo's dad quietly asked me to leave. He led me to the front door. He said it wasn't my fault. But he said the kids were too frightened of Slappy now. There was no way I could do my show.

I saw Margo hurrying over to me. But I turned and ran out the door.

I had never been so upset. I didn't know what to do. A light rain had started to come down. I watched rainwater flow down the curb and into the sewer drain. I wanted to flow away with it.

Now I threw myself onto my bed.

I kept picturing little Alicia, screaming and crying, trying to twist out of Slappy's grasp.

Mom knocked hard on my bedroom door. "Amy? Amy — what are you doing? What's wrong?"

"Go away!" I wailed. "Just go away."

But she opened the door and stepped into the room. Sara came in behind her, a confused expression on her face.

"Amy — the show didn't go well?" Mom asked softly.

"Go away!" I sobbed. "Please!"

"Amy, you'll do better next time," Sara said, stepping up to the bed. She put a hand on my trembling shoulder.

"Shut up!" I cried. "Shut up, Miss Perfect!"

I didn't mean to sound so angry. I was out of control.

Sara stepped back, hurt.

"Tell us what happened," Mom insisted. "You'll feel better if you tell us."

I pulled myself up until I was sitting on the edge of the bed. I wiped my eyes and brushed my wet hair off my face.

And then, suddenly, the whole story burst out of me.

I told how Slappy grabbed Alicia's hand and wouldn't let go. And how all the kids were crying. And the parents were all screaming and making a fuss. And how I had to leave without doing my act.

And then I leaped to my feet, threw my arms around my mom, and started to sob again.

She petted my hair, the way she used to do when I was a little girl. She kept whispering, "Ssshh shhhh shhhh."

Slowly, I began to calm down.

"This is so weird," Sara murmured, shaking her head.

"I'm a little worried about you," Mom said, holding my hands. "The little girl got her hand caught. That's all. You don't really believe that the dummy grabbed her hand — do you?"

Mom stared at me hard, studying me.

She thinks I'm crazy, I realized. She thinks I'm totally messed up.

She doesn't believe me.

I decided I'd better not insist that my story was true. I shook my head. "Yeah. I guess her hand got caught," I said, lowering my eyes to the floor.

"Maybe you should put Slappy away for a while," Mom suggested, biting her bottom lip.

"Yeah. You're right," I agreed. I pointed. "I already put him in the closet."

"Good idea," Mom replied. "Leave him in there for a while. I think you've been spending too much time with that dummy."

"Yeah. You need a new hobby," Sara chimed in.

"It wasn't a hobby!" I snapped.

"Well, leave him in the closet for a few days — okay, Amy?" Mom said.

I nodded. "I never want to see him again," I muttered.

I thought I heard a sigh from inside the closet. But, of course, that was my imagination.

"Get yourself cleaned up," Mom instructed. "Wash your face. Then come to the kitchen and I'll make you a snack."

"Okay," I agreed.

Sara followed Mom out the door. "Weird," I heard Sara mutter. "Amy is getting so weird."

Margo called after dinner. She said she felt terrible about what had happened. She said her dad didn't blame me. "He wants to give you another chance," Margo told me. "Maybe with older kids."

"Thanks," I replied. "But I put Slappy away for a while. I don't know if I want to be a ventriloquist anymore."

"At the party today — what happened?" Margo asked. "What went wrong?"

"I don't really know," I said. "I don't really know."

That night, I went to bed early. Before I turned out the light, I glanced at the closet door. It was closed tightly.

Having Slappy shut up in the closet made me feel safer.

I fell asleep quickly. I slept a deep, dreamless sleep.

When I awoke the next morning, I sat up and rubbed my eyes.

Then I heard Sara's angry screams down the hall.

"Mom! Dad! Mom! Hurry!" Sara was shouting. "Come see what Amy did now!"

I shut my eyes, listening to my sister's screams.

What now? I thought with a shudder. What now?

"Ohh!" I let out a low cry when I saw that my closet door was open a crack.

My heart pounding, I climbed out of bed and began running down the hall to Sara's room. Mom, Dad, and Jed were already on their way.

"Mom! Dad! Look what she did!" Sara screamed.

"Oh, no!" I heard Mom and Dad shriek.

I stopped in the doorway, peered in — and gasped.

Sara's bedroom walls! They were smeared with red paint!

Someone had taken a thick paintbrush and had scrawled AMY AMY AMY AMY in huge red letters all over Sara's walls.

"Noooo!" I moaned. I covered my mouth with both hands to stop the sound.

My eyes darted from wall to wall, reading my name over and over.

AMY AMY AMY AMY.

Why *my* name?

I suddenly felt sick. I swallowed hard, trying to force back my nausea.

I blinked several times, trying to blink the ugly red scrawls away.

AMY AMY AMY AMY.

"Why?" Sara asked me in a trembling voice. She adjusted her nightshirt and leaned against her dresser. "Why, Amy?"

I suddenly realized that everyone was staring at me.

"I — I — I — " I sputtered.

"Amy, this cannot continue," Dad said solemnly. His expression wasn't angry. It was sad.

"We'll get you some help, dear," Mom said. She had tears in her eyes. Her chin trembled.

Jed stood silently with his arms crossed in front of his pajama shirt.

"Why, Amy?" Sara demanded again.

"But — I *didn't!*" I finally choked out.

"Amy — no stories," Mom said softly.

"But, Mom — I didn't do it!" I insisted shrilly.

"This is serious," Dad murmured, rubbing his whiskery chin. "Amy, do you realize how serious this is?"

Jed reached out two fingers and rubbed them over one of the red paint scrawls. "Dry," he reported.

"That means it was done early in the night," Dad said, his eyes locked on me. "Do you realize how bad this is? This isn't just mischief."

I took a deep breath. My whole body was shaking. "Slappy did it!" I blurted out. "I'm not crazy, Dad! I'm not! You've got to believe me! Slappy did it!"

"Amy, please — " Mom said softly.

"Come with me!" I cried. "I'll prove it. I'll prove that Slappy did it. Come on!"

I didn't wait for them to reply. I turned and bolted from the room.

I flew down the hall. They all followed silently behind me.

"Is Amy sick or something?" I heard Jed ask my parents.

I didn't hear the answer.

I burst into my room. They hurried close behind.

I stepped up to the closet and pulled the door open.

"See?" I cried, pointing to Slappy. "See? That proves it! Slappy did it!"

# 14

I pointed triumphantly at Slappy. "See? See?"

The dummy sat crossed-legged on the closet floor. His head stood erect on his narrow shoulders. He appeared to grin up at us.

Slappy's left hand rested on the closet floor. His right hand was in his lap.

And in his right hand he clutched a fat paintbrush.

The bristles on the brush were caked with red paint.

"I *told* you Slappy did it!" I cried, stepping back so the others could get a better view.

But everyone remained silent. Mom and Dad frowned and shook their heads.

Jed's giggle broke the silence. "This is dumb," he told Sara.

Sara lowered her eyes and didn't reply.

"Oh, Amy," Mom said, sighing. "Did you really think you could blame it on the dummy by putting the paintbrush in his hand?"

"Huh?" I cried. I didn't understand what Mom was saying.

"Did you really expect us to believe this?" Dad asked softly. His eyes stared hard into mine.

"Did you think you could put the brush into Slappy's hand, and make us think he painted your name on Sara's walls?"

"But I *didn't*!" I shrieked.

"When did he learn how to spell?" Jed chimed in.

"Be quiet, Jed," Dad said sharply. "This is serious. It isn't a joke."

"Sara, take Jed out of here," Mom instructed. "The two of you go to the kitchen and get breakfast started."

Sara began to guide Jed to the door. But he pulled away. "I want to stay!" he cried. "I want to see how you punish Amy."

"Get!" Mom cried, shooing him away with both hands.

Sara tugged him out of the room.

I was shaking all over. I narrowed my eyes at Slappy. Had his grin grown even wider?

I stared at the paintbrush in his hand. The red paint on the bristles blurred, blurred until I saw only red.

I blinked several times and turned back to my parents. "You really don't believe me?" I asked softly, my voice trembling.

They shook their heads. "How can we believe you, dear?" Mom replied.

"We can't believe that a wooden dummy has been doing these horrible things in Sara's room," Dad added. "Why don't you tell us the truth, Amy?"

"But I *am!*" I protested.

How could I prove it to them? How?

I let out an angry cry and slammed the closet door shut.

"Let's try to calm down," Mom urged quietly. "Let's all get dressed and have some breakfast. We can talk about this when we're feeling better."

"Good idea," Dad replied, still squinting at me through his glasses. He was studying me as if he'd never seen me before.

He scratched his bald head. "Guess I'll have to call a painter for Sara's room. It'll take at least two coats to cover up the red."

They turned and made their way slowly from my room, talking about how much it was going to cost to have my sister's room painted.

I stood in the center of the room and shut my eyes. Every time I closed them, I saw red. All over Sara's wall:

AMY AMY AMY AMY.

"But I didn't do it!" I cried out loud.

My heart pounding, I spun around. I grabbed the knob and jerked open the closet door.

I grabbed Slappy by the shoulders of his gray jacket and pulled him up from the floor.

The paintbrush fell from his hand. It landed with a thud beside my bare foot.

I shook the dummy angrily. Shook him so hard that his arms and legs swung back and forth, and his head snapped back.

Then I lifted him so that we were eye to eye.

"Admit it!" I screamed, glaring into his grinning face. "Go ahead! Admit that you did it! Tell me that you did it!"

The glassy blue eyes gazed up at me.

Lifelessly.

Blankly.

Neither of us moved.

And then, to my horror, the wooden lips parted. The red mouth slowly opened.

And Slappy let out a soft, evil, *"Hee hee hee."*

# 15

"I can't come over," I told Margo glumly. I was sprawled on top of my bed, the phone pressed against my ear. "I'm not allowed out of my room all day."

"Huh? Why?" Margo demanded.

I sighed. "If I told you, Margo, you wouldn't believe me."

"Try me," she replied.

I decided not to tell her. I mean, my whole family thought I was crazy. Why should my best friend think it, too?

"Maybe I'll tell you about it when I see you," I said.

Silence at the other end.

Then Margo uttered, "Wow."

"Wow? What does wow mean?" I cried.

"Wow. It must be pretty bad if you can't talk about it, Amy."

"It — it's just weird," I stammered. "Can we change the subject?"

Another silence. "Daddy has a birthday party for six-year-olds coming up, Amy. And he wondered — "

"No. Sorry," I broke in quickly. "I put Slappy away."

"Excuse me?" Margo reacted with surprise.

"I put the dummy away," I told her. "I'm finished with that. I'm not going to be a ventriloquist anymore."

"But, Amy — " Margo protested. "You *loved* playing with those dummies. And you said you wanted to make some money, remember? So Daddy — "

"No," I repeated firmly. "I changed my mind, Margo. I'm sorry. Tell your dad I'm sorry. I — I'll tell you about it when I see you."

I swallowed hard. And added: "*If* I ever see you."

"You sound terrible," Margo replied softly. "Should I come over to your house? I think I could get my dad to drop me off."

"I'm totally grounded," I said unhappily. "No visitors."

I heard footsteps in the hall. Probably Mom or Dad checking up on me. I wasn't allowed to be on the phone, either.

"Got to go. Bye, Margo," I whispered. I hung up the phone.

Mom knocked on my bedroom door. I recognized her knock. "Amy, want to talk?" she called in.

"Not really," I replied glumly.

"As soon as you tell the truth, you can come out," Mom said.

"I know," I muttered.

"Why don't you just tell the truth now? It's such a beautiful day," Mom called in. "Don't waste the whole day in your room."

"I — I don't feel like talking now," I told her.

She didn't say anything else. But I could hear her standing out there. Finally I heard her footsteps padding back down the hall.

I grabbed my pillow and buried my face in it.

I wanted to shut out the world. And think.

Think. Think. Think.

I wasn't going to confess to a crime I didn't do. No way.

I was going to find a way to prove to them that Slappy was the culprit. And I was going to prove to them that I wasn't crazy.

I had to show them that Slappy wasn't an ordinary dummy.

He was alive. And he was evil.

But how could I prove it?

I climbed to my feet and began pacing back and forth. I stopped at the window and gazed out at the front yard.

It *was* a beautiful spring day. Bright yellow

tulips bobbed in the flower patch in front of my window. The sky was a solid blue. The twin maple trees in the center of the yard were starting to unfurl fresh leaves.

I took a deep breath. The air smelled so fresh and sweet.

I saw Jed and a couple of his friends. They were Rollerblading down the sidewalk. Laughing. Having a good time.

And I was a prisoner. A prisoner in my room.

All because of Slappy.

I spun away from the window and stared at the closet door. I had shoved Slappy into the back of the closet and shut the door tightly.

I'm going to catch you in the act, Slappy, I decided.

That's how I'm going to prove I'm not crazy.

I'm going to stay up all night. I'm going to stay up *every* night. And the first time you creep out of that closet, I'll be awake. And I'll follow you.

And I'll make sure that everyone sees what you are doing.

I'll make sure that everyone sees that *you* are the evil one in this house.

I felt so upset. I knew I wasn't really thinking clearly.

But having a plan made me feel a little better.

Taking one last glance at the closet door, I crossed the room to my desk and started to do my homework.

Mom and Dad let me come out for dinner.

Dad had grilled hamburgers in the backyard, the first barbecue of spring. I loved grilled hamburgers, especially when they're charred real black. But I could barely taste my food.

I guess I felt too excited and nervous about trapping Slappy.

No one talked much.

Mom kept chattering to Dad about the vegetable garden and what she wanted to plant. Sara talked a little about the mural she had started to paint in her room. Jed kept complaining about how he wrecked his knee Rollerblading.

No one spoke to me. They kept glancing over the table at me. Studying me like I was some kind of zoo animal.

I asked to be excused before dessert.

I usually stay up till ten. But a little after nine, I decided to go to bed.

I was wide awake. Eager to trap Slappy.

I turned out the light and tucked myself in. Then I lay staring up at the shifting shadows on the bedroom ceiling, waiting, waiting . . .

Waiting for Slappy to come creeping out of the closet.

I must have fallen asleep.

I tried not to. But I must have drifted off anyway.

I was startled awake by sounds in the room.

221

I raised my head, instantly alert. And listened.

The scrape of feet on my carpet. A soft rustling.

A shiver of fear ran down my back. I felt goosebumps up and down my arms.

Another low sound. So near my bed.

I reached forward quickly. Clicked on the bed table lamp.

And cried out.

# 16

"Jed — what are you *doing* in here?" I shrieked.

He stood blinking at me in the center of the room. One leg of his blue pajama pants had rolled up. His red hair was matted against one side of his head.

"What are you doing in my room?" I demanded breathlessly.

He squinted at me. "Huh? Why are you yelling at me? You *called* me, Amy."

"I — I *what?*" I sputtered.

"You called me. I heard you." He rubbed his eyes with his fingers and yawned. "I was asleep. You woke me up."

I lowered my feet to the floor and stood up. My legs felt shaky and weak. Jed had really scared me.

"I was asleep, too," I told him. "I didn't call you."

"Yes, you did," he insisted. "You told me to

come to your room." He bent to pull down the pajama leg.

"Jed, you just woke *me* up," I replied. "So how could I call you?"

He scratched his hair. He yawned again. "You mean I dreamed it?"

I studied his face. "Jed — did you sneak into my room to play some kind of prank?" I demanded sternly.

He wrinkled his face up, tried to appear innocent.

"*Did* you?" I demanded. "Were you going into the closet to do something with Slappy?"

"No way!" he protested. He started to back out of the room. "I'm telling the truth, Amy. I thought you called me. That's all."

I squinted hard at him, trying to decide if he was telling the truth. I let my eyes wander around the room. Everything seemed okay. Dennis lay in the armchair, his head in his lap.

The closet door remained closed.

"It was a dream, that's all," Jed repeated. "Good night, Amy."

I said good night. "Sorry I got upset, Jed. It's been a bad day."

I listened to him pad back to his room.

The cat poked his head into my room, his eyes gleaming like gold. "Go to sleep, George," I whispered. "You go to sleep, too, okay?" He obediently turned and disappeared.

I clicked off the bed table lamp and settled back into bed.

Jed was telling the truth, I decided. He seemed as confused as I was.

My eyes suddenly felt heavy. As if there were hundred-pound weights over them. I let out a loud yawn.

I felt so sleepy. And the pillow felt so soft and warm.

But I couldn't let myself fall back to sleep.

I had to stay awake. Had to wait for Slappy to make his move.

Did I drift back to sleep? I'm not sure.

A loud *click* made my eyes shoot open wide.

I raised my head in time to see the closet door start to open.

The room lay in darkness. No light washed in from the window. The door was a black shadow, sliding slowly, slowly.

My heart began to pound. My mouth suddenly felt dry as cotton.

The closet door slid slowly, silently.

A low *creak*.

And then a shadow stepped out from behind the dark door.

I squinted hard at it. Not moving a muscle.

Another *creak* of the door.

The figure took another silent step. Out of the closet. Another step. Another. Making its way past my bed, to the bedroom door.

Slappy.

Yes!

Even in the night blackness I could see his large, rounded head. I watched his skinny arms dangle at his sides, the wooden hands bobbing as he moved.

The heavy leather shoes slid over my carpet. The thin, boneless legs nearly collapsed with each shuffling step.

Like a scarecrow, I thought, gripped with horror.

He walks like a scarecrow. Because he has no bones. No bones at all.

Up and down, his whole body bobbed as he crept away.

I waited until he slithered and scraped out the door and into the hall. Then I jumped to my feet.

I took a deep breath and held it.

Then I tiptoed through the darkness after him.

Here we go! I told myself. *Here we go!*

# 17

I stopped at the bedroom door and poked my head into the hall. Mom keeps a small night-light on all night just outside her bedroom door. It cast dim yellow light over the other end of the hall.

Peering into the light, I watched Slappy pull himself silently toward Sara's room. The big shoes shuffled along the carpet. Slappy's body bobbed and bent. The big, wooden hands nearly dragged along the floor.

When my chest started to ache, I realized I hadn't taken a breath. As silently as I could, I let out a long whoosh of air. Then I took another deep breath and started to follow Slappy down the hall.

I had a sudden impulse to shout: "Mom! Dad!"

They would burst out of their room and see Slappy standing there in the middle of the hall.

But, no.

I didn't want to shout for them now. I wanted to see where Slappy was heading. I wanted to see what he planned to do.

I took a step. The floorboard creaked under my bare foot.

Did he hear me?

I pressed my back against the wall, tried to squeeze myself flat in the deep shadows.

I peered through the dim yellow light at him. He kept bobbing silently along. His shoulders rode up and down with each shuffling step.

He was just outside Sara's room when he turned around.

My heart stopped.

I ducked low. Dropped back into the bathroom.

Had he seen me?

Had he turned around because he knew I was there?

I shut my eyes. Waited. Listened.

Listened for him to come scraping back. Listened for him to turn around and come back to get me.

Silence.

I swallowed hard. My mouth felt so dry. My legs were trembling. I grabbed the tile wall to steady myself.

Still silent out there.

I gathered up my courage and slowly, slowly poked my head out into the hall.

Empty.

I squinted toward Sara's room in the yellow light.

No one there.

He's in Sara's room, I told myself. He's doing something terrible in Sara's room. Something I'll be blamed for.

Not *this* time, Slappy! I silently vowed.

This time you're going to be caught.

Pressing against the wall, I crept down the hall. I stopped in Sara's doorway.

The night-light was plugged in across from Sara's room. The light was brighter here.

I squinted into her bedroom. I could see the mural she had started to paint. A beach scene. The ocean. A broad, yellow beach. Kites flying over the beach. Kids building a sand castle in one corner. The mural was tacked up, nearly covering the entire wall.

Where was Slappy?

I took a step into the room — and saw him.

Standing at her paint table.

I saw his big wooden hand fumble over the table of supplies. Then he grabbed a paintbrush in one hand.

He raised and lowered the brush, as if pretending to paint the air.

Then I saw him dip the paintbrush in a jar of paint.

Slappy took a step toward the mural. Then another step.

He stood for a moment, admiring the mural.

He raised the paintbrush high.

That's when I burst into the room.

I dove toward the dummy just as he raised the paintbrush to the mural.

I grabbed the paintbrush with one hand. Wrapped my other hand around his waist. And tugged him back.

The dummy kicked both legs and tried to punch me with his fists.

"Hey — !" a startled voice shouted.

The light clicked on.

Slappy went limp on my arm. His head dropped. His arms and legs dangled to the floor.

Sitting up in bed, Sara gaped at me in horror.

I saw her eyes stop at the paintbrush in my hand.

"Amy — what are you *doing?*" she cried.

And, then, without waiting for an answer, Sara began to shout: "Mom! Dad! Hurry! She's in here again!"

## 18

Dad came rumbling in first, adjusting his pajama pants. "What's going on? What's the problem?"

Mom followed right behind him, blinking and yawning.

"I — I took this from Slappy," I stammered, holding up the paintbrush. "He — he was going to ruin the mural."

They stared at the paintbrush in my hand.

"I heard Slappy sneak out of the closet," I explained breathlessly. "I followed him into Sara's room. I grabbed him just before — before he did something terrible."

I turned to Sara. "You saw Slappy — right? You saw him?"

"Yeah," Sara said, still in bed, her arms crossed over her chest. "I see Slappy. You're carrying him on your arm."

The dummy hung over my arm, its head nearly hitting the floor.

"No!" I cried to Sara. "You saw him sneak into

231

your room — right? That's why you turned on the light?"

Sara rolled her eyes. "I saw *you* come into my room," she replied. "You're *carrying* the dummy, Amy. You're holding the dummy — and the brush."

"But — but — but — " I sputtered.

My eyes darted from face to face. They all stared back at me as if I had just landed on Earth in a flying saucer.

No one in my family was going to believe me. No one.

The next morning, Mom hung up the phone as I came down for breakfast. "You're wearing shorts to school?" she asked, eyeing my outfit — olive-green shorts and a red, sleeveless T-shirt.

"The radio said it's going to be hot," I replied.

Jed and Sara were already at the table. They glanced up from their cereal bowls, but didn't say anything.

I poured myself a glass of grape juice. I'm the only one in my family who doesn't like orange juice. I guess I *am* totally weird.

"Who were you talking to on the phone?" I asked Mom. I took a long drink.

"Uh . . . Dr. Palmer's secretary," she replied hesitantly. "You have purple above your lip," she told me, pointing.

I wiped the grape juice off with a napkin. "Dr. Palmer? Isn't she a shrink?" I asked.

Mom nodded. "I tried to get an appointment for today. But she can't see you until Wednesday."

"But, Mom — !" I protested.

Mom placed a finger over her mouth. "Sssshhh. No discussion."

"But, Mom — !" I repeated.

"Ssshhh. Just talk to her once, Amy. You might enjoy it. You might think it's helpful."

"Yeah. Sure," I muttered.

I turned to Sara and Jed. They stared down at their cereal bowls.

I sighed and set the juice glass down in the sink.

I knew what this meant. It meant that I had until Wednesday to prove to my family that I wasn't a total wack job.

In the lunchroom at school, Margo begged me to tell her what was going on with me. "Why were you locked up in your room all day yesterday?" she demanded. "Come on, Amy — spill."

"It's no big deal," I lied.

No way I was going to tell her.

I didn't need the story going around school that Amy Kramer believes her ventriloquist dummy is alive.

I didn't need everyone whispering about me and staring at me the way everyone in my family did.

"Dad wants to know if you'll change your mind about the birthday party," Margo said. "If you want to perform with Slappy, you can — "

"No. Forget it!" I interrupted. "I put Slappy in the closet, and he's staying there. Forever."

Margo's eyes went wide. "Okay. Okay. Wow. You don't have to bite my head off."

"Sorry," I said quickly. "I'm a little stressed out these days. Here. Want this?" I handed her the brownie Mom had packed.

"Thanks," Margo replied, surprised.

"Later," I said. I crinkled up my lunch bag, tossed it in the trash, and hurried away.

In my room that night, I couldn't concentrate on my homework. I kept staring at the calendar.

Monday night. I had only two nights to prove that I wasn't crazy, that Slappy really was doing these horrible things.

I slammed my history book shut. No way I could read about the firing on Fort Sumter tonight.

I paced back and forth for a while. Thinking. Thinking hard. But getting nowhere.

What could I do?

What?

After a while, my head felt about to split open. I reached up both hands and tugged at my hair.

"Aaaaagh!" I let out a furious cry. Of anger. Of frustration.

Maybe I'll just get rid of Slappy, I decided.

Maybe I'll take him outside and toss him in the trash.

And that will end the whole problem.

The idea made me feel a little better.

I turned and took two steps toward the closet.

But I stopped with a gasp when I saw the doorknob slowly turn.

As I stared in shock, the closet door swung open.

Slappy stepped out.

He slumped forward and stopped a few feet in front of me.

His blue eyes glared up at me. His grin grew wider.

"Amy," he rasped, "it's time you and I had a little talk."

# 19

"Amy, now you are my slave," Slappy said. His threat came out in a harsh, cold rasp. The eerie voice made me shiver.

I stared back at him. I couldn't reply.

I gaped into those glassy blue eyes, that red-lipped smirk.

"You read the ancient words that bring me to life," the dummy whispered. "And now you will serve me. You will do everything I ask."

"No!" I finally managed to choke out. "No! Please — !"

"Yes!" he cried. The grinning wooden head bobbed up and down, nodding. "Yes, Amy! You are my slave now! My slave forever!"

"I w-won't!" I stammered. "You can't make me — " My voice caught in my throat. My legs wobbled like rubber. My knees buckled, and I nearly fell.

Slappy raised one hand and grabbed my wrist. I felt the cold, wooden fingers tighten around me.

"You will do as I tell you — from now on," the dummy whispered. "Or else . . ."

"Let go of me!" I cried. I struggled to tug my arm free. But his grasp was too tight. "Or else *what?*" I cried.

"Or else I will destroy your sister's mural," Slappy replied. His painted grin grew wider. The cold eyes glared into mine.

"Big deal," I muttered. "Do you really think I'll be your slave because you wreck her painting? You've already wrecked Sara's room — haven't you? That doesn't mean I'll be your slave!"

"I'll keep on destroying things," Slappy replied, tightening his grip on my wrist, tugging me down toward him. "Maybe I'll start wrecking your brother's things, too. And you will be blamed, Amy. You will be blamed for it all."

"Stop — " I cried, trying to twist free.

"Your parents are already worried about you — aren't they, Amy?" the dummy rasped in that harsh, cold whispery voice. "Your parents already think you're crazy!"

"Stop! Please — !" I pleaded.

"What do you think they'll do when you start wrecking everything in the house?" Slappy demanded. "What do you think they'll do to you, Amy?"

"Listen to me!" I shrieked. "You can't — "

He jerked my arm hard. "They'll send you away!" he rasped, his eyes flashing wildly. "That's what your parents will do. They'll send you away. And you'll never see them again — except on visiting days!"

He tilted back his wooden head and uttered a shrill laugh.

A low moan escaped my throat. My entire body shuddered with terror.

Slappy tugged me closer. "You will be an excellent slave," he whispered in my ear. "You and I will have many good years together. You will devote your life to me."

"No!" I cried. "No, I won't!"

I sucked in a deep breath. Then I swung my arm hard, as hard as I could.

I caught the dummy by surprise.

Before he could let go of my wrist, I pulled him off balance.

He let out a startled grunt as I lifted him off the floor.

*He's just a dummy*, I told myself. *Just a dummy. I can handle him. I can beat him.*

His hand fell off my wrist.

I ducked low. Grabbed his boneless arm with both hands. Swung my shoulder. Flipped him over my back.

He landed hard on his stomach. His head made a loud *clonk* as it hit the floor.

Breathing hard, my heart thudding wildly, I dove.

*I can handle him. I can beat him.*

238

I tried to pin him to the floor with my knees.

But he spun away and scrambled up, faster than I could believe.

I cried out as he swung his wooden fist.

I tried to dodge away. But he was too fast.

The heavy fist hit me square in the forehead.

My face felt as if it had exploded. Pain shot down my body.

Everything went bright red.

And, holding both sides of my head, I crumpled to the floor.

# 20

*I can handle him. I can beat him.*

The words repeated in my mind.

I blinked my eyes. Raised my head.

I refused to give up.

Through the haze of red, I reached up with both hands.

I grabbed Slappy by the waist and pulled him down.

Ignoring my throbbing forehead, I wrestled him to the ground. He kicked both feet and thrashed his arms wildly. He swung at me, trying to land another blow.

But I dug my knee into his middle. Then I wrapped my hands around his thrashing arms and pinned them to the floor.

"Let go, slave!" he squealed. "I command you — let go!" He struggled and squirmed.

But I held tight.

His eyes darted frantically from side to side.

His wooden jaw clicked open and shut, open and shut, as he strained to squirm free.

"I command you to let go, slave! You have no choice! You must obey me!"

I ignored his shrill cries and swung his arms behind his back. Holding them tightly in place, I climbed to my feet.

He tried to kick me with both shoes. But I let go of the arms and grabbed his legs.

I swung him upside down. Once again, his head hit the floor with a *clonk*.

It didn't seem to hurt him a bit.

"Let go! Let go, slave! You will pay! You will pay dearly for this!" He screamed and protested, squirming and swinging his arms.

Breathing hard, I dragged him across the rug — and swung him into the open closet.

He dove quickly, trying to escape.

But I slammed the door in his face. And turned the lock.

With a sigh, I leaned my back against the closet door and struggled to catch my breath.

"Let me out! You can't keep me in here!" Slappy raged.

He began pounding on the door. Then he kicked the door.

"I'll break it down! I really will!" he threatened. He pounded even harder. The big wooden hands thudded against the wooden door.

I turned and saw the door start to give.

He's going to break it open! I realized.

*What can I do? What can I do now?* I tried to fight back my panic, struggled to think clearly.

Slappy furiously kicked at the door.

I need help, I decided.

I bolted into the hall. Mom and Dad had their bedroom door closed, I saw. Should I wake them up?

No. They wouldn't believe me.

I'd drag them into my room. Slappy would be slumped lifelessly on the closet floor. Mom and Dad would be even more upset about me.

Sara, I thought. Maybe I can convince Sara. Maybe Sara will listen to me.

Her door was open. I burst into her bedroom.

She stood at the mural, brush in hand, dabbing yellow paint on the beach.

She turned as I ran in, and her face tightened in anger. "Amy — what do *you* want?" she demanded.

"You — you've got to believe me!" I sputtered. "I need your help! It wasn't me who did those horrible things. It really wasn't, Sara. It was Slappy. Please — believe me! It was Slappy!"

"Yes. I know," Sara replied calmly.

# 21

"Huh?" My mouth dropped open. I stared at her in surprise. "What did you say?"

Sara set down the paintbrush. She wiped her hands on her gray smock. "Amy — I know it's Slappy," she repeated in a whisper.

"I — I — " I was so stunned, I couldn't speak. "But, Sara — you — "

"I'm sorry. I'm so sorry!" she cried with emotion. She rushed forward and threw her arms around me. She hugged me tightly.

I still didn't believe what she had said. My head was spinning.

I gently pushed her away. "You knew all this time? You knew it was Slappy and not me?"

Sara nodded. "The other night, I woke up. I heard someone in my room. I pretended to be asleep. But I had my eyes open partway."

"And — ?" I demanded.

"I saw Slappy," Sara confessed, lowering her eyes. "I saw him carrying a red paintbrush. I saw

243

him painting AMY AMY AMY AMY all over my walls."

"But you didn't tell Mom and Dad?" I cried. "You made them think it was me? And the whole time, you knew the truth?"

Sara kept her eyes on the floor. Her black hair fell over her face. She brushed it back with a quick, nervous sweep of one hand.

"I — I didn't want to believe it," she confessed. "I didn't want to believe that a dummy could walk on its own, that it could be . . . alive."

I glared at her. "And, so — ?"

"So I accused you," Sara said with a sob. "I guess the truth was just too scary. I was too frightened, Amy. I *wanted* to believe it was you doing those horrible things. I wanted to pretend it wasn't the dummy."

"You *wanted* to get me in trouble," I accused. "That's why you did it, Sara. That's why you lied to Mom and Dad. You *wanted* to get me in trouble."

She finally raised her face to me. I saw two tears trailing down her cheeks. "Yeah, I guess," she murmured.

She wiped the tears off with her hands. Her green eyes locked on mine. "I — I guess I'm a little jealous of you," she said.

"Huh?" My sister had stunned me again. I squinted at her, trying to make sense of her words. "You?" I cried. "You're jealous of *me*?"

She nodded. "Yeah. I guess. Everything is easy for you. You're so relaxed. Everyone likes your sense of humor. It's not like that for me," Sara explained. "I have to paint to impress people."

I opened my mouth, but no sound came out. This had to be the biggest surprise of all. Sara jealous of *me*?

Didn't she know how jealous I was of *her*?

I suddenly had a funny feeling in my chest. My eyes brimmed with tears. Strong emotion swept over me like an ocean wave.

I rushed forward and hugged Sara.

For some reason, we both started laughing. I can't explain it. We stood there in the middle of her room, laughing like lunatics.

I guess we were just so glad that the truth was out.

Then Slappy's painted face flashed back into my mind. And I remembered with a chill why I had burst into my sister's room.

"You have to help me," I told her. "Right now."

Sara's smile vanished. "Help you do what?" she demanded.

"We have to get rid of Slappy," I told her. "We have to get rid of him for good."

I tugged her hand. She followed me down the hall.

"But — how?" she asked.

Stepping into my room, we both cried out at once.

We heard a final kick — and the closet door swung open.

Slappy burst out, his eyes wild with rage.

"Guess what, slaves?" he rasped. "Slappy wins!"

# 22

"Grab him!" I cried to my sister.

I reached out both arms and made a frantic dive for the dummy. But he scampered to the side and slipped away from my tackle.

His blue eyes flashed excitedly. His red lips twisted in an ugly grin.

"Give up, slaves!" he rasped. "You cannot win!"

Sara held back, hands against the door frame. I could see the fear in her eyes.

I made another grab for Slappy. Missed again.

"Sara — help me!" I pleaded.

Sara took a step into the room.

I leaped at Slappy, grabbed one boneless ankle.

With a grunt, he pulled out of my grasp. He darted toward the door — and ran right into Sara.

The collision stunned them both.

Sara staggered back.

Slappy teetered off balance.

I threw myself at him, caught his arms, and pulled them behind his back.

He squirmed and twisted. He kicked out furiously.

But Sara grabbed both of his big leather shoes. "Tie him in a knot!" she cried breathlessly.

He kicked and thrashed.

But we held tight.

I twisted his arms behind him. Twisted them around each other. Twisted. Twisted. Then tied them in as tight a knot as I could.

Slappy squirmed and bucked, grunting loudly, his wooden jaws clicking.

When I glanced up from my work on the arms, I saw that Sara had wrapped his legs in a knot, too.

Slappy tilted back his head and uttered a roar of rage. His eyes slid up into his head so that only the whites showed. *"Put me down, slaves! Put me down at once!"*

With one hand, I grabbed a wad of tissues from my bed table and jammed it into Slappy's mouth.

He uttered a grunt of protest, then went silent.

"Now what?" Sara cried breathlessly. "Where should we put him?"

My eyes shot around the room. No, I decided. I don't want him in my room. I don't want him in the house.

"Outside," I instructed my sister, holding on to the knotted arms with both of my hands. "Let's get him outside."

Struggling to hold on to the bucking legs, Sara glanced at the clock. "It's after eleven. What if Mom and Dad hear us?"

"I don't care!" I cried. "Hurry! I want him out of here! I never want to see him again!"

We dragged Slappy out into the hall. Mom and Dad's door remained closed.

Good, I thought. They hadn't heard our struggle.

Sara carried him by the knotted legs. I held on to the arms.

Slappy had stopped struggling and squirming. I think he was waiting to see what we were going to do with him. The wad of tissues had silenced his cries.

I didn't know where to take him. I only knew I wanted him out of the house.

We carried him through the darkened living room and out the front door. We stepped into a hot, sticky night, more like summer than spring. A pale sliver of a moon hovered low in a blue-black sky.

There was no breeze. No sounds of any kind. Nothing moved.

Sara and I carried the dummy to the driveway. "Should we take him somewhere on our bikes?" she suggested.

"How will we balance him?" I asked. "Besides, it's too dark. Too dangerous. Let's just carry him a few blocks and dump him somewhere."

"You mean in a trash can or something?" Sara asked.

I nodded. "That's where he belongs. In the trash."

Luckily, the dummy didn't weigh much at all. We made our way to the sidewalk, then carried him to the end of the block.

Slappy remained limp, his eyes rolled up in his head.

At the corner, I spotted two circles of white light approaching. Car headlights. "Quick — !" I whispered to Sara.

We slipped behind a hedge just in time. The car rolled by without slowing.

We waited for the glow of red taillights to disappear in the darkness. Then we continued down the next block, carrying the dummy between us.

"Hey — how about those?" Sara asked, pointing with her free hand.

I squinted to see what she had spotted. A row of metal trash cans lined up at the curb in front of a dark house across the street.

"I oks good," I said. "Let's shove him in and clamp down the lid. Maybe the trash guys will haul him away tomorrow."

I led the way across the street — and then stopped. "Sara — wait," I whispered. "I have a better idea."

I dragged the dummy toward the corner. I motioned to the metal drain down at the curb.

"The sewer?" Sara whispered.

I nodded. "It's perfect." Through the narrow opening at the curb, I could hear running water far down below. "Come on. Shove him in."

Slappy still didn't move or protest in any way.

I lowered his head to the drain opening. Then Sara and I pushed him in headfirst.

I heard a *splash* and a hard *thud* as he hit the sewer floor.

We both listened. Silence. Then the soft trickle of water.

Sara and I grinned at each other.

We hurried home. I was so happy, I skipped most of the way.

The next morning, Sara and I came to the kitchen for breakfast together. Mom turned from the counter, where she was pouring herself a cup of coffee.

Jed was already at the table, eating his Frosted Flakes. "What's *he* doing down here?" Jed asked.

He pointed across the table.

At Slappy. Sitting in the chair.

# 23

Sara and I both gasped.

"Yes. Why is that dummy down here?" Mom asked me. "I found him sitting there when I came in this morning. And why is he so dirty? Where has he been, Amy?"

I could barely choke out a word. "I . . . uh . . . I guess he fell or something," I finally mumbled.

"Well, take him back upstairs," Mom ordered. "He's supposed to be kept in the closet — remember?"

"Uh . . . yeah. I remember," I said, sighing.

"You'll have to clean him up later," Mom said, stirring her coffee. "He looks as if he's been wallowing in the mud."

"Okay," I replied weakly.

I hoisted Slappy up and slung him over my shoulder. Then I started to my room.

"I — I'll come with you," Sara stammered.

"What for?" Mom demanded. "Sit down, Sara,

and eat your breakfast. You're both going to be late."

Sara obediently sat down across from Jed. I made my way down the hall.

I was halfway to my room when Slappy raised his head and whispered in my ear, "Good morning, slave. Did you sleep well?"

I tossed him into the closet and locked the door.

I could hear him laughing inside the closet. The evil laugh made me shake all over.

*What am I going to do now?* I asked myself. *What can I do to get rid of this creature?*

The day dragged by. I don't think I heard a word my teacher said.

I couldn't get Slappy's evil, grinning face out of my mind. His raspy voice rattled in my ears.

*I won't be your slave!* I silently vowed. *I'll get you out of my house — out of my life — if it's the last thing I do!*

That night, I lay wide awake in my bed. How could I sleep, knowing that evil dummy sat in the closet a few feet away?

The night was hot and steamy. I had pushed the window open all the way, but there was no breeze. A fly buzzed by my head, the first fly of spring.

Staring up at the twisting shadows on the ceiling, I brushed the fly away with one hand. As soon as the buzzing vanished, another sound took its place.

A click. A low squeak.

The sound of the closet door opening.

I raised myself up off the pillow. Squinting into the darkness, I saw Slappy creep out of the closet.

He took a few shuffling steps, his big shoes sliding silently over my carpet. He turned.

Was he coming toward my bed?

No.

His head and shoulders bobbed as he pulled himself to the door. Then out into the hall.

He's going to Sara's room, I knew.

But what was he going to do there? Did he plan to pay us back for what we did to him last night?

What new horror was he going to create?

I lowered my feet to the floor, climbed out of bed, and followed him out into the hall.

# 24

My eyes adjusted quickly to the dim yellow light from the night-light at the other end of the hall. I watched Slappy slither toward my sister's room. He moved as silently as a shadow.

I held my breath and kept my back against the wall as I followed behind him. When he turned into Sara's room, I stepped away from the wall and started to run.

I reached the bedroom doorway in time to see Slappy pick up a wide paintbrush from Sara's supply table. He took a step toward the mural on the wall.

One step.

And then another small figure leaped out of the darkness.

The lights flashed on.

"Dennis!" I cried.

"*Stand back!*" Dennis ordered in a high, shrill voice. He lowered his wooden head and charged at Slappy.

Sara sat up in her bed and uttered a frightened cry.

I could see the stunned expression on Slappy's face.

Dennis flew at Slappy. He slammed his head into Slappy's middle.

Slappy let out a loud *"Oooof!"* He staggered back. Fell.

A loud *thud* rang through the room as the back of Slappy's head hit Sara's iron bedpost.

I raised both hands to my cheeks and gasped as Slappy's head cracked open.

The wooden head split down the middle.

I watched the evil face crack apart. The wide, shocked eyes slid in different directions. The red lips cracked and fell away.

The head dropped to the floor in two pieces. And then the body collapsed in a heap beside them.

My hands still pressed against my face, my heart pounding, I took a few steps into the room.

Dennis ran past me, out to the hall.

But my eyes were locked on the two pieces of Slappy's head. I stared in horror as an enormous white worm crawled out of one of the pieces. The fat worm slithered and curled to the wall — and vanished into a crack in the molding.

Sara climbed out of bed, breathing hard, her face bright red from the excitement.

The closet door swung open. Mom and Dad came bursting out.

"Girls — are you okay?" Dad cried.

We nodded.

"We saw the whole thing!" Mom exclaimed. She threw her arms around me. "Amy, I'm so sorry. I'm so sorry. We should have believed you. I'm so sorry we didn't believe you."

"We believe you now!" Dad declared, staring down at Slappy's broken head, his crumpled body. "We saw everything!"

It was all planned. Sara and I had worked it out before dinner.

Sara convinced Mom and Dad to hide in the closet. Mom and Dad were really creeped out by the way I was acting. They were willing to do anything.

So Sara pretended to go to sleep. Mom and Dad hid in the closet.

I left the closet door unlocked to make it easier for Slappy to get out.

I knew Slappy would creep into Sara's room. I knew Mom and Dad would finally see that I'm not crazy.

And then Jed burst out dressed as Dennis, with Dennis's head propped up on top of his turtleneck sweater.

We knew that would shock Slappy. We knew it would give us a chance to grab him.

We didn't know what a great job Jed would do. We didn't know that Jed would actually destroy the evil dummy. We didn't know that Slappy's head would crack apart. That was just good luck.

"Hey — where *is* Jed?" I asked, my eyes searching the room.

"Jed? Jed?" Mom called. "Where are you? You did a great job!"

No reply.

No sign of my brother.

"Weird," Sara muttered, shaking her head.

We all trooped down the hall into Jed's room.

We found him in bed, sound asleep. He groggily raised his head from the pillow and squinted at us. "What time is it?" he asked sleepily.

"It's nearly eleven," Dad replied.

"Oh, no!" Jed cried, sitting up. "I'm sorry! I forgot to wake up! I forgot I was supposed to dress up like Dennis!"

I felt a shiver run down my back. I turned to my parents. "Then who fought Slappy?" I asked. "Who fought Slappy?"

# NIGHT OF THE LIVING DUMMY III

# 1

The stairs up to my attic are narrow and steep. The fifth step is loose and wobbles when you stand on it. All the other stairs creak and groan.

My whole house creaks and groans. It's a big, old house. And it's kind of falling apart. Mom and Dad don't really have the money to repair it.

"Trina — hurry!" my brother, Dan, whispered. His words echoed in the steep attic stairwell. Dan is ten, and he is always in a hurry.

He's short and very skinny. I think he looks like a mouse. He has short brown hair, dark eyes, and a pointy little chin. And he's always scurrying around like a mouse searching for a place to hide.

Sometimes I call him Mouse. You know. Like a nickname. Dan hates it. So I only call him Mouse when I want to make him mad.

Dan and I don't look at all like brother and sister. I'm tall and I have curly red hair and green eyes. I'm a little chubby, but Mom says not to worry about it. I'll probably slim down by the time I'm thirteen, next August.

Anyway, no one would ever call me Mouse! For one thing, I'm a lot braver than Dan.

You have to be brave to go up to our attic. Not because of the creaking stairs. Or the way the wind whistles through the attic windows and makes the panes rattle. Not because of the dim light up there. Or the shadows. Or the low ceiling covered with cracks.

You have to be brave because of the eyes.

The dozens of eyes that stare at you through the darkness.

The eyes that never blink. The eyes that stare with such eerie, heavy silence.

Dan reached the attic ahead of me. I heard him take a few steps over the squeaking, wooden floorboards. Then I heard him stop.

I knew why he stopped. He was staring back at the eyes, at the grinning faces.

I crept up behind him, moving on tiptoe. I leaned my face close to his ear. And I shouted, "BOO!"

He didn't jump.

"Trina, you're about as funny as a wet sponge," he said. He shoved me away.

"I think wet sponges are funny," I replied. I admit it. I like to annoy him.

"Give me a break," Dan muttered.

I grabbed his arm. "Okay." I pretended to break it in two.

I know it's dumb. But that's the way my brother and I kid around all the time.

Dad says we didn't get our sense of humor from him. But I think we probably did.

Dad owns a little camera store now. But before that he was a ventriloquist. You know. He did a comedy act with a dummy.

Danny O'Dell and Wilbur.

That was the name of the act. Wilbur was the dummy, in case you didn't guess it.

Danny O'Dell is my dad. My brother is Dan, Jr. But he hates the word junior, so no one ever calls him that.

Except me. When I want to make him *really* mad!

"Someone left the attic light on," Dan said, pointing to the ceiling light. The only light in the whole attic.

Our attic is one big room. There are windows at both ends. But they are both caked with dust, so not much light gets through.

Dan and I made our way across the room. The dummies all stared at us, their eyes big and blank. Most of them had wide grins on their wooden faces. Some of their mouths hung open. Some of their heads tilted down so we couldn't see their faces.

Wilbur — Dad's first dummy, the original Wilbur — was perched on an old armchair. His hands were draped over the chair arms. His head tilted against the chair back.

Dan laughed. "Wilbur looks just like Dad taking a nap!"

I laughed, too. With his short brown hair, his black eyeglasses, and his goofy grin, Wilbur looked *a lot* like Dad!

The old dummy's black-and-yellow checked sports jacket was worn and frayed. But Wilbur's face was freshly painted. His black leather shoes were shiny.

One wooden hand had part of the thumb chipped out. But Wilbur looked great for such an old dummy.

Dad keeps all of the dummies in good shape. He calls the attic his Dummy Museum. Spread around the room are a dozen old ventriloquist's dummies that he has collected.

He spends all of his spare time fixing them up. Painting them. Giving them fresh wigs. Making new suits and pants for them. Working on their insides, making sure their eyes and mouths move correctly.

These days, Dad doesn't get to use his ventriloquist skills very often. Sometimes he'll take one of the dummies to a kid's birthday party and put on a show. Sometimes people in town will invite him to perform at a party to raise money for a school or library.

But most of the time the dummies just sit up here, staring at each other.

Some of them are propped against the attic wall. Some are sprawled out on the couch. Some of them sit in folding chairs, hands crossed in their laps. Wilbur is the only one lucky enough to have his own armchair.

When Dan and I were little, we were afraid to come up to the attic. I didn't like the way the dummies stared at me. I thought their grins were evil.

Dan liked to stick his hand into their backs and move their mouths. He made the dummies say frightening things.

*"I'm going to get you, Trina!"* he would make Rocky growl. Rocky is the mean-faced dummy that sneers instead of smiles. He's dressed like a tough guy in a red-and-white striped T-shirt and black jeans. He's really evil-looking. *"I'm coming to your room tonight, Trina. And I'm going to GET you!"*

"Stop it, Dan! Stop it!" I would scream. Then I would go running downstairs and tell Mom that Dan was scaring me.

I was only eight or nine.

I'm a lot older now. And braver. But I still feel a little creeped out when I come up here.

I know it's dumb. But sometimes I imagine the dummies sitting around up here, talking to each other, giggling and laughing.

Sometimes late at night when I'm lying in bed, the ceiling creaks over my head. Footsteps! I picture the dummies walking around in the attic, their heavy black shoes clonking over the floorboards.

I picture them wrestling around on the old couch. Or playing a wild game of catch, their wooden hands snapping as they catch the ball.

Dumb? Of course it's dumb.

But I can't help it.

They're supposed to be funny little guys. But they scare me.

I hate the way they stare at me without blinking. And I hate the red-lipped grins frozen on their faces.

Dan and I come up to the attic because Dan likes to play with them. And because I like to see how Dad fixes them up.

But I really don't like to come up to the attic alone.

Dan picked up Miss Lucy. That's the only girl dummy in the group. She has curly blond hair and bright blue eyes.

My brother stuck his hand into the dummy's back and perched her on his knee. "Hi, Trina," he made the dummy say in a high, shrill voice.

Dan started to make her say something else.

But he stopped suddenly. His mouth dropped open — like a dummy's — and he pointed across the room.

"Trina — l-look!" Dan stammered. "Over there!"

I turned quickly. And I saw Rocky, the mean-looking dummy, blink his eyes.

I gasped as the dummy leaned forward and sneered. *"Trina, I'm going to GET you!"* he growled.

# 2

I uttered a startled cry and jumped back.

I swung around, ready to run to the attic steps — and I saw Dan laughing.

"Hey — !" I cried out angrily. "What's going on here?"

I turned back to see Dad climb to his feet behind Rocky's chair. He carried Rocky in one arm. Dad's grin was as wide as a dummy's!

"Gotcha!" he cried in Rocky's voice.

I turned angrily on my brother. "Did you know Dad was back there? Did you know Dad was here the whole time?"

Dan nodded. "Of course."

"You two are both dummies!" I cried. I flung my red hair back with both hands and let out an exasperated sigh. "That was so stupid!"

"You fell for it," Dan shot back, grinning at Dad.

"Who's the dummy here?" Dad made Rocky say. "Hey — who's pulling *your* string? I'm not a dummy — knock on wood!"

Dan laughed, but I just shook my head.

Dad refused to give up. "Hey — come over here!" he made Rocky say. "Scratch my back. I think I've got termites!"

I gave in and laughed. I'd heard that joke a million times. But I knew Dad wouldn't stop trying until I laughed.

He's a really good ventriloquist. You can never see his lips move. But his jokes are totally lame.

I guess that's why he had to give up the act and open a camera store. I don't know for sure. It all happened before I was born.

Dad set Rocky back on his chair. The dummy sneered up at us. Such a bad-news dummy. Why couldn't he smile like the others?

Dad pushed his eyeglasses up on his nose. "Come over here," he said. "I want to show you something."

He put one hand on my shoulder and one hand on Dan's shoulder and led us to the other end of the big attic room. This is where Dad has his workshop — his worktable and all his tools and supplies for fixing up the dummies.

Dad reached under the worktable and pulled up a large brown-paper shopping bag. I could tell by the smile on his face what he had in the bag. But I didn't say anything to ruin his surprise.

Slowly, carefully, Dad reached into the shopping bag. His smile grew wider as he lifted out a dummy. "Hey, guys — check this out!" Dad exclaimed.

The dummy had been folded up inside the bag. Dad set it down flat on the worktable and carefully unfolded the arms and legs. He looked like a surgeon starting an operation.

"I found this one in a trash can," he told us. "Do you believe someone just threw it away?"

He tilted the dummy up so we could see it. I followed Dan up to the worktable to get a better look.

"The head was split in two," Dad said, placing one hand at the back of the dummy's neck. "But it took two seconds to repair it. Just a little glue."

I leaned close to check out Dad's new treasure. It had wavy brown hair painted on top of its head. The face was kind of strange. Kind of intense.

The eyes were bright blue. They shimmered. Sort of like real eyes. The dummy had bright red painted lips, curved up into a smile.

An ugly smile, I thought. Kind of gross and nasty.

His lower lip had a chip on one side so that it didn't quite match the other lip.

The dummy wore a gray double-breasted suit over a white shirt collar. The collar was stapled to his neck.

He didn't have a shirt. Instead, his wooden chest had been painted white. Big black leather shoes — very scuffed up — dangled from his skinny gray pants legs.

"Can you believe someone just tossed him into the trash?" Dad repeated. "Isn't he great?"

"Yeah. Great," I murmured. I didn't like the new dummy at all. I didn't like his face, the way his blue eyes gleamed, the crooked smile.

Dan must have felt the same way. "He's kind of tough-looking," he said. He picked up one of the dummy's wooden hands. It had deep scratches all over it. The knuckles appeared cut and bruised. As if the dummy had been in a fight.

"Not as tough-looking as Rocky over there," Dad replied. "But he does have a strange smile." He picked at the small chip in the dummy's lip. "I can fill that in with some liquid wood filler. Then I'll give the whole face a fresh paint job."

"What's the dummy's name?" I asked.

Dad shrugged. "Beats me. Maybe we'll call him Smiley."

"Smiley?" I made a disgusted face.

Dad started to reply. But the phone rang downstairs. One ring. Two. Three.

"I guess your mom is still at that school meeting," Dad said. He ran to the stairs. "I'd better answer it. Don't touch Smiley till I get back." He vanished down the stairs.

I picked up the dummy's head carefully in both hands. "Dad did a great gluing job," I said.

"He should do *your* head next!" Dan shot back. Typical.

"I don't think Smiley is a good name for him," Dan said, slapping the dummy's hands together.

"How about Dan Junior?" I suggested. "Or Dan the Third?"

He ignored me. "How many dummies does Dad have now?" He turned back toward the others across the attic and quickly counted them.

I counted faster. "This new one makes thirteen," I said.

Dan's eyes went wide. "Whoa. That's an unlucky number."

"Well, if we count you, it's fourteen!" I said. Gotcha, Danny Boy!

Dan stuck out his tongue at me. He set the dummy's hands down on its chest. "Hey — what's that?" He reached into the pocket of the gray suit jacket and pulled out a folded-up slip of paper.

"Maybe that has the dummy's name on it," I said. I grabbed the paper out of Dan's hands and raised it to my face. I unfolded it and started to read.

"Well?" Dan tried to grab it back. But I swung out of his reach. "What's the name?"

"It doesn't say," I told him. "There are just these weird words. Foreign, I guess."

I moved my lips silently as I struggled to read them. Then I read the words out loud: *"Karru marri odonna loma molonu karrano."*

274

Dan's mouth dropped open. "Huh? What's *that* supposed to mean?" he cried.

He grabbed the paper from my hand. "I think you read it upside down!"

"No way!" I protested.

I glanced down at the dummy.

The glassy blue eyes stared up at me.

Then the right eye slowly closed. The dummy *winked* at me.

And then his left hand shot straight up — and slapped me in the face.

# 3

"Hey — !" I shouted. I jerked back as pain shot through my jaw.

"What's your problem?" Dan demanded, glancing up from the slip of paper.

"Didn't you *see*?" I shrieked. "He — he *slapped* me!" I rubbed my cheek.

Dan rolled his eyes. "Yeah. For sure."

"No — really!" I cried. "First he winked at me. Then he slapped me."

"Tell me another one," Dan groaned. "You're such a jerk, Trina. Just because you fall for Dad's jokes doesn't mean I'm going to fall for yours."

"But I'm telling the truth!" I insisted.

I glanced up to see Dad poke his head up at the top of the stairs. "What's going on, guys?"

Dan folded up the slip of paper and tucked it back into the dummy's jacket pocket. "Nothing much," he told Dad.

"Dad — the new dummy!" I cried, still rubbing my aching jaw. "He *slapped* me!"

Dad laughed. "Sorry, Trina. You'll have to do better than that. You can't kid a kidder."

That's one of Dad's favorite expressions: "You can't kid a kidder."

"But, Dad — " I stopped. I could see he wasn't going to believe me. I wasn't even sure I believed it myself.

I glanced down at the dummy. He stared blankly up at the ceiling. Totally lifeless.

"I have news, guys," Dad said, sitting the new dummy up. "That was my brother — your uncle Cal — on the phone. He's coming for a short visit while Aunt Susan's away on business. And he's bringing your cousin Zane with him. It's Zane's spring vacation from school, too."

Dan and I both groaned. Dan stuck his finger in his mouth and pretended to puke.

Zane isn't our favorite cousin.

He's our *only* cousin.

He's twelve, but you'd think he was five or six. He's pretty nerdy. His nose runs a lot. And he's kind of a wimp.

Kind of a *major* wimp.

"Hey, stop groaning," Dad scolded. "Zane is your only cousin. He's family."

Dan and I groaned again. We couldn't help it.

"He isn't a bad kid," Dad continued, narrowing his eyes at us behind his glasses. That meant he was being serious. "You two have to promise me something."

"What kind of promise?" I asked.

"You have to promise me that you'll be nicer to Zane this time."

"We were nice to him last time," Dan insisted. "We *talked* to him, didn't we?"

"You scared him to death last time," Dad said, frowning. "You made him believe that this old house is haunted. And you scared him so badly, he ran outside and refused to come back in."

"Dad, it was all a joke," I protested.

"Yeah. It was a scream!" Dan agreed. He poked me in the side with his elbow. "A scream. Get it?"

"Not funny," Dad said unhappily. "Not funny at all. Listen, guys — Zane can't help it if he's a little timid. He'll outgrow it. You just have to be nice to him."

Dan snickered. "Zane is afraid of your dummies, Dad. Can you believe it?"

"Then don't drag him up here and scare the life out of him," Dad ordered.

"How about if we just play one or two little jokes on him?" Dan asked.

"No tricks," Dad replied firmly. "None."

Dan and I exchanged glances.

"Promise me," Dad insisted. "I mean it. Right now. Both of you. Promise me there will be no tricks. Promise me you won't try to scare your cousin."

"Okay. I promise," I said. I raised my right hand as if I were swearing an oath.

"I promise, too," Dan said softly.

I checked to see if his fingers were crossed. They weren't.

Dan and I had both made a solemn promise. We both promised not to terrify our cousin. And we meant it.

But it was a promise we couldn't keep.

Before the week was over, our cousin Zane would be terrified.

And so would we.

# 4

I was playing the piano when Zane arrived. The piano is tucked away in a small room in the back of the house. It's a small black upright piano, kind of beat-up and scratched. Dad bought it from my old music teacher who moved to Cleveland.

Two of the pedals don't work. And the piano really needs to be tuned. But I love to play it — especially when I'm stressed out or excited. It always helps to calm me down.

I'm pretty good at it. Even Dan agrees. Most of the time he pushes me off the piano bench so he can play "Chopsticks." But sometimes he stands beside me and listens. I've been practicing some nice Haydn pieces and some of the easy Chopin *études*.

Anyway, I was in the back of the house banging away on the piano when Zane and Uncle Cal arrived. I guess I was a little nervous about seeing Zane again.

Dan and I were really mean to him during his last visit. Like Dad said, Zane has always been scared of this old house. And we did everything we could to make him even *more* scared.

We walked around in the attic every night, howling softly like ghosts, making the floor creak. We crept into his bedroom closet in the middle of the night and made him think his clothes were dancing. We rigged a pair of Mom's panty hose so they cast a ghostly shadow of legs onto his bedroom floor.

Poor Zane. I think Dan and I went a little too far. After a few days, he jumped at every sound. And his eyes kept darting from side to side like a frightened lizard's.

I heard him tell Uncle Cal that he never wanted to come back here.

Dan and I laughed about that. But it wasn't very nice.

So I was a little nervous about seeing Zane again. I was playing the piano so loudly, I didn't hear the doorbell. Dan had to come running in and tell me Uncle Cal and Zane had arrived.

I jumped up from the piano bench. "How does Zane look?" I asked my brother.

"Big," Dan replied. "He grew. A lot. And he let his hair grow long."

Zane was always a pretty big guy. That's why Dan and I thought his being a total wimp was so funny.

He's big and beefy. Not tall. He's built kind of like a bulldog. A big blond bulldog.

I guess he's actually good-looking. He has round blue eyes, wavy blond hair, and a nice smile. He looks as if he works out or plays sports. He really doesn't look like the wimp type at all.

That's why it's such a riot to see him quivering in fear. Or wailing like a baby. Running to his mom or dad in terror.

I followed Dan through the back hall. "Did Zane say anything to you?" I asked.

"Just hi," Dan replied.

"A friendly 'hi' or an unfriendly 'hi'?" I demanded.

Dan didn't have time to answer. We had reached the front hall.

"Hey — !" Uncle Cal greeted me, stretching out his arms for a hug. Uncle Cal looks a lot like a chipmunk. He's very small. He has a round face, a twitchy little nose, and two teeth that poke out from his upper lip.

"You're getting so tall!" he exclaimed as I hugged him. "You've grown a lot, Trina!"

Why do grown-ups *always* have to comment on how tall kids are getting? Can't they think of anything else to say?

I saw Dad lugging their two heavy suitcases up the stairs.

"I didn't know if you'd be hungry or not," Mom

told Uncle Cal. "So I made a bunch of sandwiches."

I turned to say hi to Zane. And a flash of white light made me cry out in surprise.

"Don't move. One more," I heard Zane say.

I blinked rapidly, trying to clear the light from my eyes. When I finally focused, I saw that Zane had a camera up to his face.

He clicked it. Another bright flash of light.

"That's good," he said. "You looked really surprised. I only like to take candid shots."

"Zane is really into photography," Uncle Cal said, grinning proudly.

"I'm blind!" I cried, rubbing my eyes.

"I needed extra flash because this house is so dark," Zane said. He lowered his head to the camera and fiddled with his lens.

Dad came shuffling down the stairs. Zane turned and snapped his picture.

"Zane is really into photography," Uncle Cal repeated to my father. "I told him maybe you've got an old camera or two at the shop that he could have."

"Uh . . . maybe," Dad replied.

Uncle Cal makes a lot more money than Dad. But whenever he visits, he always tries to get Dad to give him stuff.

"Nice camera," Dad told Zane. "What kind of photos do you like to take?"

"Candid shots," Zane replied, pushing back his blond hair. "And I take a lot of still lifes." He stepped into the hall and flashed a close-up of the banister.

Dan leaned close and whispered in my ear, "He's still a pain. Let's give him a really good scare."

"No way!" I whispered back. "No scares this time. We promised Dad — remember?"

"I've set up a darkroom in the basement," Dad told Zane. "Sometimes I bring developing work home from the store. You can use the darkroom this week, if you want to."

"Great!" Zane replied.

"I told Zane maybe you have some sheets of developing paper you can spare," Uncle Cal said to Dad.

Zane raised his camera and flashed another picture. Then he turned to Dan. "Are you still into video games?" he asked.

"Yeah," Dan replied. "Mostly sports games. I have the new *NBA Jams*. And I'm saving my allowance to get the new thirty-two-bit system. You still play?"

Zane shook his head. "Not since I got my camera. I don't really have time for games anymore."

"How about some sandwiches, everyone?" Mom asked, moving toward the dining room.

"I think I'd like to unpack first," Uncle Cal told her. "Zane, you should unpack, too."

We all split up. Dan and Dad disappeared somewhere. Uncle Cal and Zane went up to their rooms to unpack — our big old house has a lot of extra bedrooms.

I was heading into the kitchen to help Mom with the sandwiches when I heard Zane scream.

A shrill scream from upstairs.

A scream of horror.

Mom gasped and dropped the sandwich tray she was carrying.

I spun around and went running to the front hall.

Dad was already halfway up the stairs. "What's wrong?" he called. "Zane — what's the matter?"

When I reached the second floor, I saw Dan step out of his room. Zane stood in the hallway. Someone lay stretched across the floor at his feet.

Even from halfway down the hall, I could see that Zane was trembling.

I hurried over to him.

Who was sprawled on the floor like that, legs and arms all twisted?

"Zane — what happened? What happened?" Dad and Uncle Cal both shouted.

Zane stood there shaking all over. The camera seemed to tremble, too, swinging on its strap over his chest.

I glanced down at the body on the floor.

A ventriloquist's dummy.

Rocky.

Rocky sneered up at the ceiling. His red-and-white striped shirt had rolled up halfway, revealing his wooden body. One leg was bent under him. Both arms were stretched out over the floor.

"That d-dummy — " Zane stammered, pointing down at Rocky. "It — it *fell* on me when I opened the bedroom door."

"Huh? It *what?*" Uncle Cal cried.

"It dropped down on me," Zane repeated. "When I pushed the door. I didn't mean to scream. It just scared me, that's all. It was so heavy. And it fell near my head."

I turned and saw Dad glaring angrily at Dan.

Dan raised both hands in protest. "Hey — don't look at *me!*" he cried.

"Dan, you made a promise," Dad said sharply.

"I didn't do it!" Dan cried. "It had to be Trina!"

"Hey — no way!" I protested. "No way! I didn't do it!"

Dad narrowed his eyes at me. "I suppose the dummy climbed up on top of the door by himself!" he said, rolling his eyes.

"It was just a joke," Uncle Cal chimed in. "You're okay — right, Zane?"

"Yeah. Sure." Zane's cheeks were red. I could see he was embarrassed by all the fuss. "I just wasn't expecting something to fall on me. You know." He stared at the floor.

"Let's finish unpacking," Uncle Cal suggested. "I'm starting to get hungry." He turned to Dad. "Do you have any extra pillows? There's only one on my bed. And I like to sleep with a *lot* of pillows."

"I'll see if we have any more," Dad replied. He frowned at me. "You and Dan — take Rocky up to the attic. And no more little jokes. You promised — remember?"

I picked Rocky up carefully and slung him over my shoulder. "Get the attic door for me," I instructed Dan.

We made our way down the hall. "What is your problem, Mouse?" I whispered to my brother.

"Don't call me Mouse," he replied through gritted teeth. "You know I hate it."

"Well, I hate broken promises," I told him. "You can't wait one minute to start scaring Zane? You're going to get us in major trouble."

"Me?" Dan put on his innocent act. "I didn't hide the dummy up there. *You* did — and you know it!"

"Did not!" I whispered angrily.

"Hey, guys, can I come with you?" I turned to see Zane right behind us. I hadn't realized he'd followed us.

"You want to come up to the Dummy Museum?" I asked, unable to hide my surprise. Last visit, Zane had been afraid of the dummies.

"Yeah. I want to take some pictures," he replied. He raised his camera in both hands.

"Cool," Dan said. "That's a cool idea." I could see that he was trying to be friendly to Zane.

I didn't want to be left out. "It's neat that you're into photography," I told Zane.

"Yeah. I know," he replied.

Dan led the way up the attic stairs. Halfway up, I turned back. I saw Zane lingering at the bottom.

"Are you coming up or not?" I called down. My voice echoed in the narrow, dark stairwell.

I caught a look of fear on Zane's face. He was trying to be brave, I realized. Trying not to be afraid the way he was last time.

"Coming," he called up. I saw him take a deep breath. Then he came running up the stairs.

He stayed close to Dan and me as we crossed the attic. The eyes peered out at us darkly from around the big room.

I clicked on the light. The dummies all came into view. Propped on chairs and the old couch, leaning against the wall, they grinned at us.

I carried Rocky over to his folding chair. I slid him off my shoulder and set him down. I crossed his arms in his lap and straightened his striped shirt. The mean-looking dummy sneered up at me.

"Uncle Danny has a few new guys," Zane said from across the room. He stood close to Dan in front of the couch. He held the camera in his hands, but he didn't take any pictures. "Where does he find them?"

"He found the newest one in a trash can," I replied, pointing to the mean-looking dummy.

Dan picked up Miss Lucy and held it up to Zane. "Hiya, Zane! Take my picture!" Dan made Miss Lucy say in a high, shrill voice.

Zane obediently raised the camera to his eye. "Say cheese," he told Miss Lucy.

"Cheese," Dan said in Miss Lucy's high voice.

Zane flashed a picture.

"Give me a big wet kiss!" Dan made Miss Lucy say. He shoved the dummy's face close to Zane's.

Zane backed away. "Yuck."

"Put the dummy down," I told my brother. "We'd better get back downstairs. They're all probably waiting for us."

"Okay, okay," Dan grumbled. He turned to set Miss Lucy down. Zane wandered down the row of dummies, studying them.

I bent down and straightened Wilbur's bow tie. The old dummy was starting to look really ragged.

I was still working on the bow tie when I heard a hard *slap*.

And I heard Zane's startled cry of pain.

"Owwww!"

# 6

I spun around and saw Zane rubbing his jaw.

"Hey — that dummy *slapped* me!" he cried angrily.

He pointed to a red-haired dummy on the arm of the couch.

"I-I don't *believe* it!" Zane exclaimed. "It swung its arm up, and it — it *slapped* me!"

Dan stood behind the couch. I saw a smile spread over his face. Then he burst out laughing. "Get serious," he told Zane. "That's impossible."

"You did it!" Zane accused my brother, still rubbing his jaw. "You moved the dummy!"

"No way!" Dan backed away till he bumped the wall. "How could I? I was behind the couch the whole time."

I stepped quickly up to the couch. "Which dummy was it?" I demanded.

Zane pointed to a dummy with red hair and bright red freckles painted all over his grinning face. "That guy."

291

"Arnie," I reported. "One of Dad's first dummies."

"I don't care what his name is," Zane snapped. "He slapped me!"

"But that's dumb," I insisted. "It's just a ventriloquist's dummy, Zane. Here. Look."

I picked Arnie up. The old dummy was heavier than I remembered. I started to hand him to Zane. But my cousin backed away.

"Something weird is going on here," Zane said, keeping his eyes on the dummy. "I'm going to tell Uncle Danny."

"No. Don't tell Dad," I pleaded. "Give us a break, Zane. It'll get us in big trouble."

"Yeah. Don't tell," Dan chimed in. "The dummy probably just slipped or something. You know. It fell over."

"It reached up," Zane insisted. "I saw it swing its arm and — "

He was interrupted by Mom's voice from downstairs. "Hurry up, kids. Get down here. We're all waiting for you."

"Coming!" I shouted. I dropped Arnie back onto the arm of the couch. He fell into the dummy next to him. I left him like that and followed Dan and Zane to the stairs.

I held Dan back and let Zane go down by himself. "What are you trying to prove?" I angrily asked my brother. "That wasn't funny."

"Trina, I didn't do it. I swear!" Dan claimed, raising his right hand. "I swear!"

"So what are you saying?" I demanded. "That the dummy really reached up and slapped him?" Dan twisted his face. He shrugged. "I don't know. I just know that I didn't do it. I didn't swing that dummy's arm."

"Don't be stupid," I replied. "Of course you did." I shoved my brother toward the stairs.

"Hey — give me a break," he muttered.

"You're a total liar," I told him. "You think you can scare Zane — and me. But it isn't worth it, Dan. We promised Dad, remember? Remember?"

He ignored me and started down the stairs.

I felt really angry. I knew that Dan had perched the dummy on top of the bedroom door so that it would fall on Zane. And I knew that he had swung the dummy's arm to slap Zane.

I wondered how far Dan would go to frighten our cousin.

I knew I had to stop him. If Dan kept this up, he'd get us both grounded for life. Or worse.

But what could I do?

I was still thinking about it in bed later that night. I couldn't get to sleep. I lay there, staring up at the ceiling, thinking about Dan and what a liar he was.

Dummies are made of wood and cloth, I told myself. They don't swing their arms and slap people.

And they don't get up and walk around the

293

house and climb up onto doors on their own. They don't walk on their own. . . .

They don't . . .

I finally started to drift off to sleep when I heard light footsteps on my bedroom carpet.

And then a hoarse whisper close to my ear: *"Trina . . . Trina . . . "*

# 7

*"Trina . . . Trina . . . "*

The hoarse whisper — so near my ear — made me shoot straight up in bed.

I leaped to my feet. Pulled the covers with me. Lurched forward.

And nearly knocked Zane onto his back.

"Zane?"

He stumbled backwards. "Sorry!" he whispered. "I thought you were awake."

"Zane!" I repeated. My heart thudded in my chest. "What are you *doing* in here?"

"Sorry," he whispered, backing up some more. He stopped a few inches in front of my dresser. "I didn't mean to scare you. I just — "

I held my hand over my heart. I could feel it start to slow back down to normal. "Sorry I jumped out at you like that," I told him. "I was half asleep, I guess. And when you whispered my name . . . "

I clicked on the bed-table lamp. I rubbed my eyes and squinted at Zane.

He was wearing baggy blue pajamas. One pajama leg had rolled up nearly to his knee. His blond hair had fallen over his face. He had such a frightened, little-boy expression on his face. He looked about six years old!

"I tried to wake up Dad," he whispered. "But he's such a sound sleeper. I kept knocking on his bedroom door and calling to him. But he didn't hear me. So I came in here."

"What's your problem?" I asked, stretching my arms over my head.

"I-I heard voices," he stammered, glancing to the open bedroom door.

"Excuse me? Voices?" I pushed my hair back. Straightened my long nightshirt. Studied him.

He nodded. "I heard voices. Upstairs. I mean, I *think* they were upstairs. Funny voices. Talking very fast."

I squinted at him. "You heard voices in the *attic?*"

He nodded again. "Yeah. I'm pretty sure."

"I'm pretty sure you were dreaming." I sighed. I shook my head.

"No. I was wide awake. Really." He picked up a little stuffed bear from my dresser. He squeezed it between his hands.

"I never sleep very well in new places," he told

me. "I *never* sleep very well in this house!" He let out an unhappy laugh. "I was wide awake."

"There's no one in the attic," I said, yawning. I tilted my ear to the ceiling. "Listen," I instructed. "Silent up there. No voices."

We both listened to the silence for a while.

Then Zane set down the stuffed bear. "Do you think I could have a bowl of cereal?" he asked.

"Huh?" I gaped at him.

"A bowl of cereal always helps calm me down," he said. An embarrassed smile crossed his face. "Just a habit from when I was a kid."

I squinted at my clock radio. It was a little after midnight. "You want a bowl of cereal *now*?"

He nodded. "Is that okay?" he asked shyly.

Poor guy, I thought. He's really freaked out.

"Sure," I said. "I'll come down to the kitchen with you. Show you where everything is."

I found my flip-flops and slipped my feet into them. I keep them under my bed. I don't like walking barefoot on the floorboards in the hall. There are a lot of nails that poke up from the floor.

Mom and Dad keep saying they're going to buy carpet. But money is tight. I don't think carpet is tops on their list.

Zane appeared a little calmer. I smiled at him and led the way into the hall.

He's not such a bad guy, I thought. He's a little wimpy — but so what? I decided to have a serious

297

talk with Dan first thing in the morning. I planned to make Dan *promise* he wouldn't pull any more scares on Zane.

The long hall was so dark, Zane and I both held onto the wall as we made our way to the stairs. Mom and Dad used to keep a little night-light at the end of the hall. But the bulb burned out, and they never replaced it.

Holding onto the banister, we made our way slowly down the steps. Pale light from outside cast long blue shadows over the living room. In the dim light, our old furniture rose up like ghosts around the room.

"This house always creeps me out," Zane whispered, staying close by my side as we crossed through the front room.

"I've lived here all my life, and sometimes I'm scared of it, too," I confessed. "Old houses make so many strange sounds. Sometimes I think I hear the house groaning and moaning."

"I really did hear voices," Zane whispered.

We crept through the shadows to the kitchen. My flip-flops slapped on the linoleum. Silvery moonlight washed through the curtains over the kitchen window.

I started to fumble on the wall for the light switch.

But I stopped when I saw the dark figure slumped at the kitchen table.

298

Zane saw him, too. I heard Zane gasp. He jerked back into the doorway.

"Dad? Are you still up?" I called. "Why are you sitting in the dark?"

My hand found the light switch. I clicked on the kitchen light.

And Zane and I both let out a scream.

# 8

I recognized the red-and-white striped shirt. I didn't even have to see the face.

Rocky leaned over the table, his wooden head propped in his hands.

Zane and I crept closer to the table. I moved to the other side. The dummy sneered at me. His glassy eyes were cold and cruel.

Such a nasty expression.

"How did *he* get down here?" Zane asked. He stared hard at the dummy, as if expecting the dummy to answer.

"Only one way," I murmured. "He sure didn't walk."

Zane turned to me. "You mean Dan?"

I sighed. "Of course. Who else? Mister Dumb Jokes."

"But how did your brother know we'd be coming down to the kitchen tonight?" Zane asked.

"Let's go ask him," I replied.

I knew Dan was awake. Probably sitting on the

edge of his bed, waiting eagerly to hear us scream from the kitchen. Giggling to himself. So pleased with himself.

So pleased that he broke his promise to Dad. And gave Zane and me a little scare.

I balled both hands into tight fists. I could feel the anger rising in my chest.

When I get really furious like that, I usually go to the back room and pound the piano. I pound out a Sousa march or a hard, fast rock song. I pound the keys till I start to calm down.

Tonight, I decided, I would pound my brother instead.

"Come on," I urged Zane. "Upstairs."

I took one last glance at Rocky, slouched over the kitchen table. The dummy stared blankly back at me.

I really hate that dummy, I thought. I'm going to ask Dad to put him away in a closet or a trunk.

I forced myself to turn away from the sneering, wooden face. Then I put both hands on Zane's shoulders and guided him back to the stairs.

"I'm going to tell Dan that we're both fed up with his dumb jokes," I whispered to my cousin. "Enough is enough. We'll make him promise to stop leaving that dummy everywhere we go."

Zane didn't reply. In the dim light, I could see the grim expression on his face.

I wondered what he was thinking about. Was he remembering his last visit to our house? Was he remembering how Dan and I terrified him then?

Maybe he doesn't trust me, either, I told myself.

We climbed the stairs and crept down the dark hallway to my brother's room.

The door was half open. I pushed it open the rest of the way and stepped inside. Zane kept close behind me.

I expected Dan to be sitting up, waiting for us. I expected to see him grinning, enjoying his little joke.

Silvery moonlight flooded in through his double windows. From the doorway, I could see him clearly. Lying on his side in bed. Covers up to his chin. Eyes tightly closed.

Was he faking? Was he really awake?

"Dan," I whispered. "Da-an."

He didn't move. His eyes didn't open.

"Dan — I'm coming to *tickle* you!" I whispered. He could never keep a straight face when I threatened him. Dan is *very* ticklish.

But he didn't move.

Zane and I crept closer. Up to the bed. We both stood over my brother, staring hard at him, studying him in the silvery light.

He was breathing softly, in a steady rhythm. His mouth was open a little. He made short whistling sounds. Mouse sounds. With his pointy chin and upturned nose, he really did look like a little mouse.

I leaned over him. "Da-an, get ready to be tickled!" I whispered.

I leaned back, expecting him to leap out at me, to shout "Boo!" or something.

But he continued sleeping, whistling softly with each breath.

I turned to Zane, who hung back in the center of the room. "He's really asleep," I reported.

"Let's go back to our rooms," Zane replied in a soft whisper. He yawned.

I followed him to the bedroom door. "What about your cereal?" I asked.

"Forget it. I'm too sleepy now."

We were nearly to the door when I heard someone move in the hall.

"Ohhh." I let out a low moan as a face appeared in the doorway.

Rocky's face.

He had followed us upstairs!

# 9

I grabbed Zane's arm. We both shouted cries of
surprise.

The dummy moved quickly into the room.

I cut my cry short as I saw that he wasn't walking on his own. He was being carried.

Dad had the dummy by the back of the neck.

"Hey — what's going on?" Dan called sleepily
from behind us. He raised his head from the pillow
and squinted at us. "Huh? What's everybody
doing in my room?"

"That's what *I'd* like to know," Dad said
sharply. He gazed suspiciously from Zane to
me.

"You — you woke me up," Dan murmured. He
cleared his throat. Then he propped himself up on
one elbow. "Why are you carrying that dummy,
Dad?"

"Perhaps one of you would like to answer that
question," Dad growled. He had pulled a robe over
his pajamas. His hair was matted to his forehead.

He wasn't wearing his glasses, so he squinted at us.

"What's going on? I don't understand," Dan said sleepily. He rubbed his eyes.

Was he putting on an act? I wondered. His innocent-little-boy act?

"I heard noises downstairs," Dad said, shifting Rocky to his other hand. "I went down to see what was going on. I found this dummy sitting at the kitchen table."

"I didn't put him there!" Dan cried, suddenly wide awake. "Really. I didn't!"

"Neither did Zane or me!" I chimed in.

Dad turned to me. He sighed. "I'm really sleepy. I don't like these jokes in the middle of the night."

"But I didn't do it!" I cried.

Dad squinted hard at me. He really couldn't see at all without his glasses. "Do I have to punish you and your brother?" he demanded. "Do I have to ground you? Or keep you from going away to camp this summer?"

"*No!*" Dan and I both cried at once. Dan and I were both going to summer camp for the first time this year. It's all we've talked about since Christmas.

"Dad, I was asleep. Really," Dan insisted.

"No more stories," Dad replied wearily. "The next time one of my dummies is somewhere he shouldn't be, you're both in major trouble."

"But, Dad — " I started.

"One last chance," Dad said. "I mean it. If I see Rocky out of the attic again, you've both *had* it!" He waved Zane and me to the door. "Get to your rooms. Now. Not another word."

"Do you believe me or not?" Dan demanded.

"I don't believe that Rocky has been moving around the house on his own," Dad replied. "Now lie down and get back to sleep, Dan. I'm giving you one last chance. Don't blow it."

Dad followed Zane and me into the hall. "See you in the morning," he murmured. He made his way to the attic stairs to take Rocky back up to the Dummy Museum. I heard him muttering to himself all the way up the stairs.

I said good night to Zane and headed to my room. I felt sleepy and upset and worried and confused — all at once.

I knew that Dan *had* to be the one who kept springing Rocky on Zane. But why was he doing it? And would he quit now — before Dad grounded us or totally ruined our summer?

I fell asleep, still asking myself question after question.

The next morning, I woke up early. I pulled on jeans and a sweatshirt and hurried downstairs for breakfast.

And there sat Rocky at the kitchen table.

# 10

I peered around the kitchen. No one else around.

How lucky that I was the first one downstairs!

I grabbed Rocky up by the back of the neck. Then I tucked him under one arm and dragged him up to the attic as fast as I could.

When I returned to the kitchen a few moments later, Mom had already started breakfast.

Whew! A close call.

"Trina — you're up early," Mom said, filling the coffee maker with water. "Are you okay?"

I glanced at the table. I had the sick feeling that Rocky would be sitting there sneering at me.

But of course he was upstairs in the attic. I had just carried him up there.

The table stood empty.

"I'm fine," I told her. "Just fine."

It was definitely Be Kind to Zane Day.

After breakfast, Dad hurried off to the camera

store. A short while later, Mom and Uncle Cal left for the mall to do some shopping.

It was a bright morning. Yellow sunlight streamed in through the windows. The sky stretched clear and cloudless.

Zane brought down his camera. He decided it was a perfect day to take some photographs.

Dan and I expected him to go outside. But our cousin wanted to stay indoors and shoot.

"I'm very interested in moldings," he told us.

We followed him around the house. Dan and I had made a solemn vow to be nice to Zane and not to scare him.

After breakfast, when Zane was upstairs getting his camera, I grabbed my brother. I pinned him against the wall. "No tricks," I told him.

Dan tried to wriggle away. But I'm stronger than he is. I kept him pinned against the wall.

"Raise your right hand and swear," I instructed him.

"Okay, okay." He gave in easily. He raised his right hand, and he repeated the vow I recited. "No tricks against Zane. No making fun of Zane. No dummies — *anywhere!*"

I let him go as Zane returned with his camera.

"You have some awesome moldings," Zane said, gazing up at the living room ceiling.

"Really?" I replied, trying to sound interested. What could be interesting about a molding?

Zane tilted up his camera. He focused for what

seemed like hours. Then he clicked a photo of the molding above the living room curtains.

"Do you have a ladder?" he asked Dan. "I'd really like to get a closer shot. I'm afraid my zoom lens will distort it."

And so Dan hurried off to the basement to get Zane a ladder.

I was proud of my brother. He didn't complain about having to go get the ladder. And he'd lasted a whole ten minutes without cracking any molding jokes or making fun of Zane.

Which wasn't easy.

I mean, what kind of a nerd thinks it's cool to take photos of ceilings and walls?

Meanwhile, we had no school, and it was the sunniest, warmest, most beautiful day of March outside. Almost like spring. And Dan and I were stuck holding the ladder for Zane so he could use his macro lens and get a really tight molding shot.

"Awesome!" Zane declared, snapping a few more. "Awesome!"

He climbed down the ladder. He adjusted the lens. Fiddled with some other dials on the camera.

"Want to go outside or something?" I suggested.

He didn't seem to hear me. "I'd like to get a few more banister shots," he announced. "See the way the sunlight is pouring through the wooden bars? It makes a really interesting pattern on the wall."

I started to say something rude. But Dan caught my eye. He shook a finger at me. A warning.

I bit my lip and didn't say anything.

This is sooooo boring, I thought. But at least we're keeping out of trouble.

We stood beside Zane as he photographed the banister from all angles. After about the tenth shot, his camera began to hum and whir.

"End of the roll," he announced. His eyes lit up. "Know what would be really cool? To go down into the basement to the darkroom and develop these right now."

"Cool," I replied. I tried to sound sincere. Dan and I were both trying so hard to be nice to this kid!

"Uncle Danny said I could use his darkroom downstairs," Zane said, watching the camera as it rewound the film roll. "That would be awesome."

"Awesome," I repeated.

Dan and I exchanged glances. The most beautiful day of the *century* — and we were heading down to a dark closet in the basement.

"I've never watched pictures get developed," Dan told our cousin. "Can you show me how to do it?"

"It's pretty easy," Zane replied, following us down the basement stairs. "Once you get the timing down."

We made our way through the laundry room, past the furnace, to the darkroom against the far wall. We slipped inside, and I clicked on the special red light.

"Close the door tightly," Zane instructed. "We can't let in any light at all."

I double-checked the darkroom door. Then Zane set to work. He arranged the developing pans. He poured bottles of chemicals into the pans. He unspooled the film roll and began to develop.

I'd watched Dad do it a hundred times before. It really was kind of interesting. And it was cool when the image began to appear and then darken on the developing paper.

Dan and I stood close to Zane, watching him work.

"I think I got some very good angles on the living room moldings," Zane said. He dipped the large sheet of paper in one pan. Then he pulled it up, let it drip for a few seconds, and lowered it into the pan beside it.

A grin spread over his face. "Let's take a look."

He leaned over the table. Raised the sheet of paper. Held it up to the red light.

His grin faded quickly. "Hey — who shot this?" he demanded angrily.

Dan and I moved closer to see the photo.

"Who shot this?" Zane repeated. He furiously picked up another sheet from the developing pan. Another one. Another one.

311

"How did these get on the roll?" he cried. He shoved them all toward Dan and me.

Photos of Rocky.

Close-up portraits.

Photo after photo of the sneering dummy.

"Who shot them? Who?" Zane demanded angrily, shoving the wet photos in our faces.

"I didn't!" Dan declared, pulling back.

"I didn't either!" I protested.

But then, who did? I asked myself, staring hard at the ugly, sneering face on each sheet.

Who did?

# 11

"What's going on up here, guys?"

The dummies stared back at me blankly. None of them replied.

"What's the story?" I demanded. My eyes moved from one dummy to the next. "Come on, guys. Speak up or I'll come back here with a buzz saw and give you all haircuts!"

Silence.

I paced back and forth in front of them, gazing at them sternly, my arms crossed in front of my chest.

It was late in the afternoon. The sun had begun to lower itself behind the trees. Orange light washed in through the dusty attic windows.

I had crept up to the attic to search for clues. Something weird was going on.

How did all those photos of Rocky get onto Zane's roll of film? Who took those photos?

The same person who kept carrying Rocky

downstairs and sitting him where he would frighten Zane.

"It was Dan — right, guys?" I asked the wide-eyed dummies. "Dan came up here — right?"

I searched the floor. The couch. Under all the chairs.

I didn't find a single clue.

Now I was questioning the dummies. But of course they weren't being very helpful.

Stop wasting time and get back downstairs, I told myself.

I turned and started to the stairs — when I heard soft laughter.

"Huh?" I uttered a startled cry and spun around.

Another quiet laugh. A snicker.

And then a hoarse voice: *Is your hair red? Or are you starting to rust?*"

"Excuse me?" I cried, raising a hand to my mouth. My eyes swept quickly from dummy to dummy.

Who said that?

*"Hey, Trina — you're pretty. Pretty ugly!"*
That was followed by another soft snicker. Evil laughter.

*"I like your perfume. What is it — flea and tick spray?"*

My eyes stopped on the new dummy, the one Dad called Smiley. He sat straight up in the center

314

of the couch. The voice seemed to be coming from him.

*"Pinch me. I'm having a nightmare. Or is that really your face?"*

I froze. A cold shiver ran down my back.

The hoarse voice *did* come from the new dummy!

He stared blankly at me. His mouth hung open in a stiff, unpleasant grin.

But the voice came from Smiley. The rude insults came from Smiley.

But that's impossible! I told myself.

Impossible!

Ventriloquist's dummies can't talk without a ventriloquist.

"Th-this is crazy!" I stammered out loud.

And then the dummy started to move.

# 12

I let out a scream.

Dan popped up from behind the couch.

The dummy toppled onto its side.

"You-you-you — !" I sputtered, pointing furiously at my brother.

My heart was pounding. I felt cold all over. "That's not funny! You — you scared me to death!" I shrieked.

To my surprise, Dan didn't laugh. His eyes were narrowed. His mouth hung open. "Who was making those jokes?" he demanded. His eyes darted from dummy to dummy.

"Give me a break!" I shot back. "Are you going to tell me it wasn't you?"

He scratched his short brown hair. "I didn't say a word."

"Dan, you're the biggest liar!" I cried. "How long have you been up here? What are you doing here? You were spying on me — right?"

He shook his head and stepped out from behind

the couch. "What are *you* doing up here, Trina?" he asked. "Did you come up to get Rocky? To take Rocky downstairs again and try to scare Zane?"

I let out an angry growl and shoved Dan with all my might.

He stumbled backwards and fell onto the couch. He cried out as he landed on top of the new dummy. He and the dummy appeared to wrestle for a moment as Dan struggled to climb to his feet.

I stepped up close to the couch and blocked his way. As he tried to get up, I pushed him back down.

"You know I'm not the one who's been moving Rocky around," I shouted. "We all know *you've* been doing it, Dan. And you're going to get the two of us in real trouble with Dad."

"You're wrong!" Dan declared angrily. His little mouse face turned bright red. "Wrong! Wrong! Wrong!"

He burst up from the couch. The dummy bounced on the cushion. Its head turned. It appeared to grin up at me.

I turned to my brother. "If you weren't planning more trouble, what were you doing up here?"

"Waiting," he replied.

"Excuse me? Waiting for whom?" I demanded, crossing my arms over my chest.

"Just waiting," he insisted. "Don't you *get* it, Trina?"

I kicked at a ball of dust on the floor. It stuck to the toe of my sneaker. "Get it? Get what?"

"Don't you see what's going on?" Dan demanded. "Haven't you caught on yet?"

I bent down and pulled the dust ball off my sneaker. Now it stuck to my fingers. "What is in your little mouse brain?" I asked. I rolled my eyes. "This should be good."

My brother stepped up beside me. He lowered his voice to a whisper. "Zane is doing it all," he said.

I laughed. I wasn't sure I'd heard him.

"No. Really." He grabbed my arm. "I know I'm right, Trina. Zane is doing everything. Zane is moving the dummy, bringing it downstairs, then pretending to be scared. Zane made it slap him. Zane carried it to the kitchen table both of those times."

I shoved Dan's hand off my arm. Then I spread my hand over his forehead and pretended to check his temperature. "You are totally losing it," I told him. "Go lie down. I'll tell Mom you're running a high fever."

"*Listen to me!*" Dan screeched. "I'm serious! I'm right. I know I'm right!"

"Why?" I demanded. "Why would Zane do that, Dan? Why would he scare himself?"

"To pay us back for last time," Dan replied. "Don't you get it? Zane is trying to get us in trouble."

I dropped down onto the couch beside Smiley. I thought hard about what my brother was saying. "You mean Zane wants Dad to think that you and I are using the dummies to scare Zane."

"Yes!" Dan cried. "But Zane is doing it all. He's scaring himself. And making it look as if we're doing it — to get us in big trouble."

I fiddled with the dummy's hand as I thought about it some more. "Zane scare himself? I don't think so," I replied finally. "What gave you this idea? What proof do you have?"

Dan dropped down on the couch arm. "First of all," he started, "you didn't carry Rocky downstairs all those times, did you?"

I shook my head. "No way."

"Well, neither did I," Dan declared. "So who does that leave? Rocky isn't walking around by himself — right?"

"Of course not. But — "

"It was the camera that gave it away," Dan said. "The photos Zane developed of Rocky were the biggest clue."

I let the dummy hand fall to the couch. "What do you mean?" I asked. I really wasn't following my brother's thinking at all.

"That camera is never out of Zane's sight," Dan replied. "Most of the time, he keeps it around his neck. So who else could have snapped all those photos of Rocky?"

I swallowed hard. "You mean that Zane — ?"

Dan nodded. "Zane was the only one who could have taken those pictures of Rocky. He sneaked up to the attic. He snapped them. Then he acted scared and angry when he developed them."

"But it was all an act?" I asked.

"For sure," Dan replied. "It's all been an act. To scare us. And to get us in trouble with Dad. Zane is trying to pay us back for how we scared him last time."

I still had my doubts. "It isn't like Zane," I argued. "He's so wimpy, so quiet and shy. He's not the kind of boy who plays tricks on people."

"He's had months to plan it!" Dan exclaimed. "Months to plan his revenge. We can prove it, Trina. We can hide up here and wait for him. That's why I was up here. Hiding behind the couch."

"To catch him in the act?"

Dan nodded. He whispered even though we were alone. "After everyone goes to bed tonight, let's sneak up here and wait. Wait and see if Zane comes."

"Okay," I agreed. "It's worth a try . . . I guess."

Was Dan right?

Would we catch Zane in the act?

I couldn't wait for everyone to go to sleep. I was dying to find out.

# 13

Gusts of wind rattled the attic windowpanes. Heavy clouds covered the moon.

We crept up the attic stairs into the darkness. Up a step. Then stop. Up a step. Then stop. Trying to be silent.

The old house moaned and groaned beneath us. The attic stretched blacker than the stairway.

I reached for the light switch. But Dan slapped my hand away. "Are you crazy?" he whispered. "It has to be dark. Totally dark. Or else Zane will know that someone is up here."

"I know that," I whispered sleepily. "I just wanted to take one look at the dummies. You know. Make sure they're all here."

"They're all here," Dan replied impatiently. "Just keep moving. We'll hide behind the couch."

We crept on tiptoe over the attic floorboards. I couldn't see a thing. The heavy clouds kept any light from washing in through the windows.

Finally, my eyes adjusted to the darkness. I

could see the arms of the couch. I saw dummy heads. Dummy shoulders. Shadows against shadows.

"Dan — where are you?" I whispered.

"Back here. Hurry." His whisper came from behind the couch.

I could feel the dummy eyes on me as I made my way around the couch. I thought I heard a soft snicker. The evil laughter again.

But that had to be my imagination.

I trailed my hand over the couch arm. Felt a wooden dummy hand resting on the arm. The dummy hand felt surprisingly warm.

Humanly warm.

*Don't start imagining things, Trina,* I scolded myself.

That dummy hand is warm because it's *hot* up in this attic.

The wind rattled the glass. Strong gusts roared against the roof, so low over our heads.

I heard a loud groan. A soft chuckle. A strange whistling sound.

Ignoring all the attic noises, I ducked down on the floor beside my brother. "Well? Here we are," I whispered. "Now what?"

"Sssshhhh." In the darkness, I could see him raise a finger to his lips. "Now we wait. And listen."

We both turned and rested our backs against

the back of the couch. I raised my knees and wrapped my arms around them.

"He isn't coming," I whispered. "This is a waste of time."

"Ssshhh. Just wait, Trina," Dan scolded. "Give him time."

I yawned. I felt so sleepy. The heat of the attic was making me even sleepier.

I shut my eyes and thought about Zane.

At dinner, he couldn't wait to pass around the photographs of Rocky. "I don't know who took these shots," Zane complained to my dad. "But they wasted half a roll of film."

Dad glared angrily at Dan and me. But he didn't make a fuss. "Can we talk about it after dinner?" he suggested quietly.

"I'm kind of scared," Zane told Dad in a trembling voice. "So many weird things have been happening. It's like the dummies have lives of their own." He shook his head. "Wow. I hope I don't have nightmares tonight."

"Let's not talk about the dummies now," Mom chimed in. "Zane, tell us about your school. Who is your teacher this year? What are you studying?"

"Could I have a second helping of potatoes?" Uncle Cal interrupted. He reached for the bowl. "They're so good. I may have to make a pig of myself."

Dad took another quick glance at the close-up

snapshots of Rocky. He flashed Dan and me another angry scowl. Then he set the photos down on the floor.

After dinner, Dan and I were careful to keep as far away from Dad as we could. No way we wanted to hear another lecture about how we were terrifying our poor cousin. And how we'd be punished if we didn't stop it at once.

Now it was a little before midnight. And we were huddled in the dark attic. Listening to the swirling wind and the moans and groans of the house. Backs pressed against the couch. Waiting . . .

I kept my eyes closed. Thinking hard. Thinking about Zane. About Rocky.

Dan and I aren't alone up here, I thought drowsily. There are thirteen wooden dummies up here with us. Thirteen pairs of eyes staring into the heavy darkness. Thirteen frozen grins. Except for Rocky's sneer, of course.

Empty, lifeless bodies . . .

Heavy, wooden heads and hands . . .

Thinking about the dummies, the dummies all around, I guess I drifted off to sleep.

Did I dream about the dummies?

Maybe I did.

I don't know how long I slept.

I was awakened by footsteps. Soft, shuffling footsteps across the attic floor.

And I knew the dummies had come alive.

324

# 14

I jerked my head up, listening hard.

My hands were still wrapped around my knees. Both hands had fallen asleep. They tingled. The back of my neck ached. My mouth felt dry and sour.

I uttered a silent gasp as I heard the shuffling, scraping footsteps move closer.

Not dummies walking around, I realized.

A single figure. One. One person. Moving slowly, carefully toward the couch.

Why did I think I heard dummies moving? It must have been a picture left over from my dream.

I shook my hands, trying to make them stop tingling.

I was wide awake now. Totally alert.

The footsteps scraped closer.

Could it be Dan? Where was Dan?

Had he climbed up while I slept? Was he making his way back to the couch?

No.

Squinting into the darkness, I saw Dan beside me.

He had climbed to his knees. He saw me move. He waved his hand and signaled for me to be silent.

Dan gripped the back of the couch with both hands. Then he leaned forward and peered out into the room.

I crawled to the other end of the couch. Then, keeping low, I poked my head out and squinted into the deep shadows. All grays and blacks.

The wind howled around the house. Across the big attic room, the windowpanes rattled and shook.

I wanted to jump out. To scream and jump out. And flash on the light.

But I felt Dan's hand on my arm. He must have read my thoughts. He raised a finger to his lips.

We both waited. Frozen there behind the couch. Crouching low. Listening to each footstep. Each creak of the floorboards.

The dark figure stopped in front of the folding chair next to the couch. He stood inches from Dan and me. If I wanted to, I could reach out and grab his leg.

I struggled to see his face. But it was hidden by the couch. And I didn't dare raise myself up higher.

I heard the *clonk* of wood against wood. Two dummy hands hitting each other.

I heard the rustle of heavy cloth. The *thud* of leather shoes bumping each other.

The intruder had picked up a dummy off the chair.

Squinting into the deep blackness, I could see him swing the dummy over his shoulder. I could see the dummy arms swaying, swaying at his back.

The dark figure turned away quickly. And began walking to the attic stairs.

I crept out from behind the couch. Moving on tiptoe, I began to follow the intruder.

Pressed against the wall, tiptoeing as silently as I could, I moved across the room. I held my breath. I could hear Dan close behind me.

I reached the light switch just as the intruder made it to the stairs.

My hand fumbled against the wall as I reached.

Reached . . . reached for the light switch with a trembling hand.

Yes!

I flicked on the light. And Dan and I both shrieked at the same time.

## 15

"Zane!"

My brother and I both screamed his name.

Zane's eyes bulged. His mouth opened in a high, frightened wail.

I saw his knees bend. I think he nearly crumpled to the floor.

He uttered several squeaks. Then his mouth hung open. I could see he was gasping for breath.

"Zane — we caught you!" I managed to choke out.

He had Rocky draped over his shoulder.

"What — what — ?" Zane struggled to speak, but no words came out. He sputtered and started to choke. The sneering dummy bounced on his shoulder.

"Zane — we figured it out," Dan told him. "Your little tricks aren't going to work."

Our cousin was still sputtering and coughing.

"We know it's been you all along," Dan told him.

He stepped over and slapped Zane hard on the back a few times.

After a few seconds, Zane stopped sputtering.

Dan picked Rocky up off Zane's shoulder and started to carry him back to his chair.

"How-how-how did you know?" Zane stammered.

"We just figured it out," I told him. "What's the big idea, anyway?"

Zane shrugged. He lowered his eyes to the floor. "You know. Just having some fun."

I glared at him. "Some fun?" I cried angrily. "You tried to get us in huge trouble. You — you could have ruined our whole summer!"

Zane shrugged again. "It was kind of my turn. You know?"

"Well, we're even now," Dan chimed in.

"Right," I agreed quickly. "We're all even now — right, Zane?"

He nodded. "Yeah. I guess." A grin spread slowly over his face. "I had you guys going, didn't I? With that stupid dummy popping up everywhere you looked."

Dan and I didn't grin back.

"You fooled us," I murmured.

"You fooled everyone," my brother added.

Zane grinned. A gleeful grin. I could see how pleased he was with himself. "I guess Dan and I deserved it," I confessed.

"Guess you did," Zane shot back. Would he ever stop grinning?

"So now that we're even, do we have a truce?" I demanded. "No more joking around with the dummies? No more trying to scare each other or get anyone in trouble?"

Zane bit his lower lip. He thought about it a long, long time. "Okay. Truce," he said finally.

We all shook hands solemnly. Then we slapped each other high fives. Then the three of us started laughing. I'm not sure why. The laughter just burst out of us.

Crazy giggling.

I guess because it was so late and we were so sleepy. And we were so glad we could be friends now. We didn't have to play tricks on each other anymore.

As we made our way down the stairs, I felt really happy.

I thought all the scary stuff with the dummies was over.

I had no way of knowing that it was just beginning.

# 16

The next morning, Dan, Zane, and I went for a long bike ride. The strong winds had faded away during the night. A soft breeze, warm and fresh-smelling, followed us as we pedaled along the path.

The trees were still winter bare. The ground glistened with a silvery morning frost. But the sweet, warm air told me that spring was on its way.

We biked slowly, following a dirt path that curved into the woods. The sun, still low in the sky, warmed our faces. I stopped to unzip my jacket. And pointed to a patch of green daffodil leaves just beginning to poke up from the ground.

"Only three more months of school!" Dan cried. He raised both fists in the air and let out a cheer.

"We're going to camp this summer for the first time," I told Zane. "Up in Massachusetts."

"For eight weeks!" Dan added happily.

Zane brushed back his blond hair. He leaned

over the handlebars of my dad's bike and began pedaling harder. "I don't know what I'm doing this summer," he said. "Probably just hanging out."

"What do you *want* to do this summer?" I asked him.

He grinned at me. "Just hang out."

We all laughed. I was in a great mood and so were the guys.

Dan kept pulling wheelies, leaning way back and raising his front tire off the ground. Zane tried to do it — and crashed into a tree.

He went sailing to the ground, and the bike fell on top of him. I expected him to whine and complain. That's his usual style. But he picked himself up, muttering, "Smooth move, Zane."

"I want to see that one again!" Dan joked.

Zane laughed. "You try it!"

He brushed the dirt off his jeans and climbed back onto the bike. We pedaled on down the path, joking and laughing.

I think we were in such great moods because of the truce. We could finally relax and not worry about who was trying to terrify who.

The dirt path ended at a small, round pond. The pond gleamed in the sunlight, still half-frozen from the long winter.

Zane climbed off his bike and rested it on the tall grass. Then he stepped up to the edge of the pond to take photos.

"Look at the weeds poking up from the melting ice!" he exclaimed, clicking away. "Awesome. Awesome!" He knelt down low and snapped a bunch of weed photos.

Dan and I exchanged glances. I couldn't see what was so special about the weeds. But I guess that's why I'm not a photographer.

As Zane stood up, a tiny brown-and-black chipmunk scampered along the edge of the pond. Zane swung his camera and clicked off a couple of shots.

"Hey! I think I got him!" he declared happily.

"Great!" I cried. Everything seemed great this morning.

We hung out at the pond for a while. We took a short walk through the woods. Then we started to get hungry for lunch. So we rode back to the house.

We were about to return the bikes to the garage when Zane spotted the old well at the back of our yard. "Cool!" he cried, his blue eyes lighting up. "Let's check it out!"

Holding his camera in one hand, he hopped off his bike and went running across the grass to the well.

It's a round, stone well with green moss covering the smooth gray stones. It used to have a pointed red roof over it. But the roof blew off during a bad storm, and Dad hauled it away.

When we were little, Dan and I used to scare each other by pretending that monsters and trolls lived down inside it. But we hadn't paid much attention to the old well in years. Dad kept saying he was going to tear it down and cover it up. But he never got around to it.

Zane clicked a bunch of photos. "Is there still water down there?" he asked.

I shrugged. "I don't know."

Dan grabbed Zane around the waist. "We could toss you down and see if you make a splash!" he declared.

Zane wrestled himself out of my brother's grasp. "I've got a better idea." He picked up a stone and dropped it down the well.

After a long wait, we heard a splash far down below.

"Cool!" Zane exclaimed. He took several more pictures until he had finished the roll.

Then we made our way inside the house for lunch. We hurried upstairs to clean up.

Zane stopped at the doorway to his room.

I saw his eyes bulge and his mouth drop open. I saw his face go white.

Dan and I ran up next to him.

We stared into the bedroom — and cried out in horror.

# 17

"The r-room — it's been *trashed!*" Dan stammered.

The three of us huddled in the doorway, staring into the bedroom. Staring at an unbelievable mess.

At first I thought maybe Zane had left the windows open all night, and the strong winds had blown everything around.

But that didn't make any sense.

All of the clothes had been pulled out of the closet and tossed over the floor. The dresser drawers had all been pulled out and dumped over the carpet.

The bookshelves had been emptied. Books littered the floor, the bed — they were tossed everywhere. One bed table was turned on its side. The other stood upside down on top of the bed. A lamp lay on the floor in front of the closet. Its shade was ripped and broken.

"Look — !" Zane pointed into the center of the room.

Sitting on a tangled hill of clothes was Rocky. The dummy sat straight up, his legs crossed casually in front of him. He sneered at us as if daring us to enter.

"I-I really don't believe this!" I cried, tugging at the sides of my hair.

"*What* don't you believe?"

Mom's voice made me jump.

I turned to see her coming out of her bedroom. She tucked her blue sweater into her jeans as she walked toward us.

"Mom — !" I cried. "Something terrible has happened!"

Her smile faded. "What on earth — ?" she started.

I stepped aside so she could see into Zane's room.

"Oh, no!" Mom cried out and raised both hands to her cheeks. She swallowed hard. "Did someone break in?" Her voice sounded tiny and frightened.

I peered quickly into my room across the hall. "No. I don't think so," I reported. "This is the only room that's messed up."

"But — but — " Mom sputtered. Then her eyes stopped on Rocky on top of the pile of clothes. "What is *he* doing down here?" Mom demanded.

"We don't know," I told her.

"But who *did* this?" Mom cried, still pressing her hands against her cheeks.

"We didn't!" Dan declared.

"We've been outside all morning," Zane added breathlessly. "It wasn't Trina, or Dan, or me. We weren't home. We were riding bikes."

"But — someone had to do this!" Mom declared. "Someone deliberately tore this room apart."

But who was it? I wondered. My eyes darted around the mess, landing on the sneering dummy.

Who was it?

# 18

We all pitched in and helped get the room back together. It took the rest of the afternoon.

The lamp in front of the closet was broken. Everything else just had to be picked up and put back where it belonged.

We worked in silence. None of us knew what to say.

At first, Mom wanted to call the police. But there was no sign that someone had broken into the house. All the other rooms were perfectly okay.

Dad returned home from the camera shop while we were still cleaning up. He, of course, was furious. "What do I have to do? Bolt the attic door?" he shouted at Dan and me.

He grabbed up Rocky and slung the dummy over his shoulder. "This isn't a joke anymore," Dad said, narrowing his eyes at both of us. "This isn't funny. This is serious."

"But we didn't do it!" I protested for the hundredth time.

"Well, the dummy didn't do it," Dad shot back. "That's one thing I know for sure."

I don't know *anything* for sure, I thought. I stared at Rocky's sneering face as Dad started down the hall to the attic stairs. Then I bent down to pick up the broken lamp from the floor.

That night I dreamed once again about ventriloquist's dummies.

I saw them dancing. A dozen of them. All of Dad's dummies from upstairs.

I saw them dancing in Zane's room. Dancing over the tangled piles of clothes and books. Dancing over the bed. Over the toppled bed table.

I saw Rocky dancing with Miss Lucy. I saw Wilbur doing a frantic, crazy dance on top of the dresser. And I saw Smiley, the new dummy, clapping his wooden hands, bobbing his head, grinning, grinning from the middle of the room as the other dummies danced around him.

They waved their big hands over their heads. Their skinny legs twisted and bent.

They danced in silence. No music. No sound at all.

And as their bodies twisted and swayed, their faces remained frozen. They grinned at one another with blank, unblinking eyes. Grinned their frightening, red-lipped grins.

Bobbed and bent, tilted and swayed, grinning, grinning, grinning the whole time in the eerie silence.

And then the grins faded as I pulled myself out of the dream.

I opened my eyes. Slowly woke up.

Felt the heavy hands on my neck.

Stared up into Rocky's ugly face.

Rocky on top of me. The dummy on top of my blanket. Over me.

Reaching. Reaching his heavy wooden hands for my throat!

# 19

I opened my mouth in a shrill scream of horror.

My hands shot out. I grabbed the dummy's hands.

I thrashed my legs. Kicked off the blanket. Kicked at the dummy.

The big eyes stared at me as if startled.

I grabbed his head. Shoved him down.

I sat up, my entire body trembling. Then I grabbed the dummy's waist.

And flung him to the floor.

The ceiling light flashed on. Mom and Dad burst into my room together.

"What's happening?"

"Trina — what's wrong?"

They both stopped short when they saw the dummy sprawled on the floor beside my bed.

"He — he — " I gasped, pointing down at Rocky. I struggled to catch my breath. "Rocky — he jumped on me. He tried to choke me. I-I woke up and — "

Dad let out a loud growl and tore at his hair. "This has got to stop!" he bellowed.

Mom dropped down beside me on the bed and wrapped me in a hug. I couldn't stop my shoulders from trembling.

"It was so scary!" I choked out. "I woke up — and there he was!"

"This is out of control!" Dad screamed, shaking his fist in the air. "Out of control!"

Mom calmed me down. Then she and I both had to calm Dad down.

Finally, after everyone was calm, they turned out the light and made their way out of the room. They closed the door. I heard Dad carrying Rocky back up to the attic.

Maybe Dad *should* get a lock for the attic door, I thought.

I shut my eyes and tried not to think about Rocky, or Zane, or the dummies — or anything at all.

After a while, I must have drifted back to sleep.

I don't know how much time passed.

I was awakened by a knock on the door. Two sharp knocks and then two more.

I sat straight up with a gasp.

I knew that Rocky had come back.

The bedroom door creaked open slowly.

I took a deep breath and held it, staring through the dark.

"Trina — ?" a voice whispered. "Trina — are you awake?"

As the door opened, a rectangle of gray light spilled into the room from the hallway. Dan poked his head in, then took a few steps across the floor.

"Trina? It's me."

I let out my breath in a long *whoosh*. "Dan — what do you want?" My voice was hoarse from sleep.

"I heard everything," Dan said, stepping up beside the bed. He pulled down one pajama sleeve. Then he raised his eyes to me. "Zane put Rocky on your bed. Zane did it!" Dan whispered.

"Huh? Why do you say that? We all have a truce — remember? Zane agreed the tricks were all over."

"Right," Dan whispered. "And now Zane thinks

he can *really* scare us. Because we don't suspect him any longer. Zane hasn't given up, Trina. I'm sure of it."

I bit my lower lip. I tried to think about what Dan was saying. But I was so sleepy!

Dan leaned close and whispered excitedly. "This morning before we went biking, Zane went up to his room — remember? He said he forgot his camera. So . . . he had time to mess up his room. Before he left the house."

"Yeah. Maybe," I murmured.

"And tonight he brought Rocky down and set him up on your bed. I'm sure of it," Dan insisted. "I'm sure it's Zane. We have to hide up in the attic again. Tomorrow night. We'll catch Zane again. I know we will."

"Hide up there again? No way!" I cried. "It's hot up there. And too creepy. And I'm staying as far away from those dummies as I can."

My brother sighed. "I know I'm right," he whispered.

"I don't know *what* I know," I replied. "I don't know anything about anything." I slid under the covers, pulled the blanket over my head, and tried to get back to sleep.

The next night, Mom and Dad had a dinner party in honor of Zane and Uncle Cal. They invited the Birches and the Canfields from down the street, and Cousin Robin and her husband Fred.

Fred is a great guy. Everyone calls him Froggy because he can puff out his cheeks like a frog. Froggy is short and very round and really looks like a frog.

He always makes me laugh. He knows a million great jokes. Robin is always trying to get him to shut up. But he never does.

Mom and Dad don't have many dinner parties. So they had to work all day to get the dining room ready. To set the table. And to cook the dinner.

Mom made a leg of lamb. Dad cooked up his specialty — Caribbean-style scalloped potatoes. Very spicy.

Mom bought flowers for the table. She and Dad brought out all the fancy plates and glasses that we usually see only on holidays.

The dining room really looked awesome as we all sat down to dinner. Dan, Zane, and I were down at the far end of the table. Froggy sat at our end. I guess, because he's just a big kid.

Froggy told me a moron joke. Someone asks a moron: "Can you stand on your head?" And the moron says, "No, I can't. It's up too high."

I started to laugh when I saw Zane jump up from the table. "Where are you going?" I called after him.

Zane turned back at the dining room doorway. "To get my camera," he replied. "I want to take some pictures of the table before it gets all messed up."

He disappeared upstairs.

A few seconds later, we all heard him scream.

Chairs scraped the floor as everyone jumped up. We all went running up the stairs.

I reached Zane's room first. From the doorway, I saw him standing in the center of the room.

I saw the sick look on Zane's face.

And then I saw the camera in his hand.

Or what was left of the camera.

It looked as if it had been run over by a truck. The film door had been twisted off and lay on the floor. The lens was smashed. The whole camera body was bent and broken.

Zane turned the camera over in his hands, gazing down at it sadly, shaking his head.

I raised my eyes to the bed. And saw Rocky sitting on the bedspread. A roll of gray film unspooled across his lap.

Dad burst into the room. All of our other guests pushed in after him.

"What happened?" someone asked.

"Is that Zane's camera?"

"What's going on?"

"That's what happens when you try to take my picture!" Froggy joked.

No one laughed. It wasn't funny.

Dad's face turned dark red as he took the camera from Zane's hand. Dad examined it carefully. His expression remained grim.

"This isn't mischief anymore," he murmured. I could barely hear him over all the other voices in the room. Everyone had begun talking at once.

"This cannot be allowed," Dad said solemnly. He raised his eyes to Dan, then me. He stared at us both for the longest time without saying anything.

Zane let out a long sigh. I turned and saw that he was about to cry.

"Zane — " I started.

But he uttered an angry shout. Then he pushed past Froggy and Mr. and Mrs. Birch. And went running from the room.

"Someone here has done a very sick thing," Dad said sadly. He raised the camera to his face, running a finger over the broken lens. "This is a very expensive camera. It was Zane's most prized possession."

All of our guests became very quiet.

Dad kept his eyes on Dan and me. He started to say something else.

But then we all heard the deafening crash from downstairs.

# 21

"What is going *on* here?" Dad cried. He tossed the broken camera onto the bed and darted from the room.

The others went hurrying after him. All talking at once. I heard their shoes pounding down the stairs.

I turned to Dan. "Still think Zane is doing these things?"

Dan shrugged. "Maybe."

"No way," I told him. "No way Zane is going to smash his own camera. He loved his camera. No way he would smash it just to get you and me in trouble."

Dan raised troubled eyes to me. "Then I don't get it," he said in a tiny voice. I could see the fear on his face.

I heard startled shouts and cries of alarm from downstairs. "Let's check out the *next* disaster," I said, rolling my eyes.

We reached the bedroom door at the same time

and squeezed through together. Then I led the way along the hall and down the stairs.

I fought back my own fear as we approached the dining room.

Something very strange was going on in this house, I knew. Dad was right when he said it was no joke.

Tearing Zane's room apart wasn't a joke. It was evil.

Wrecking Zane's camera was evil, too.

Thinking about Rocky gave me a chill. The dummy was always there. Whenever something evil happened, there sat Rocky.

Trina, don't be crazy! I scolded myself. Don't start thinking that a wooden ventriloquist's dummy can be evil.

That's crazy thinking. That's really messed up.

*But what could I think?*

My throat tightened. My mouth suddenly felt very dry.

I took a deep breath and led the way into the dining room.

I saw Dad in the kitchen doorway. He had his arm around Mom's shoulders. Mom had her head buried against Dad's shirtsleeve.

Was she crying?

Yes.

The guests all stood against the wall, shaking their heads, their expressions grim and confused. They muttered quietly, staring at the disaster.

The disaster. The terrible disaster.

The dining room table.

I saw the overturned platters first. Dad's scalloped potatoes smeared over the tablecloth. Clumps of potatoes stuck to the wall and the front of the china hutch.

The salad poured over the floor and the chairs. The bread ripped into small chunks, the chunks tossed over the table. The flowers ripped off their stems. The vase on its side, water pouring over the tablecloth, puddling on the floor.

The glasses all turned over. A bottle of red wine tipped over, a dark red stain spreading over the tablecloth.

I heard Mom's sobs. I heard the sounds of Dad's muttered attempts to calm her down. I saw the other guests shaking their heads, their faces so upset, so concerned, so puzzled.

And then Dan grabbed my shoulder and pointed me toward the head of the table. And I saw two dummies sitting there on dining room chairs.

Wilbur and the new dummy. Wilbur and Smiley.

They sat at the table, grinning at each other, wine glasses in their hands. As if celebrating. As if toasting each other.

# 22

That night, Dan and I hid behind the couch in the attic once again. The attic stretched dark and silent. So dark, I could barely see my brother sitting beside me.

We were both in pajamas. The air was hot and dry. But my hands and my bare feet felt cold and clammy.

We talked softly, our legs stretched out on the floor, resting against the back of the couch. As we talked, we waited — and listened. Listened to every sound.

It was nearly midnight, but I didn't feel sleepy. I felt alert. Ready for anything.

Ready to catch Zane in the act once again.

This time, I brought my little flash camera with me. When Zane crept up here to carry one of the dummies downstairs, I'd snap his photo. Then I'd have proof to show Mom and Dad.

Yes, I finally decided that Dan was right. Zane had to be the one who was destroying our house.

Destroying our house and trying to scare everyone into thinking the dummies had come to life.

"But why?" I whispered to Dan. "Did we scare Zane so badly the last time he was here? So badly that he'll do *anything* to pay us back?"

"He's sick," Dan muttered. "That's the only answer. He's totally messed up."

"So messed up that he wrecked his own camera," I murmured, shaking my head.

"So messed up that he ran downstairs and trashed the dining room," Dan added.

The dining room. That's what convinced me that Zane was guilty.

All of us were upstairs in Zane's room, examining his broken camera.

Zane was the only other person downstairs.

Zane was the only person in the house who could have trashed the dining room and wrecked the dinner.

Of course he acted horrified and shocked. Of course he acted as if he didn't have a clue about what had happened.

What a sad, sad night.

The dinner guests didn't know what to say to Mom and Dad. It was such a frightening mystery. No one had an answer.

The guests helped clean up the mess. The food was ruined. It couldn't be eaten. No one felt like eating, anyway.

Everyone left as soon as the dining room was cleaned and cleared.

As the last guest left, I turned to Dan. "Uh-oh," I whispered. "Family Conference Time. We're in for a major lecture now."

But I was wrong. Mom hurried up to her room. And Dad said he was too disgusted to talk to anyone.

Uncle Cal asked if Dad would like him to take the car and pick up some fried chicken or hamburgers or something.

Dad just scowled at him and stomped away. He carried Smiley and Wilbur up to the attic. I heard him slam the attic door. Then he disappeared into the bedroom to help comfort Mom.

Zane turned to his dad. "I-I can't believe my good camera is smashed," he whimpered.

Uncle Cal placed a hand on Zane's shoulder. "I'll bet your uncle Danny has a new camera at his shop that he'll want to give you."

"But I liked my *old* camera!" Zane wailed.

And that's when I decided he was guilty. He's a phony, I decided. He's carrying on like this — putting on a show for Dan and me.

But I wasn't going to fall for it. No way.

I made sure I had film in my little camera. Then I grabbed Dan and we crept up to the attic to wait. To wait in the darkness and catch Zane.

To end the disasters in our house once and for all.

We didn't have to wait long.

After about half an hour, I heard the tap of soft footsteps on the attic floor.

I sucked in my breath. My whole body tensed, and I nearly dropped the camera.

Beside me, Dan raised himself to his knees.

My heart pounding, I crept to the edge of the couch.

*Tap tap.* Shuffling footsteps on the bare floorboards.

I saw a dark figure bend down and lift a dummy off a chair.

"It's Zane," I whispered to Dan. "I knew it!"

In the heavy darkness, I could see him carrying the dummy to the stairs.

I stood up. My legs trembled. But I moved quickly.

I raised the camera. Stepped in front of the couch.

Pushed the shutter button.

The room flashed in an explosion of white light.

I clicked off another one.

Another bright white flash.

And in the flash, I saw Rocky dangling over Zane's shoulder.

No.

Not Zane!

Not Zane. Not Zane.

In the flash of light, I saw Rocky dangling over *another dummy's* shoulder!

Smiley! The new dummy.

The new dummy was shuffling toward the stairs, carrying Rocky away.

## 23

The dummy turned.

My hand fumbled for the light switch. I clicked on the light.

I stood frozen in front of the couch. Too startled to move.

"Smiley — stop!" I screamed.

The dummy's grin faded. The eyes narrowed at me. "I'm not Smiley," he croaked. He had a hoarse, raspy voice. "My name is Slappy."

He turned back to the stairs.

"Stop him!" I cried to my brother.

We both made a dive for the dummy.

Slappy spun around. He pulled Rocky off his shoulder — and heaved him at Dan.

I grabbed Slappy around the waist and tackled him to the floor.

He swung both hands hard. One of them slammed into my forehead.

"Unh." I let out a groan as the pain shot through me.

My hands slid off the dummy's slender waist. Slappy jumped nimbly to his feet, his grin wide and leering.

He was enjoying this!

He kicked me in the side with the toe of his big leather shoe.

My head still throbbing, I rolled out of the way. And turned back in time to see Dan grab the dummy from behind.

Dan drove his head into the dummy's back. They both dropped hard to the floor.

"Let go of me, slave!" Slappy demanded in his ugly, hoarse voice. "You are my slave now! Let go of me! I order you!"

I pulled myself to my knees as Dan and Slappy wrestled over the floor.

"He's so . . . *strong!*" Dan called out to me.

Slappy rolled on top of him. Started to pound him with his wooden fists.

I grabbed Slappy by the shoulders and tugged with all my strength. Slappy swung his arms, thrashing at my brother.

I pulled hard, trying to tug him off Dan's stomach.

"Let go! Let go!" the dummy shrieked. "Let go, slave!"

"Get off him!" I cried.

We were making such a racket, I didn't hear the attic door open downstairs. And I didn't hear the footsteps running up the stairs.

A face appeared. And then a large body.

"Dad!" I cried breathlessly. "Dad — look!"

"What on earth — !" Dad exclaimed.

"Dad — it's alive! The dummy is alive!" I shrieked.

"Huh?" Squinting through his glasses, Dad lowered his gaze to the dummy on the floor.

The dummy sprawled lifelessly on its back beside Dan. One arm was twisted beneath its back. Both legs were bent in two.

The mouth hung open in its painted grin. The eyes stared blankly at the ceiling.

"It *is* alive!" Dan insisted. "It really is!"

Dad stared down at the still, silent dummy.

"The dummy picked up Rocky!" Dan declared in a high, excited voice. "He said his name was Slappy. He picked up Rocky. He was carrying him downstairs."

Dad *tsk-tsk*ed and shook his head. "Give it up, Dan," he murmured angrily. "Just stop it right now." He raised his eyes to Dan, then to me. "I knew you two were the troublemakers."

"But, Dad — " I protested.

"I'm not an idiot," Dad snapped, scowling at me. "You can't expect me to believe a dumb story about a dummy coming to life and carrying another dummy around. Have you both lost your minds entirely?"

"It's true," Dan insisted.

We both gazed down at Slappy. He sure didn't

look alive. For a moment, I had the frightening feeling that I'd dreamed the whole scene.

But then I remembered something. "I have proof!" I cried. "Dad, I can prove to you that Dan and I aren't lying."

Dad rubbed the back of his neck. "I'm so tired," he moaned. "It's been such a long, horrible day. Please. Give me a break, Trina."

"But I took some pictures!" I told him. "I have pictures of Slappy carrying Rocky!"

"Trina, I'm warning you — " Dad started.

But I spun away, searching for my camera. Where was it? Where?

It took me a few seconds to spot it on the floor against the wall back by the couch. I hurried across the room to grab it.

And stopped halfway.

The back of the camera — it had sprung open. The film was exposed. The pictures were ruined.

The camera must have flown out of my hand when I tried to tackle Slappy, I realized. I picked it up and examined it sadly.

No pictures. No proof.

I turned back to find Dad scowling at me. "No more wasting my time, Trina. You two are grounded until further notice. I'm so disgusted with both of you. Your mother and I will think of other punishments after your cousin leaves."

Then Dad waved a hand at Slappy and Rocky. "Put them away. Right now. And stay out of the attic. Stay away from my dummies. That's all I have to say to you. Good night."

Dad turned away sharply and stomped down the stairs.

I glanced at Dan and shrugged. I didn't know what to say.

My heart was pounding. I was so angry. So upset. So *hurt*. My chest felt about to explode.

I bent down to pick up Slappy.

The dummy winked at me.

His ugly grin grew wider. And then he puckered his red lips and made disgusting, wet kissing sounds.

# 24

"Don't touch me, slave," Slappy growled.

I gasped and jumped back. I still couldn't believe this was happening. I wrapped my arms around myself to stop my body from trembling.

"You — you really are alive?" Dan asked softly.

"You bet your soft head I am!" the dummy roared.

"What do you want?" I cried. "Why are you doing this to us? Why are you getting us in all this trouble?"

The ugly grin spread over his face. "If you treat me nice, slaves, maybe I won't get you in any more trouble. Maybe you'll get lucky." He tapped his head and added, "Knock on wood."

"We're not your slaves!" I insisted.

He tossed back his head and let out a dry laugh. "Who's the dummy here?" he cried. "You or me?"

"You carried Rocky downstairs all those times?" Dan asked. I could see that my brother was having a hard time believing this, too.

"You don't think that bag of kindling can move on his own, do you?" Slappy sneered. "I had some fun with that ugly guy. I put him at the scene of the crimes to throw you off the track. To keep you slaves guessing."

"And you smashed Zane's camera and ruined the dinner party?" I demanded.

He narrowed his eyes to evil slits. "I'll do much worse if you slaves don't obey me."

I could feel the anger rising through my body. "You — you're going to ruin everything!" I screamed at him. "You're going to ruin our lives! You're going to keep us from going to camp this summer!"

Slappy snickered. "You won't be going to camp. You'll be staying home to take good care of *me*!"

And then I exploded.

"Nooooo!" I uttered a long wail of protest.

I grabbed his head in both hands. I started to tug.

I remembered his head had been split in two when Dad found him. I planned to pull his head apart — to split it in two again!

He kicked his legs frantically and thrashed his arms.

His heavy shoes kicked at my legs.

But I held on tight. Pulling. Pulling. Struggling to pull his head apart.

"Let me try! Let me try!" Dan called.

I let out a sigh and dropped the dummy to the

floor. "It's no use," I told Dan. "Dad did too good a job. It's glued tight."

Slappy scrambled to his feet. He shook his head. "Thanks for the head massage, slave! Now rub my back!" He laughed, an ugly dry laugh that sounded more like a cough.

Dan stared at the dummy in wide-eyed horror. "Trina — what are we going to do?" he cried, his voice just above a whisper.

"How about a game of Kick the Dummy Down the Stairs?" Slappy suggested, leering at us. "We'll take turns being the dummy. You can go first!"

"We — we have to do something!" Dan stammered. "He's a *monster!* He's evil! We have to get rid of him!"

But how? I wondered.

How?

And then I had an idea.

# 25

Slappy must have read my thoughts. He turned and started to run.

But I dove fast — and wrapped my hands around his skinny legs.

He let out a harsh, angry cry as I began twisting his legs around each other, struggling to tie them in a knot.

He swung an arm. The wooden hand caught me on the ear.

But I held on.

"Dan — grab his arms! Hurry!"

My brother moved quickly. Slappy tried to bat him away. But Dan ducked low. And when he came up, he grabbed Slappy's wrists and held on.

"Let me go, slaves!" the dummy rasped. "Let me go now. You'll be sorry! You'll pay!"

I saw the fear on Dan's face.

Slappy swung a hand free. He tried to swipe at Dan's throat.

364

But Dan reached out and grabbed onto the loose arm again.

I felt eyes on me. I glanced up to see the other dummies around the room. They appeared to watch us struggle. A silent, still audience.

I pulled a red kerchief off a dummy's neck. And I stuffed it into Slappy's mouth to keep him quiet.

"Downstairs! Hurry!" I instructed my brother.

The dummy twisted and squirmed, trying to break free.

But I had his legs tied around each other. And Dan kept a tight grip on his arms.

We began making our way to the attic stairs.

"Where are we taking him?" Dan demanded.

"Outside," I replied. The dummy bucked and squirmed. I nearly dropped him.

"In our pajamas?" Dan asked.

I nodded and began backing down the stairs. Slappy struggled hard to get free. I nearly lost my balance and toppled over backwards.

"We're not going far," I groaned.

Somehow we made it all the way downstairs. I had to let go with one hand to open the front door. Slappy bucked his knees, trying to untangle his legs.

I pushed the door open. Grabbed the legs again.

Dan and I carried the squirming dummy outside.

A cold, clear night. A light, silvery frost over the grass. A half moon high over the trees.

"Ohhh." I let out a moan as my bare feet touched the frozen grass.

"It's c-cold!" Dan stammered. "I can't hold on much longer."

I saw him shiver. The front lawn suddenly darkened as clouds rolled over the moon. My legs trembled. The damp cold seeped through my thin pajamas.

"Where are we taking him?" Dan whispered.

"Around to the back."

Slappy kicked hard. But I held on tightly.

Something scampered past my bare feet. I heard scurrying footsteps over the frosty ground.

A rabbit? A raccoon?

I didn't stop to see. Gripping Slappy's ankles with both hands, I backed up. Backed along the side of the house.

"My feet are numb!" Dan complained.

"Almost there," I replied.

Slappy uttered hoarse cries beneath the kerchief that gagged his mouth. His round eyes rolled wildly. Again, he tried to kick free.

Dan and I hauled him to the back of the yard. By the time we got to the old well, my feet were frozen numb, too. And my whole body shook from the cold.

"What are we going to do?" Dan asked in a tiny voice.

The clouds rolled away. Shadows pulled back. The silvery moonlight lit up the old stone well.

"We're going to toss him down the well," I groaned.

Dan stared at me, surprised.

"He's evil," I explained. "We have no choice."

Dan nodded.

We lifted Slappy onto the smooth stones at the top of the well. He bucked and kicked. He tried to scream through his gag.

I saw Dan shiver again.

"It's a wooden dummy," I told him. "It isn't a person. It's an evil wooden dummy."

We both shoved hard at the same time.

The dummy slid off the stone wall and dropped into the well.

Dan and I both waited until we heard the splash from far below.

Then we ran side by side back to the house.

He's gone! I thought gratefully. Joyfully. The evil thing is gone for good.

I slept really well that night. And I didn't dream about dummies.

The next morning, Dan and I met in the hall. We both were smiling. We felt so good.

I was actually singing as I followed Dan down the stairs for breakfast.

Dad greeted us at the kitchen door with an

angry frown. "What is *he* doing down here?" Dad demanded.

He pointed into the kitchen.

Pointed at the breakfast table.

Pointed to Slappy, sitting at the breakfast table, grinning his ugly painted grin, his eyes wide and innocent.

# 26

Dan's mouth dropped open.

I let out a sharp cry.

"Don't act stunned. Just get him out of here," Dad said angrily. "And why is he all wet? Did you have him out in the rain?"

I glanced out the kitchen window. Lightning flashed through a dark gray sky. Sheets of rain pounded the glass. Thunder rumbled overhead.

"Not a very nice morning," Uncle Cal said, stepping up behind Dan and me.

"I've got coffee ready," Dad told him.

"I see your friend here beat us down to breakfast," Uncle Cal said, motioning to Slappy.

The dummy's grin seemed to grow wider.

"Get him out of here, Trina," Dad repeated sharply. "Anyone want pancakes this morning?" He moved to the cabinet and started searching for a frying pan.

"Make a few extra for me. I'm starving," Uncle

369

Cal said. "I'll go see if Zane is up." He turned and hurried out of the kitchen.

Dad leaned into the cabinet, banging pots and pans, searching for the one he always used for pancakes.

"Dad, I have to tell you something," I said softly. I couldn't hold it in any longer. I had to tell Dad the truth. I had to tell him the whole story.

"Dad, Slappy is evil," I told him. "He's alive, and he's evil. Dan and I threw him down the well last night. We had to get rid of him. But now — he's back. You have to help us, Dad. We have to get rid of him — now."

I took a deep breath and let it out. It felt so good to get the story off my chest.

Dad pulled his head from the cabinet and turned to me. "Did you say something, Trina? I was making such a racket, I couldn't hear you."

"Dad, I-I — " I stammered.

"Get that dummy *out* of here — now!" Dad shouted. He stuck his head back into the cabinet. "How can a whole frying pan disappear into thin air?"

I let out a disappointed sigh. A loud burst of thunder made me jump.

I motioned with my head for Dan to help me. We lifted Slappy off the chair. I held him around the waist, as far away from me as possible.

370

His gray suit was sopping wet. Water dripped off his black leather shoes.

We were halfway up the attic stairs when Slappy blinked and let out a soft chuckle. "Nice try, slaves," he rasped. "But give up. I'm never going away. Never!"

# 27

What a dreary morning.

Rain pounded the windows. Lightning crackled through the charcoal-gray sky. Thunder boomed so close it rocked the house.

I felt as if the storm were inside my head. As if the heavy, heavy storm clouds were weighing me down. As if the thunder erupted inside my brain, drowning out my thoughts.

Dan and I slumped on the couch in the den, watching the storm through the venetian blinds over the big window. We were trying to come up with an idea, a way to get rid of Slappy.

The room was chilly. Damp, cold air leaked through the old window. I rubbed the sleeves of my sweater, trying to warm myself.

We were alone in the house. Mom, Dad, Uncle Cal, and Zane had gone into town.

"I tried to tell Dad," I said. "You heard me, Dan. I tried to tell him about Slappy. But he didn't hear me."

"Dad wouldn't believe you anyway, Trina," Dan replied glumly. He sighed. "Who *would* believe it?"

"How can a wooden dummy come to life?" I asked, shaking my head. "How?"

And then I remembered.

And then I had an idea.

I jumped up from the couch. I tugged my brother by the arm. "Come on."

He pulled back. "Where?"

"To the attic. I think I know how to put Slappy to sleep — for good."

I stopped at the attic door and held Dan back. "Be very quiet," I instructed him. "Maybe Slappy is asleep. If he's asleep, my plan will go a whole lot better."

Thunder roared as I opened the door. I led the way up the stairs, moving slowly, carefully, one step at a time. I could hear the rain pounding down on the roof. And I could see the flicker of lightning on the low ceiling.

I stopped as I reached the top of the stairs and turned toward the dummy collection. A flash of lightning through the window cast the shadows of their heads on the wall. As the lightning flickered, the shadows all seemed to be moving.

Dan stepped up behind me. "Here we are. Now what?" he whispered.

I raised a finger to my lips and began to tiptoe

across the floor. Thunder boomed. It sounded so much louder up here under the roof!

When Dan and I dragged Slappy up here this morning, we had tossed him down on the floor. We were too freaked and frightened to spend the time propping him up on his chair. We just wanted to dump him and get away from the attic.

I saw Slappy in the flickering white lightning. Lying on his back in the center of the floor. The other dummies sat around him, grinning their silent grins.

I took a step closer. And then another. Moving as silently as I could.

I peered down at the evil dummy. His arms were at his sides. His legs were twisted around each other.

And his eyes were closed.

Yes!

His eyes were closed. He was asleep.

I took another few steps toward Slappy. But I felt Dan's hand on my arm, tugging me back. "Trina — what are you going to do?" he whispered.

My eyes darted to Slappy. Still asleep. Thunder roared all around. It sounded as if we were standing in the middle of it.

"Remember those weird words I read?" I whispered to my brother, keeping my eyes on the evil dummy. "Remember those weird words on that slip of paper?"

Dan thought for a moment. Then he nodded.

"Well, maybe it was those words that brought him to life," I whispered. "Maybe it's some kind of secret chant."

Dan shrugged. "Maybe." He didn't sound too hopeful.

"I saw you tuck that slip of paper back into Slappy's jacket pocket," I told my brother. "I'm going to take it out and read the words again. Maybe the same words that bring him to life will also put him back to sleep."

Of *course* it was a crazy idea.

But a dummy coming to life was crazy, too. And a dummy trying to turn you into his slave was crazy.

It was *all* crazy. So maybe my idea was just crazy enough to work.

"Good luck," my brother whispered, his eyes on the sleeping dummy on the floor.

I made my way over to Slappy.

I knelt down on my knees beside him.

I took a deep breath and held it. Then slowly, slowly, I began to reach my hand down to his jacket pocket.

I knew the slip of paper was inside that pocket. Could I pull it out without waking up Slappy?

I lowered my hand. Lowered it.

My fingers touched the top of the jacket pocket.

Still holding my breath, I began to slip two fingers inside.

*"Gotcha!"* Slappy shrieked as his hands shot up. He grabbed both of my wrists and began to squeeze.

# 28

I was so stunned, I nearly fell on top of him.

As I struggled to keep my balance, his wooden hands dug into my wrists. They tightened around me, cutting into my skin.

"Let go of me!" I screamed. I struggled to pull my arms away. But he was too strong. Too strong.

The hard fingers dug into my wrists. They squeezed harder, harder — until they cut off all circulation.

"Let go of me! Let go!" My cry came out a shrill wail.

"I give the orders, sssssslave!" Slappy hissed. "You will obey me. Obey me *forever!* Or you will pay!"

"Let go! Let me go!" I shrieked. I tugged. I struggled to my feet. I jerked my arms up and down.

But Slappy didn't loosen his hold.

His whole body bounced in the air. Hit the floor. Bounced back up as I pulled.

But his hands gripped even harder.

I couldn't free myself. And the pain — the intense pain — shot down my arms. Down my sides. Down my whole body.

"Pick me up, sssslave!" the dummy hissed. "Pick me up and put me on my chair."

"Let go!" I cried. "You're breaking my wrists! Let go!"

The dummy uttered a cold laugh in reply.

The pain shot through my body. My legs wobbled. I dropped back to my knees.

I turned in time to see Dan dive toward us.

I thought he was going to grab the dummy's hand and try to set me free.

Instead, Dan grabbed for the jacket pocket.

Slappy let go of my wrists. But not in time.

Dan pulled the slip of paper from the pocket.

Slappy swiped at Dan's hand, trying to grab the paper away.

But Dan swung around. He unfolded the paper and raised it to his face. And then he shouted out the mysterious words that were written there:

"*Karru marri odonna loma molonu karrano.*"

Would it work?

Would it put Slappy back to sleep?

# 29

I rubbed my aching wrists and stared down at the grinning dummy.

He gazed back at me. And then winked.

His laughter roared over the thunder, over the hard, steady drumming of rain on the roof.

"You cannot defeat me that way, slave!" Slappy cried gleefully.

I took a step back. A chill ran down my back, making my whole body shudder.

My plan hadn't worked.

My only plan. My last, desperate plan. A total failure.

I caught the disappointment on Dan's face. The slip of paper fell from his fingers and floated to the floor.

"You will pay for this!" Slappy threatened. "You will pay for your foolish attempt to defeat me."

He pushed his hands against the floor and started to climb to his feet.

I backed up.

And saw the other dummies move.

All of them. They were sliding off their chairs. Lowering themselves from the couch.

They stretched their skinny arms. Flexed their big, wooden hands.

Their heads bobbed, their knees bent as they started to shuffle toward us.

They had all come to life! Twelve dummies, brought to life by those strange words Dan had cried out.

Twelve dummies staggering toward Dan and me.

We were trapped between them. Trapped in the circle as they shuffled, dragging their heavy shoes. Their eyes wide. Locked on Dan and me.

As they staggered and shuffled. Moving stiffly, grinning, grinning so coldly.

Closing in on Dan and me.

# 30

Wilbur limped toward us, his big, chipped hands stretched out, ready to grab us. Lucy's big blue eyes gleamed coldly as she staggered toward us. Arnie let out a high-pitched giggle as he pulled himself closer.

Closer.

Dan and I spun around. But we had nowhere to turn. Nowhere to escape.

The dummies' big shoes scraped heavily over the wooden floorboards. Their knees bent with each step. They looked as if they would tumble to the floor.

But they kept coming. Lurching forward. Bodies bending. Heads bobbing.

Alive. Wooden creatures. Alive!

Dan raised his hands over his face as if to shield himself.

I took a step back. But the dummies behind me were closing in, too.

I took a long, deep breath and held it.

Then I waited.

Waited for their wooden hands to grab us.

I uttered a loud gasp as Wilbur and Arnie staggered right past me.

The dummies all brushed past Dan and me.

As if we weren't there.

I stared in shock as they circled Slappy. I saw Rocky grab Slappy by the collar. I saw Lucy grab Slappy's shoes.

Then the circle of dummies moved in closer. Tighter.

I couldn't see what they were doing to Slappy. But I saw their skinny arms jerking and tugging. I saw them all struggling together.

Wrestling with him.

Were they pulling him apart?

I couldn't see. But I heard Slappy's scream of terror.

Dan and I clung to each other, watching the strange sight. It looked like a football huddle. A huddle of dummies.

The dummies grunted and groaned, muttering in low tones as they worked over Slappy.

We couldn't see Slappy in the middle.

We heard only one scream.

We didn't hear him scream again.

And then I heard the attic door open.

Footsteps on the stairs!

Someone was coming up.

# 31

I poked Dan and turned him to the stairs.

We both cried out as Zane climbed up to the attic and squinted across the long room at us.

Did he see the struggling dummies? Did he see that they were all alive?

I turned back — in time to see the dummies all collapse in a heap.

"Whoa!" I cried, my heart pounding. I blinked several times. I didn't believe what I saw.

The twelve dummies lay lifeless on the floor, arms and legs in a wild tangle. Mouths open. Eyes gazing up blankly at the low ceiling.

Slappy lay sprawled in the middle. His head tilted to one side. I saw the blank stare in his eyes. Saw the open-mouthed, wooden grin.

He was completely lifeless now. As lifeless as all the others.

Had the other dummies somehow destroyed his evil?

Would Slappy remain a lifeless block of wood forever?

I didn't have time to think about it. Zane came hurrying across the attic, an angry scowl on his face. His eyes were on the pile of dummies.

"Caught you!" Zane cried to Dan and me. "Caught you both! Planning your next trick! I *knew* you two were the ones! I'm telling Uncle Danny what you're doing!"

# 32

Of course no one believed Dan and me.

Of course everyone believed Zane.

We were in the worst trouble of our lives. Dan and I were grounded forever. We probably won't be allowed to leave the house until we are in our forties!

The next day, Zane and Uncle Cal were at the front door, saying good-bye. It's a terrible thing to say — but Dan and I were *not* sad to see Zane go.

"I hope I never have to come back here," he whispered to me in the hall. Then he put on a big, phony smile for Mom and Dad.

"Zane, what kind of camera would you like?" Dad asked, putting a hand on Zane's shoulder. "You have a birthday coming up. I'd like to send you a new camera for your birthday."

Zane shrugged his big shoulders. "Thanks," he told my Dad. "But I'm really not into photography anymore."

Mom and Dad raised their eyebrows in surprise.

"Well, what *would* you like for your birthday, Zane?" Mom asked. "Is there something else you're interested in?"

Zane shyly lowered his eyes to the floor. "Well . . . I'd kind of like to try being a ventriloquist — like you, Uncle Danny."

Dad beamed happily.

That creep Zane had said just the right thing.

"Maybe you have a spare dummy you can lend Zane," Uncle Cal suggested.

Dad rubbed his chin. "Well . . . maybe I do." He turned to me. "Trina, run up to the attic. And pick out a good dummy for Zane to take home. Not one of the old ones. But a nice one that Zane can enjoy."

"No problem, Dad," I replied eagerly. I hurried up to the attic. I hoped they didn't see the enormous grin on my face.

Can you guess which dummy I picked out for Zane?

I know it's horribly mean. But I really had no choice — did I?

"Here's a good one, Zane," I said a few seconds later. I placed the grinning dummy in Zane's arms. "His name is Slappy. I think you two will be very happy together."

I hope Zane has fun learning to be a ventriloquist.

But I have the feeling he may have a few problems. Because as Zane carried Slappy into the car,
I saw the dummy wink at me.

# ABOUT THE AUTHOR

R.L. STINE is the author of the series *Fear Street*, *Nightmare Room*, and *Give Yourself Goosebumps*, as well as the phenomenally successful *Goosebumps* series. His thrilling teen titles have sold more than 250 million copies internationally — enough to earn him a spot in the *Guinness Book of World Records*! Mr. Stine lives in New York City with his wife, Jane, and his son, Matt.